MW01716118

The men of SWAT Team Bravo relaxed. But they kept their MP-5 submachine guns slung across their chests in the West German counterterrorist GSG-9 webbing. Just in case. So did the two men who handled the long-rifle portion of the mission: their guns were match grade 7.62 mm SG-1 sniper rifles, capable of firing full automatic like incredibly accurate M-60 machine guns.

Two sedans drove up to the checkpoint. The cops gave them the usual bit about emergency in progress, need to enter, have a nice night and so on, the usual treatment of nonsuspect citizens, firm and courteous.

Then the team leader saw the Colt .45 automatic emerge from the window, saw the small, round fireball, saw the Metro cop at the checkpoint go flying back from the impact of the slug on his bulletproof vest.

He didn't need to tell his people to punch up. He saw from the corner of his eye that they were already dropping their foam coffee cups and swinging their H & K automatic weapons upward.

All he had to say was two words.

He roared, "Green light!"

Even as his own MP-5 vibrated from the recoil of the fully automatic rifle, even as he saw the doors of both sedans flying open and strangely dressed men coming out with guns, the air was filled with the unearthly din of eight fully automatic police weapons going off at once.

Other titles available in this series:

Line of Fire
Miami Heat

D. A. HODGMAN

STAKEOUT SQUAD

THE COLOR OF BLOOD

A GOLD EAGLE BOOK FROM
WORLDWIDE®

TORONTO • NEW YORK • LONDON
AMSTERDAM • PARIS • SYDNEY • HAMBURG
STOCKHOLM • ATHENS • TOKYO • MILAN
MADRID • WARSAW • BUDAPEST • AUCKLAND

First edition September 1995

ISBN 0-373-63412-9

THE COLOR OF BLOOD

Printed in U.S.A.

To attorney Douglas Williams,
whose tenacious and ferocious trial advocacy has
exonerated more than one Miami-area policeman
accused of manslaughter after their weapons
ended the careers of violent criminals.

1

Radleigh Bingham was angry. The pistol in his pocket was the crystallization of his rage.

His old enemies again, the circle of insiders, the establishment types who were determined to keep him out. Escalate their private vendetta to drive him crazy, would they! He'd show them.

When he was a little kid, the teachers had given him grief, and those jerks, his parents, were always on his case. At least until his useless dad had moved away to parts unknown, and he'd been old enough to beat the crap out of Mom whenever he caught her trying to mess with his head.

Putting him away when he was fifteen. In the bughouse before he was old enough to drive a car. That was when he'd known for sure everyone was against him. Shortly after, the voices had confirmed it. The voices told him they were his only friends, and they talked to him because he was special—he was real, they told him, not like the others.

For a while, after he'd met Rosette in the halfway house and moved in with her into public housing following their release, he figured he'd found someone who understood him. The whole world had been bad to her, too. But a few weeks into being at home, she started drinking again, and that bothered him. After all, he was a working man, had obligations outside their home.

Used to be a working man, past tense. Thanks to the damn sand nigger who'd gotten him fired from the Stop 'n Grab.

It was one of those twenty-four-hour convenience stores that dotted every neighborhood here in Miami and in any other city in America. Run by a Hindu or Pakistani or whatever they were, who seemed to run every such shop you went into. Rahman Singh, damn him!

Bingham had lasted less than a week before Singh fired him. He knew from the beginning that the Indian had it in for him. He suspected there was something hidden under that turban, something electronic from the CIA, that was sending out signals that messed up his brain waves.

It had to be that. Only the day before he started, Bingham realized that he was sufficiently recovered that he no longer needed his medication. After all, they'd released him from the halfway house, hadn't they? He knew they wouldn't let them do that unless he really wasn't a paranoid schizophrenic anymore. He felt fine. If you felt fine and the state had practically said you weren't sick anymore, what was the point of still taking the medication? He had always suspected that the drug was part of their mind-control plot anyway.

That had been a Sunday, ten days ago. He reported for work the following day. From the beginning he could feel the hateful emanations from under Singh's turban, the condescending looks the man gave him.

He wondered how Singh was able to make all the customers treat him the same way, making them all give him "the look." He knew it well, had seen it in people's eyes since he was a kid. The look that said "You are not one of us. You are strange."

The week got worse and worse. By Wednesday he screamed at one woman, "What are you staring at? I know what you're up to! I know!"

There were four more incidents, followed by warnings from Singh. Radleigh Bingham knew from the beginning what was happening: it was all a plot to make him look bad, to give the dark-skinned man with the transmitter under his turban a reason to take Bingham's job away from him and throw him out into the street.

By Friday it culminated with the midget dressed up like a kid staring at him the whole time he was in the store, staring, it seemed, into his very soul. Radleigh Bingham went for him, reaching for his throat when Rahman Singh came out of nowhere behind him and grabbed him, pinning his arms, half carrying and half dragging Bingham out of the store, calling him a nut and yelling that he was fired.

All weekend he tried to buy a gun. There were plenty of gun shops in Miami. None of the gun dealers would sell him a pistol, not even the pawnshops. They all gave him the look and told him they couldn't help him.

He went back to the halfway house and broke into Old John's room. He knew Old John had a pistol he'd stolen from his son's house on a visit. It took him a while, but Bingham found the pistol hidden in the wall of a closet. It was inside a sock, a little Bryco .32 automatic with a box of gleaming little copper-coated bullets. Back at his apartment, it took Bingham a while to figure out how to load and shoot it. The gun discharged accidentally, putting a little bitty hole in the refrigerator. Rosette screamed at him, but she shut up quick when he stuffed the .32 in her face and told her what he could do.

Now it was Wednesday. The day of Rahman Singh's punishment. If his bullets could go through a refrigerator door, they could go through whatever CIA transmitter Singh had under his turban.

The store was a block ahead. His hand reached into his pocket. The feel of the gun, warm from proximity to his body, was comforting. Now he had the power.

It was just a quarter to eleven. An hour before midnight, he knew, Singh would lock the door and do business through the armored walk-up window. His timing was perfect.

Radleigh Bingham quickened his pace.

THE MAN in the Afrika Korps cap, its neck shield pulled down to cover his shaved head, crouched in the back of the stolen van. The Mini-14 rifle across his knees made him feel strong.

Next to him, a much heavier man, his red bandanna knotted at the back to cover his close-shaved scalp, fondled a Mossberg 12-gauge pump shotgun. Its tubular magazine ran to the end of its twenty-inch barrel. The weapon held eight rounds of double-O buckshot. The van was an ancient Ford Econoline, no windows except in the upper half of the back doors, and the passengers were too low to be seen.

In the front seat the third man sat nervously by the passenger's door. His jungle-camouflage boonie hat seemed to go with the olive drab shirt that he wore loose over his jeans to cover the 14-shot Browning 9 mm semiautomatic pistol tucked in his belt.

The driver was a red-faced man with a bushy, sandy beard. He was bare chested under the denim vest that he wore to conceal the Colt Commander .45 automatic tucked into his silver-buckled brown leather belt.

"Got one, a car behind us," the man in the right front said, glancing furtively into the big side-view mirror. "There's an old bag in a brown Escort behind us, an' right behind her, a white cruiser. Blue uniforms. Gotta be Miami PD, not Metro Dade. Nigger cop drivin', spic cop in the shotgun seat."

"Okay," said the one with the Afrika Korps hat and the Mini-14 rifle. "Start slowing down. There's four lanes, light traffic, plenty of room. See if you can get the bitch to pass. How we doin' for stoplights?"

"One two blocks up, another three or four blocks ahead of that," the man in the boonie hat answered. His voice was quavering with tension.

"Perfect," the man with the rifle said excitedly. "Slow down like I said. We'll let that bitch get outa there, and then, showdown!"

RADLEIGH BINGHAM STRODE purposefully into the convenience store. He swiveled his head. Rahman Singh was nowhere to be seen.

There were only two or three cars in the parking lot. In one of them, a young couple, both blond, were necking and talking. Bingham scanned the inside of the store.

An old woman and two little kids, all Hispanic, were huddled over the ice-cream cooler. A few yards away a big white guy in jeans with a black vest was thumbing through a copy of *Soldier of Fortune.* Behind the counter was a black man wearing a Cuban-style *guayabera* shirt.

Well, Bingham thought, at least they got another black man like me for the job they stole from me. Maybe I oughta tell him what they do to black people in here. Nah, never mind. He'll find out soon enough.

Bingham walked to the counter. The clerk met his eyes and flashed a friendly smile. "May I help you, sir?"

"Singh! Where's Singh?" Bingham demanded.

Something changed in the eyes of the man. It seemed to Radleigh Bingham that it was a look of recognition. Hah, he thought. This poor brother's already been fucked with by that sand nigger, recognizes why I'm pissed at him.

The man behind the counter said in a loud, clear voice, "Certainly, sir. He's in the back. I'll call him for you." He turned and said even louder, "Mr. Singh! A gentleman here to see you!"

Turning back to Bingham, he said in the same loud voice, "He's doing inventory and he may be a minute. Is there anything I can do for you?"

"You'll see," Radleigh Bingham muttered intensely. "You'll see." In his pocket, his right hand wiped the lever behind the trigger from safe to fire.

The door opened. The blond couple were coming in. They were walking toward him as if to go past. He shifted his eyes. At least they weren't staring at him, weren't giving him the look. They were casually dressed, wearing loose black vests. Christ, was everybody in Miami wearing black vests tonight?

Radleigh Bingham couldn't see that behind him the big white guy had put down his magazine and moved away from the rack toward the Hispanic woman and the two kids. He gestured and whispered to them, and with frightened looks on their faces, they ducked down behind the cover of the heavy steel ice-cream cooler. The man moved forward, his right hand disappearing under his black vest, going behind the hip.

Radleigh Bingham felt rather than saw the yellow-haired man and woman walk behind him. The black man behind the counter was in his field of view, and he saw him nod to the couple. He didn't think anything of it. They were probably regular customers he knew.

Then it happened.

A strong arm snaked around Bingham's neck from behind, jerking him off-balance. He tried to pull his gun, but two small, strong hands clamped around his wrist like a band of steel, and he couldn't get the pistol clear of the fabric.

The arm closed around the sides of his neck like a vise. He could still breathe, but he felt great pressure inside his head. He realized his eyes were bugging out.

People were shouting. It sounded like "Police! Drop your weapon! Stop resisting!"

Radleigh Bingham thrashed furiously. He felt a hot flash and a burning pain in his right thigh. He had fired the pistol in his pocket. There was a scream! He didn't realize it was his own.

The black man had jumped over the counter and was on him now. Bingham was on his knees, struggling against the inexorable pressure of the man behind him who was crushing his neck. From a corner of one bulging eye, he could see the blond woman on his right; it was she who had the death grip on his right wrist. He clawed at her with his left hand, trying to gouge her eyes and make her let go of his wrist, but the black man caught his hand and twisted it.

The room swam. He was losing consciousness. Bingham was dimly aware of two big men rushing toward them from nowhere, both white, both wearing those damn black vests, and both holding ugly black rifles or shotguns and yelling something.

And then he was not aware of anything at all.

IN THE BACK OF THE VAN, the man with the Afrika Korps hat smiled excitedly as he heard his partner in the boonie hat say, "Okay, the old bitch just swung out past us. Cop car's still right behind us. Traffic light's less than fifty yards ahead, and I think in a—yeah! It's goin' yellow now! It's red!"

"This is it," the leader barked, flipping the lever in the trigger guard of his rifle forward. "Battle stations! Everybody, weapons off safe! When I flip the door, it's the signal!"

IN THE FRONT SEAT of the Chevy Caprice that bore the door seal of the Miami Police Department, field-training Officer Umberto Rodriguez was explaining life on patrol to the rookie at the wheel, Tyray Borden.

"Thing of it is, Tyray, you have to be prepared without being paranoid. I know, I know, they told you in the academy, 'Wear your bulletproof vest.' Listen to them, and you'll wind up wearing it at home. I've been here four years and I haven't been shot at yet. Riot? Sure, wear the vest. SWAT and Stakeout? Sure, wear the vest. One of the Stakeout guys was saved this past year during that satanist thing, took a 9 mm slug right on the vest, he's just fine.

"But every day? Hey, I know what you're thinking. 'Umberto's an old fart, all burned-out, only wants to flirt with waitresses, drink coffee and eat doughnuts and do some cooping. Well, you been with me a week now, you know I don't do much snacking and I don't sleep on the job. But you also seen, I don't go up to every car with my Glock in my hand and, yeah, you're right, I don't wear a vest.

"And you know why? You're feeling why tonight. It's damn hot in Miami, Tyray! It's so hot, all the cops who wear glasses put that no-fog stuff on them, 'cause you gotta have the air-conditioning all the way up in here, and then you get out in that heat, your damn glasses fog up.

"Remember those two punks we chased the other night? Sure, we caught them, but lemme tell you something. I saw you were even more soaked with sweat than me, and you're only twenty-three. I'm going on thirty. You're gonna be before long, too. You think you're gonna be able to chase young kids in tennis shoes—and catch them—for much longer if you keep wearing that sweatbox vest?"

For the first time the young black officer behind the wheel had a chance to speak. "Hey, Umberto, I hear you, man. I didn't say you were lazy or nothing. But, man, those guys they brought in to the academy talked about how they didn't think it was gonna happen, either. Then, *blam,* they get shot in the chest and it feels like a punch, and they shot back and got the guys and just did a day in the hospital for observation 'cause they had the vest on. It ever happens to me, that's the way I want it to be, you know?"

Rodriguez sighed. Talking to these kids was like talking to walls. It was worse, actually. At least walls didn't give you stupid answers. He glanced at his watch. It would be more than an hour before they could stop for some good Cuban coffee to keep them awake.

The road was quiet. Almost no traffic. The old woman in the Ford Escort who had been in front of them turned into the left lane. They were now behind a battered old Econoline as they approached the stoplight. Habit made Rodriguez scan the streets. Nothing—almost deserted. On hot nights like this, it was as if you'd rolled up the sidewalks. People were smart enough to be inside where it was air-conditioned, even the scumbags.

"Look, Tyray," he said. "I've studied this vest thing, you know? Read a bunch of stuff from NIJ, man, National Institute of Justice. They say unless you got a good, firm vest, the blunt trauma from stopping the bullet's still gonna mess you up big-time. The vest I got says, right on it, NIJ Approved. I wore it like one night, man. That piece of shit you got, NIJ says even if it stops the bullet, it's gonna cave in your organs like it did on their lab experiments with animals."

"Yeah, well, I ain't no fifty-pound goat, neither," the black patrolman retorted. "Couple of the guys they brought in to the academy, they said their vests weren't NIJ approved, either, and when they got shot, it was like nothing, like somebody punched you in the chest or something, that's all."

The cruiser coasted to a stop behind the old Econoline van at the red light. Rodriguez sighed. "Yeah, well that's what, two, three guys? Hey, Tyray, we got over a thousand cops out here, just the city, and it's not like we get shot every day. You gotta get out from under this mind-set, like you're some kid watching TV and thinking the whole job is getting in shoot-outs and chases. Christ, all my time in the job, I never even been in—"

He stopped speaking when the door of the Econoline in front of them burst open. Umberto Rodriguez saw the men. He saw the guns.

He was reflexively reaching down to his own Glock and saying the word "Jesus" when the shooting started, when the great orange balls of flame burst toward him and his partner from the back of the van.

SERGEANT MIKE COHEN pulled his unmarked Chevy into the parking lot of the Stop 'n Grab and wedged it into the one corner where the emergency vehicles with their flashing lights hadn't hogged all the space. An EMS unit was there, with the Emergency Medical Services' huge custom van. The vehicle's Day-Glo orange highlights stood out against its white body paint, its red roof lights mingled with the red-and-blue flashers of the two Miami PD patrol cars that were on the scene.

This many units meant the scene was secured. He picked up the microphone from his dashboard bracket, keyed it to transmit and told headquarters that the Stakeout Unit Team Two leader was at the shooting scene. He locked the car behind him as he stepped out. In Miami even cops locked their cars behind them when they were going to be away from their vehicles for more than a few moments.

Cohen was only dimly aware of the stiffness in his leg. He had recovered almost completely from the 9 mm bullet he had taken there a few months ago. The night was hot and sultry. He left his jacket in the car; there was no need to cover the ParaOrdnance .45 automatic on his right hip. In front of his Pro-Line holster was clipped the badge that identified him as a Miami cop. There would be no mistaking his identity, no frightening of the citizens.

He came through the door. A slim black man was being placed on an ambulance gurney, his right leg encased in a clear plastic inflatable splint. Cohen saw uniformed patrolmen carefully secure the man's hands to the tubular steel sides of the gurney with the plastic Flex-Cuf ties that looked like big versions of the ties you wrapped garbage bags with.

The first to approach the sergeant was an overweight guy with sweat stains under the armpits of his rumpled white dress shirt and a brown tie loose around his neck. Like Cohen, he had a pistol on his right hip and a badge clipped to the belt in front of the holster. Cohen recognized him. It was Bruce Yount from the Professional Standards Unit, the Miami Police Department's internal-affairs squad.

"Hey, Sarge," Yount said sarcastically, "they ought to just assign me to Stakeout full-time to cover you guys. You're getting to be my best customers."

"Screw that," Cohen snapped. "My people okay?"

Yount raised his hands, palms up, in a conciliatory gesture. "Hey, whoa, be cool. Your guys are fine. Aren't they always? All we got hurt is an EDP, a situation that you guys were apparently aware of, with a bullet in his leg and whatever problems he's gonna have from being choked out."

A strikingly beautiful blond woman appeared behind Yount's shoulder. "The suspect shot himself in the leg while he was trying to draw his gun to shoot us, Sergeant," she said crisply. "Bob and I jumped him before he could draw. I held his hand in his pocket, and he shot himself trying to get the gun out. He tried to stick his fingers in my eyes, and Tom stopped him. Bob choked him out, and we disarmed and secured him and called for EMS."

She looked at Yount defiantly, and he dropped his gaze to the ground. She continued, "No shots were fired by any of us."

The paramedics were rolling the man on the gurney out toward the customized Dade County ambulance. Wild-eyed, the suspect was raving, "Look under his headdress! Look under his headdress! He's got a transmitter!"

Dealing with EDPs—Emotionally Disturbed Persons—did present a threat to all involved, including bystanders. But Yount was hoping for trouble, it seemed, trouble in the form of blame.

Sergeant Mike Cohen glared at the detective from the Professional Standards Unit and just shook his head.

AS SOON AS THE MEN in the back doorway of the van flipped open the doors, they began shooting.

The windshield of the police car exploded in flying glass and bullet holes, and what was left instantly became an opaque spiderweb of cracks.

The men were crouching, on their feet in the back of the van, firing downward. The one on the left with the shotgun fired a shot at the passenger cop, one at the driver, and one more at the first target, firing as fast as he could pump his arm. The gunman with the rifle pulled the trigger in quick succession, spraying right to left and back.

The first blast of buckshot caught Umberto Rodriguez full in the chest. Nine lead balls, each a third of an inch in diameter, crashed through the windshield and into his chest, shredding his heart and lungs, slamming him back in the seat. The second blast hit Tyray Borden in the chest, stopping on the vest, striking with the force of a trained boxer's punch. At the same moment, a .223-caliber bullet from the rifleman ripped painfully through the ndeltoid muscle of Officer Borden's shoulder and into the seat behind him.

Borden's reaction was instinctive. He threw himself to the left, not even realizing that his left hand had pulled open the door of the car, just as the shotgunner's third round sent another nine deadly lead pellets the size of ball bearings into Officer Rodriguez's chest. Rodriguez slumped against the side door. He was already dead when three .223 rifle bullets ripped through his chest and neck.

The roaring thunder of the gunfire continued. Tyray's Glock 17 service pistol was in his hand now. He hadn't consciously reached for it; it had just seemed to draw itself. He was on his back on the pavement. Fire lanced through his left shoulder, and he felt his now-dead left arm collapse heavily to the asphalt.

But the pistol was still in his right. The car's transmission had been in Drive, and when he'd bailed out, the engine carried the vehicle forward. He saw it bump the rear of the van, saw the man with the shotgun sway off-balance. At the same time the man with the rifle reached one arm out to grab the door of the van for balance to keep from falling onto the hood of the patrol car.

Tyray Borden thrust the gun out, extending his good arm, ignoring the pain in the shoulder, and lined up the white dot of the front sight in the three-sided white frame of the rear sight. He fired again and again, aiming at the man with the shotgun. He saw the man jerk backward, inside the van.

Another man, wearing a cowboy hat, had come from the left front door, a black automatic pistol in his hand. Borden realized now that he faced at least two targets; the man on the right side of the van with what looked like a rifle, and this guy. He knew that Rodriguez would be in a better position to deal with the rifleman, so he swung toward the guy with the cowboy hat.

The man saw Borden's movement and ducked instinctively to the side, firing, his shot going harmlessly wild. But the officer's shot also missed.

Then there was a flash to his right, and Borden felt his arm jerk as the high-velocity rifle bullet shattered his wrist. He saw his pistol flying through the air, as if in slow motion. He told his finger to pull the trigger, but the hand no longer worked and the gun was no longer there.

He realized both his arms had been blown away and he was helpless.

Umberto, he screamed in his mind. Umberto, help me!

But his partner was dead inside the police car, his heart and lungs shredded to ribbons by the buckshot.

The man with the cowboy hat came forward, bold now, the gun extended at the end of his hand.

Borden heard the man scream, "Die, you fucking nigger ZOG dog!"

Before Tyray Borden's mind could process what the strange words meant, he saw fire bloom from the muzzle of the pistol, and then everything went black.

The rookie officer did not, could not, hear what happened after that. Could not hear the rifleman in the van screaming, "They're done! Ted's hit! Come on! We're outa here!"

The man in the cowboy hat had fired six shots. Four had missed. One had broken the cop's cheekbone, skidded off and torn away part of his ear before it caromed away down the city street. The last bullet had entered his left eye, coursed through his brain and exited the back of his head to bury itself in the asphalt beneath him.

Probationary Police Officer Tyray Borden was dead before the blood poured out of his head wound into a small lake that rolled its way toward the gutter, before the doors of the white Econoline van could slam shut, before the van had spun its wheels and disappeared into the humid darkness of the Miami night.

2

Ken Bartlett sat alone in his office, contemplating the manila personnel files on his desk. His pistol, a Glock 21 .45 automatic, was in his top desk drawer. So was his badge, hooked to a belt clip. The gold shield read Miami Police Department—Lieutenant, and around it was a one-inch strip of black elastic.

The mourning band. It went around every cop's badge for a week after a brother officer was murdered in the line of duty. All cops were issued one as part of their uniform. In some departments they were the first thing to get lost.

Not in Miami. You don't lose things you use all the time.

Bartlett hated that damn mourning band. That was why the badge was in his drawer with his pistol. He didn't want to see that black band, didn't want it on his body.

It hit too close to home.

Ken Bartlett—tall, black, late thirties, good-looking—was the commander of the Miami Police Stakeout Unit. A little more than a year before, the controversial new chief of police, John Kearn, had been facing a wave of armed robberies that ended in gratuitous murder, and had responded by forming the Stakeout program. Kearn had begun his own police career as a patrolman on NYPD, and he remembered the stories of the legendary NYPD Stakeout Unit.

Trying to cope with the robbery wave in Miami, Kearn had assigned people to reach out and study stakeout operations that had worked in other cities. New York. Philadelphia. Los Angeles. The studies were compared, put in a blender, and the Miami Police Stakeout Unit was the result.

Bartlett wound up as head honcho. Under him were three sergeants and eighteen officers, divided into three equally sized teams.

In the past year, each team evolved its own individual personality. One group was involved in the unit's first shooting, in which two young teenagers were blown away. One of the kids had been armed only with a toy gun, albeit a very realistic one. The cop who shot him had never served another day of police work. Shattered by the incident, he retired on disability under what was called a "stress pension."

After that, the rest of his team seemed haunted. One more cop was placed on disability after the doctors said his newly developed cardiac arrhythmia was directly caused by the stress of spending each day waiting to get into a life-or-death shoot-out. When members of that team had to divide up into twos or threes for a particular job, Bartlett had noticed, they seemed to pair up almost at random. It was as if none of them wanted to get too close to each other.

Another of Bartlett's teams was just the opposite. They'd had several confrontations, and no one had been killed. A couple of times suspects had turned on them with guns, and shots were fired, but both times the bad guys were only wounded, not killed. They had only lost one person, an officer who requested transfer because he said the job offered no action and he thought it was a dead-end assignment. Bartlett replaced him with a cop from the SWAT team who thought that, at forty, he was too old to be kicking in doors but still cool enough to handle a close-range gunfight with armed robbers. Bartlett agreed and put him on the squad.

And then there was the other team.

Stakeout Team Two. Or, as Bartlett found himself thinking of them, the shit magnets. Whatever bad shit was going to occur at an armed robbery seemed to happen when Team Two was in the neighborhood.

Recently a lawsuit had been instituted over two women killed in a shoot-out with Team Two the previous year. He knew it would be the first of many such suits. Armed with guns, the women had been dressed as men. They had turned to fire on the cops when a couple of his Team Two officers, Tom West and Stan Baranck, blasted them to kingdom come.

During the pretrial deposition by the lawyers who brought the suit, just the past week, Bartlett was asked, "How many people have been shot and killed by your officers on Team Two?"

To his horror, Bartlett realized that he'd lost count.

He told the lawyer that he'd have to review the records and get back to him. The lawyer's eyebrows went up, and he started writing furiously on his yellow legal pad. Bartlett knew then that this one was going to come back to haunt him in court.

But the fact was, he didn't have a cop on Team Two who hadn't had to kill an armed suspect in the line of duty in the past year. Even the *sergeant* on Team Two—the supervisor who was just supposed to monitor things, not get his hands dirty—had been in three shoot-outs, killing two men and being shot once himself.

Bartlett couldn't help glancing to the drawer that hid his pistol and his black-shrouded badge. That was what it came down to on this job. Life or death. Sometimes life *and* death. A tendril of smoke coming out of the barrel of that gun, signaling the life of a human being that the cop had snuffed out because the cop had no choice. Or...the black band of mourning around the shield, for a cop who had died because he hadn't been able to defend himself in time.

The night before, two cops had been shot dead on the streets of Miami, shot to pieces, according to what the lieutenant had heard. Patrolmen blown away for no apparent reason. Hence the badge in mourning.

But that wasn't his job. Stakeout was. A trial was coming up, and he was going to have to testify about things like "the continuing pattern of excessive lethal force displayed by officers of the Stakeout Unit and particularly Stakeout Unit Team Two." That was why he had the personnel folders on his desk.

But he didn't have to open them. He knew what they contained. He knew the people they represented, the cops of Stakeout Team Two.

Ken Bartlett didn't know he was doing it, but he counted them off with his fingers as he thought of them. It was a nervous habit that other cops had noticed but never mentioned to him. A finger went up for every cop who crossed his mind.

Stan Baranck. Big white guy. Talked slow, acted quick. Family man. Religious. Like Ward Cleaver, but with a gun and a badge. Baranck had killed one of the women in the incident the city was being sued for now. Bartlett knew he'd had no choice. It was Stan Baranck who, last night when Team Two aborted not just a robbery but a premeditated murder at a Stop 'n Grab, had moved first to put the female shopper and the children out of the line of fire. Baranck had never shot a man before he'd joined the squad. He had killed more than one in the past year in face-to-face gunfights.

It amazed the police psychologists that a man like Baranck, devout and family oriented, wasn't racked with guilt for having killed that many human beings. But for Stan Baranck it was just part of the job. Line of duty. Bartlett understood, and he was one of the few people who did.

Tom West. A black man, built strong, no airs about him at all, and streetwise. He and Baranck seemed to partner up whenever Team Two had to put people in pairs. West was also deeply religious, also a man whose life centered around his family.

Lieutenant Bartlett, acutely aware of his own identity as a black man, had confronted West at the beginning, African-American to African-American, and told him that there was an excellent chance that he'd wind up having to shoot a black man. Would that be a problem?

He would never forget West's answer: that much, if not most, of the crime in his city was by blacks against blacks, and that he would protect his people up to and including pulling the trigger, and the color of the perpetrator didn't matter.

Tom West had been as good as his word.

Melinda Hoffritz. Blond, built and drop-dead gorgeous. Bright, too, with a knife-sharp mind and a zero tolerance for bullshit. A photographer for one of the big men's magazines had offered her a huge amount of money to pose nude for a pictorial roundup of what the magazine had planned to call "copchicks." Hoffritz had told the photographer and his magazine exactly where they could put their money and their cameras.

Bartlett had noticed that generally, though, she was shy and quiet in that self-effacing way that some truly beautiful women have, as if they are embarrassed by their own looks. Hoffritz was the only person on Team Two who had killed a perpetrator before joining the squad. As a young officer on patrol, she was caught up in a gun battle in which she coolly faced two punks who were blazing away at her and shot and killed them both.

Since joining Stakeout, she had killed more than that. In one terrible incident, she was taken hostage and stripped. But she overpowered her attackers and prevailed. It was the kind of trauma that would have reduced most people of either sex to quivering jelly. Not Melinda Hoffritz. She confounded the police psychologists and remained on the job. It was she who had disarmed the gunman inside the Stop 'n Grab last night.

Bob Carmody. The youngest member of the squad, a bit younger than even Hoffritz. Blond, good-looking kid, easily embarrassed and cursed with a face that flushed quickly.

Both his impeccable record during his first few years on the job and his almost supernatural skill with a handgun combined to land him a spot on this high-risk team. Carmody had turned out to be a gifted firearms instructor, the youngest man on the weapons-training unit, which was where he'd been when Bartlett had grabbed him. Carmody was one of the top two or three pistol shots on the thousand-person-plus department, and Bartlett had wanted each of his teams to have its own certified instructor.

Judging by their ratio of hits to shots fired, Bartlett had to admit that Carmody had upheld this responsibility for Team Two. In the beginning he'd feared that a man who was a good shot on the target range might just break down under the stress of the real thing.

Bartlett had been relieved to learn that his fears were unfounded. Carmody had shot more criminals in the past year than anyone else on the squad, and they were all justifiable shootings.

Like Hoffritz, Carmody was single. They gravitated to each other for paired work. They fit in perfectly for things like last night, where a couple of lovebirds needed to be in place in the parking lot, forming an outside perimeter to the stakeout that the perpetrator wouldn't look at twice.

Frank Cross. Frank was muscular and worked out daily to stay that way, and he was male-model handsome . . . and in the beginning Bartlett hadn't trusted Cross as far as he could throw the man.

Cross had been awarded a heroism medal after a shooting that saw one other cop killed and a second made a near-vegetable for life. Cross had emptied his 9 mm service pistol at the bad guy, missing every shot and just hosing the area. The citation of valor said that his barrage had driven off the attacker, saving his own life and that of the surviving wounded officer. But rumor had it that the kid had panicked, ducked, just blasted his weapon dry while aiming over his shoulder.

Bartlett hadn't wanted Cross on the squad. A man who could conceivably be a coward was too great a risk. But when the fledgling teams were formed, there were damn few Miami cops who wanted to join a unit where there was a higher-than-average chance of being in a shooting.

It wasn't collective cowardice. Rather, before Chief Kearn took over, there was a perception among the Miami Officers that any time they were involved in a controversial shooting they would be sacrificed to cover the ass of the high command. And controversial shootings were certainly predictable for a group of cops whose job description included waiting—a setup very close to ambush—for bad guys to start something that police guns would have to finish.

In short, Ken Bartlett hadn't had a whole lot of volunteers to pick from, and so he had been stuck with Frank Cross. But, Bartlett had to admit, the kid had stood up.

There was one instance when young Cross charged into the jaws of certain death to protect the surrounding citizens and brother officers, firing his .45 pistol as he went and putting down the bad guy. He'd received another heroism citation for that one.

Ken Bartlett had written up the citation himself.

Later on, in another of the bad scenes that Team Two seemed to attract like magnets, Cross and his partner were working a protection detail and got into a shoot-out with kidnappers. Cross stood up great, even though he'd been shot. The bullet that would have killed him stopped on his department-issue Second Chance vest. Bartlett still believed that Cross's partner had failed him there.

Now Bartlett didn't worry about anything in Cross's past. What was done, was done. The kid had been a stand-up cop for the Stakeout Unit, and that was what counted. The partner was another matter.

Dan Harrington. Into his forties, the oldest field cop on Team Two, Dan Harrington was a burned-out case as far as Ken Bartlett was concerned. Always glowering, never smiling. Always running in with his handcuffs to manacle the suspect and take credit for the arrest after a couple of other Stakeout cops had risked their lives to get the bad guy disarmed and down.

Harrington never socialized with the other cops, as the rest did. He lived alone and seemed to have no existence other than his eight hours a day on the job. When he refused to have an after-work beer, he'd claim indignantly that he didn't drink. But Bartlett didn't know where else he'd get those blotchy cheeks, those little ruptured blood vessels on his nose and his perennially red and rheumy eyes. He'd never caught a whiff of alcohol on Harrington's breath at work, though, so the lieutenant couldn't prove that the older cop was a closet boozer.

There were other things that worried him. When Harrington had applied for the squad, he bragged about all the shootings he'd been in, but Bartlett's investigation showed that most of the time he was safely behind cover while the other cops did the dangerous work. Maybe once, when it was safe, he'd fired his gun with enough accuracy to slightly wound a more-or-less dangerous suspect.

Since he'd been on Stakeout, Harrington had shot a few bad guys. They were all certifiable scumbags who'd needed shooting, but still, Bartlett had long had a feeling that he couldn't back up by facts, a feeling that Harrington had never taken the least risk to himself when he shot at the men he killed. He had a great explanation for not being able to properly back up Cross the night the kid was almost killed on duty.

As long as he couldn't prove anything against Harrington, Bartlett knew he had no choice but to keep him on. Still, it nagged at him that the older man was a dangerously weak link in the chain of support that kept his people alive when they went up against the most dangerous criminals in the place some people called America's most dangerous city.

Bartlett sighed in frustration. Harrington had been calling in sick again and again lately. The lieutenant suspected that he was malingering, was getting ready to file a stress pension and get out with the added bonus of a work-related disability.

Normally Bartlett would have fought phony bullshit like that tooth and nail. In this case, though, it would be a welcome excuse to get a man he considered dangerous off the job and out of the way. Harrington still wound up, by default, partnering with Frank Cross. He wondered how much longer Cross could take it.

But there were people who worked for Lieutenant Ken Bartlett who had even more serious problems, problems that weren't their own doing.

Sergeant Mike Cohen. Cohen was the leader of Team Two. He'd hated guns from the time he came on the job, never fired one except on the range until joining the Stakeout Unit. Now, a little over a year later, he had killed two men and been shot himself.

Bartlett was amazed at how many men like Cohen, West and Baranck had felt motivated to volunteer for the experimental Stakeout Unit. He had figured that the high-risk squad would draw young, bachelor adventurers, probably agnostics or atheists. Instead, a surprising number had been deeply religious family men. Go figure.

Stakeout sergeants, the way the original plan worked, were supposed to coordinate and make sure the combat cops were where they were supposed to be, that the reports were all done right, et cetera. Getting into the thick of gun battles was not in the job description.

Unfortunately the armed robbers Mike Cohen had been forced to send to the morgue with his Glock .45 had not read the job description.

The lieutenant knew his sergeant had been deeply troubled by the killings, especially the first one. More shattering yet, however, was the latest incident. Cohen had rescued a kidnap victim and gotten into a shoot-out where the bad guy's lucky bullet smashed the sergeant's pistol. He fled with the victim, helpless, hounded into a refuge where the predator shot him in the leg with a 9 mm automatic. As the killer stood over the fallen sergeant, explaining in detail that he was now going to murder him, Mike Cohen was possessed by a helpless despair he had never felt in his life.

At that moment a citizen with a gun shot the killer, ending his life instantly and saving Cohen's.

In the past few months since the incident, Bartlett knew, Mike Cohen had changed. He knew it because he and Cohen were more alike than anyone else who served under him on the Stakeout Squad.

Both of them had become cops to help people. Neither had ever really thought that his gun was more than a badge of office, and both had always secretly suspected that cops who got into shootings were cops who wanted to, and who consciously or subconsciously engineered events to go the way they did. Neither had carried guns off duty...until they became members of the Stakeout Unit.

Again Ken Bartlett's glance fell to his desk drawer. Well, he wasn't wearing it right now, but his .45 was where he could reach it. The guns tended to define the Stakeout Unit, and in fact, that had become something of an issue in the negative press coverage they had received since the beginning. All the other City of Miami cops carried 9 mm service pistols, the full-size Glock 17 if they wore uniforms and the more compact Glock 19 for plainclothes assignments. The people who had researched Philly, New York, and L.A. stakeout units had recommended that Miami Stakeout cops take a lesson from Los Angeles and use .45-caliber pistols that were more likely to stop a gunfight with one shot. As the Miami SWAT team had done before them years ago, the Stakeout officers were given their pick from confiscated .45-caliber weapons in the property room. Each had selected a .45 of a kind that fit his or her taste.

Harrington, Cohen and Bartlett went with Glock .45s because they'd already been trained by the department with that kind of pistol and knew its "manual of arms." After all, it wasn't as if they were ever going to *need* it.

That was then. This was now. Bartlett wore his .45 to work and home again and, when he went somewhere with his family on his own time, he carried the slimmer department-issue Glock 17 in a holster inside his slacks, under a polo shirt.

Cohen went further. Bartlett knew that after his service pistol had been ruined in the last shooting,

Cohen had gone to the property room and found a Canadian-made ParaOrdnance 14-shot .45 automatic with a steel frame. It was a big gun, but Cohen now carried it whenever he left the house, as well as a .38 Special revolver strapped to his ankle for backup. Although, truth to tell, a lot of Stakeout cops had been doing the same ever since the incident when Cross had been shot because his own Smith & Wesson .45 service pistol had been taken away from him during the struggle.

But Cohen seemed to have become really paranoid, and that worried the lieutenant. He'd had a heart-to-heart talk with Mike Cohen's wife after Cohen had moved out of the house.

"Ken," she had sobbed to him, "he's obsessed! He used to come home and put his gun in the lockbox like he was glad to be rid of it. Now he keeps it in his holster even when he's in the house. We have a shotgun in our bedroom closet! Loaded! The old gun that his parents gave him when he graduated from the academy—the little shiny one that he always said he would have sold but for the fact that he couldn't sell a gift from his mother and father—Ken, he's carrying that, too, in a holster on his leg! Two guns yet! And he's saying he wants me to get trained to use the shotgun when he's gone! Oh, Ken, do you see why I'm half-glad he's left the house?"

Ken Bartlett dropped his head into his hands. Just like Cohen, he had thought at first the Stakeout Squad would be a flash in the pan, an experiment that would probably end in a year, tops. Each of them would have a high-risk detail and an experimental detail in their work histories, better placing them for future promotion.

Neither of them had realized that in the inevitable gunfights that would happen when cops were arrayed against armed criminals who were likely to strike, a bond of trust and even of love would be forged between the select cops and the men who commanded them. Those bonds would be tempered in the fire of the guns when the cops under them fought to survive.

The cops under them. Subordinates to supervisors. Children to parents. After a time you became not only their commander, but their protector, looking out for them with the same defensive anger as a mother bear.

By now, for both Ken Bartlett and Mike Cohen, the Stakeout Unit was more than another assignment, another stepping stone on the career path. It had become a labor of love, a challenge, something that recommitted them to their own sense of self, of identity, of purpose. They were both in it now for the long run, whatever price they had to pay.

Bartlett stood up, stretching, tense. He couldn't help wondering about those two patrolmen who had been murdered last night.

At least, he thought, it won't involve my people. At least this is one pile of crap my shit magnets won't attract.

He didn't know how wrong he was.

3

Wallace Crowther reached up and scratched the stubble of his shaved head under his Afrika Korps hat. He looked around the luxurious, deep-carpeted living room at his cohorts. They were leaning forward in their chairs, listening raptly to the TV news. The newscaster was saying, "Police are as yet uncertain whether the discovery this morning of a murdered Florida Highway Patrol trooper in the Everglades is related to last night's ambush slaying of two City of Miami police officers...."

Crowther shuddered. It had been close. He and Tony and Dewey had been shoveling a shallow grave for their fallen comrade at the edge of the swamp. After dumping the van, they'd stuffed the body into the trunk of the second-stage getaway car, a stolen Oldsmobile. They hadn't planned for casualties. They'd had to stop at a general store to buy the shovels.

There they'd been, in the moonlight, without even a sentinel standing post, when they heard the chilling command, "Highway Patrol! Don't move!"

They froze. Turning, Crowther could see the gray-uniformed trooper in the moonlight, his straw Stetson right in place, his big Beretta automatic locked out at the end of his arms. He must have seen their car parked by the trail and followed in on foot.

He ordered them all facedown. They had no choice but to comply. If he'd just held them there and radioed for help, they would have been bought and paid for.

Crowther thought, Thank God the cop was so stupid.

Once they were down, spread-eagled, the trooper walked right up to them to search for guns. He came to Wallace Crowther first. Too afraid to challenge the drawn service automatic, Wallace Crowther lay still, felt the trooper tense as his hand found the little revolver in the waistband.

It was then that Crowther heard rather than saw the surge of movement as Tony Mann rolled over, drawing and cocking his Browning Hi-Power. Crowther felt the highway patrolman tighten up, preparing to react to the sudden, unexpected movement.

But it was too late.

Mann was firing. Crowther heard the slapping impacts of the bullets striking the trooper in the chest and neck and face, and felt the spray of hot blood that jetted from his wounds. The trooper fell heavily next to him, his gun dropping harmlessly, unfired, into the soft swamp grass.

Tony Mann rushed forward, put the gun to the trooper's head and pumped two more unnecessary bullets into the dying officer's brain.

Wallace Crowther stood up at that point, replacing his little .38 in his belt. He tried to hide the tremor in his voice when he said, "Thanks, Tony. Too bad he had to be white, though. Hate to see a good white man die, even when it has to be."

Mann snarled back, "Don't matter. Ain't no such thing as a good cop. White, nigger...it's all the same once they turn blue." He kicked the trooper's corpse viciously.

That was Tony. Wallace Crowther knew *he'd* only kill the cops of color. He revered his own white race. But Mann's hatred for the police was all consuming.

He shook his head as he recalled the rest of the night. It had been a disaster. Carrying the body back out, getting to another burial spot, this time posting a guard...ditching the bloodstained Olds and burning their bloodied clothes. They hadn't gotten in to the safehouse until the sun was coming up.

Crowther looked around the room at the others as they stared, fascinated, at the TV screen. Tony Mann, at twenty-one, two years younger than Crowther himself, lean and mean. He still wore his boonie hat, but his olive drab fatigue shirt had been burned, and now the Browning stuffed in his belt stood out starkly against his plain white T-shirt. Crowther knew why he hated cops so much. One beer-swilling night, a drunken Tony Mann had confided about his abusive father, a sheriff's deputy in Pinellas County down Tampa way. The night came when Tony, then sixteen, took his father's service revolver and shot his dad six times as he slept. The court-appointed psychiatrist had diagnosed him as psychotic, and they put him away. He had escaped from the state asylum two years ago and been free since, burning with his hatred of police.

Sitting across from Mann was burned-out Dewey Huxley. His lined face made him look like a forty-year-old convict, and the grizzly, sandy beard didn't help him look any younger, either, but Crowther knew the man was only about twenty-five. The cowboy hat covered an already receding hairline.

Dewey Huxley had thrown his blood-soaked denim vest into the fire and sat bare chested now. The lightweight Colt Commander .45 automatic was stuffed behind the big silver buckle of his hand-tooled leather dress gun belt against his bare stomach. It didn't seem to bother him.

All Crowther knew about Huxley was that he was the first to bond with their leader, had known him when they were both snot-nose little rich kids. Huxley's first arrest for drugs had occurred when he was sixteen, and he'd been doing dope ever since. It had ravaged his body and his mind alike. Dewey Huxley's parents had legally disowned him when he turned twenty-one, and he had been living off the largesse of their leader ever since. A black narcotics detective had arrested him that first time, and it was as if Huxley blamed him for everything that had gone wrong in his life since. Huxley's murderous rage was focused equally on people of color and people who wore badges.

Crowther never could get a handle on their oldest member, Theodore Scott, thirty. The barrel-chested man wore the skinhead haircut of the white supremacist, yet covered it up with that stupid red bandanna, as if he was ashamed of his decision and couldn't make up his mind. Well, no one could doubt his intentions anymore. He'd stood up as fine as any Aryan warrior, blasting both the pigs with his 12-gauge before he went down.

Crowther guessed it didn't matter anymore. They'd buried Scott last night.

He turned his glance to their leader.

Ian Altman sprawled in his oversize recliner chair, looking like a cross between an obscenely fat Buddha and Jabba the Hutt. The man stood only about five feet eight, but Crowther guessed that he weighed three-fifty if he weighed an ounce, and four hundred wouldn't be surprising. The fat rolled off his arms in ripples that hid his elbows, and spilled over his belt and onto his lap halfway down his enormous legs. The face was so bloated the lips seemed to pout like a fish, and rolls of flab obscured his jawline.

Altman was too fat to carry a gun where he could reach it. He kept a Colt Python .357 Magnum on the table next to him and carried it with him, loose in his hand, when he walked around the house. It was as if he was afraid to be without it.

Crowther only knew bits and pieces about their huge leader. The pictures of the mother and father that Altman kept all over the sumptuous home indicated that neither parent had been obese. His weight problem seemed to be due entirely to undisciplined, compulsive eating. Even now he was shoving Reese's peanut butter cups into his mouth without appearing to even know that he was eating, like a chain smoker lighting another cigarette on automatic pilot.

He'd been in some trouble as a kid. From what Crowther could gather, it had involved doing dirty things with other, smaller children in the neighborhood. Apparently the wealth of the family had allowed them to buy the kid out of trouble. Now that both parents had died off—Ian Altman had been a change-of-life baby—nothing was different. Altman had inherited his parents' hard-earned millions and their well-paid lawyers.

Crowther only had a loose handle on his leader's obsession with white supremacy. The man had grown up spoiled rotten, believing that he was better than everyone. Approaching adulthood, he had realized that his compulsive face-stuffing had made him repulsive to women and too weak and obese for anything physical. He knew he couldn't take credit for the money, and he'd never had the courage to accomplish anything with his life. The white skin was the only thing he could cling to as a badge of superiority, and the concept had slowly taken over the direction of his life, especially after his parents had died.

Crowther shrugged. He himself had come into the supremacist movement largely as a drifter. First arrested for auto theft at age fourteen, he was by sixteen a veteran of reform school. The arrests and incarceration taught him to hate police and all other authority figures. Behind the walls all the ethnics bonded with their own kind for safety, and the whites were always outnumbered by the blacks and browns. That taught Crowther the meaning of fear. And what you feared, you hated.

He grinned to himself. When you had a Charter Arms .38 loaded in your waistband and a Mini-14 with a 20-round magazine in your lap, you could afford to taste hate instead of fear.

They were a ragtag group of losers, Crowther knew. He'd seen it in the joint and on the street. Winners hung with winners, losers hung with losers. Every day some of them would bond and commit crimes. Usually they would do it stupidly and go to jail.

But they were different. Ian Altman and his money made them different.

Suddenly Crowther snapped out of his train of thought as Altman pressed the remote-control button that killed the TV. "Enough of that bullshit," the fat man said in his wheezy, high-pitched voice.

"Time to make our statement. Time to declare ourselves."

He gestured to Crowther. "Wally, you better do it. I was gonna have Ted do it, but he's dead now, dammit. You got the next-best voice. The script's right there on the table, by the tape recorder."

Crowther sat down by the machine, glanced over the script and cleared his throat. Then he pressed the buttons that put the machine on recording mode, picked up the microphone and began to read from the typewritten page.

"We announce ourselves to the world with our revolutionary act," he began, his voice loud and pompous. "We have slain the three dogs of ZOG, the Zionist Occupation Government, in the name of pure white men and women and children everywhere.

"We are the Blizzard. We are the terrible storm of white fury that will bury the dirt and the filth that contaminate this once-great nation, and blanket the land of the patriots with white purity from sea to shining sea.

"It was the police dogs of ZOG who integrated the schools with the impure filth of the lesser races so long ago. It is the police dogs of ZOG, especially the mixed-breed mongrel dogs, who enforce the hated affirmative-action laws that have made Miami a place where good white men and women cannot find work and cannot live safely.

"Our great storm will continue until all the race-mixing politicians and the mongrel dogs who do their bidding are buried. Long live white America! Long live the Blizzard!"

Crowther pressed the Off button and looked up. The fat man was smiling. A tear rolled down the bloated cheek as Ian Altman said, "That's beautiful. That's just so beautiful. . . ."

MIKE COHEN'S MIND drifted as he sat at the wheel of his Subaru, rolling slowly through the tight rush-hour traffic. He could remember when he hated guns. Now he was surrounded by three of them.

The ParaOrdnance .45 rode cocked and locked in the Pro-Line holster on his right hip, just behind the black-banded police shield that was clipped to his belt. Strapped to his ankle was the snub-nosed .38 Smith & Wesson 5-shot his parents presented him when he'd graduated from the academy. It was the traditional graduation gift for a rookie cop. All these years it had lain in the house, empty and hidden away. It was now his daily companion, a backup gun.

He patted the box on the seat behind him. It held an identical revolver, but with a frosted gray finish and fancy rosewood grips, engraved in flowery script LadySmith. It was a gift for his estranged wife.

He knew she wouldn't appreciate it.

He remembered the night their long, strong marriage had turned so bitter. It was a night where for a moment he had been certain he was going to die. He had survived, saved by an intervention he considered little short of a miracle, but now it appeared that the marriage had been mortally wounded instead.

They had been working an investigation on a series of ritual satanist sex killings. Normally that wasn't the purview of the Stakeout Unit, but two of his people were in a serendipitous position to infiltrate the Devil worshipers. Then things went swiftly to hell in a handbasket, with his officers in the clutches of satanists who had slipped away from a sophisticated police surveillance. Cohen, burned-out and haunted, searched the city for them with a sense of futility and helplessness, like a father casting a net for two hopelessly lost children.

And from the black depths of that despair came what he thought of now as "the Premonition." An overwhelming sense of dread that something terribly evil was coming to the Cohen home. He had pulled in to a pay phone and called his wife. He could remember the exact words.

"You know the combination to the wall safe, don't you? Good. All the way in the back, under the coins and the stamps, you'll find a revolver. You'll remember it when you see it. It's the one you and I took to the Patrolman's Benevolent Association firearms-training class for the police spouses, just after Jacob was born, remember?"

He instructed Sarah, "The gun is empty. There are bullets, two boxes of bullets, in the cupboard in the garage where I keep the hammer and nails. Load the gun. Take a box of extra bullets—''

She interrupted him, blurting, ''Mike, Mike, what are you talking about? You're sounding crazy!''

And he answered, ''Shut up, Sarah! God forgive me for saying this, but shut up and listen!

''Go to your sister's house with the children. If you want to tell her I'm sorry about making fun of her and her husband having all those alarms and their shotgun, go ahead. Tell her I'm sorry.

''But go! Please, Sarah, as you love me, go to your sister's house and keep the gun with you and loaded and remember how they taught you to use it.

''I love you. Tell our children I love them. I love you all more than life. Just do this, and I'll explain to you tomorrow.

''Good night.''

He hadn't explained the next day, though. He had explained that night, when Sarah rushed to the hospital to be at his bedside after he was shot through the thigh.

His premonition had come true. The final confrontation with the satanists came not far from the Cohen home, and Michael was unarmed and helpless, with a rescued victim in the car with him, his radio lost and his gun smashed by a lucky bullet, pursued by a murderous hit man. Instinct almost took him to his own home with the terror that trailed behind him. Instead, he went to another sanctuary.

It was there that he had been shot, and would have been shot again and finished had the killer not been stopped by a bullet from the gun of a righteous man.

After he'd gotten out of the hospital, Mike Cohen did something he had never done before in his life. He began to buy guns.

As a young cop, he owned the revolver and ankle holster that rode on his left leg now, the gift of his parents. The department issued him the service revolver he wore at work, taking it back and replacing it with a Glock 17 when Miami PD switched to 9 mm automatics. And they issued him his Stakeout guns, the Glock .45 and ParaOrdnance he wore now. He'd never felt a need to purchase a deadly weapon.

But that was before. The bullet in his right thigh changed things.

First he went to the Top Cop Shop, where all the officers bought their guns and any other police equipment the city didn't issue, and purchased a Sirkis 9 mm to present to the man who had saved his life.

Then he bought a shotgun for the house. A Remington 870, just like the one the department had trained him with, but in the light 20-gauge so Sarah and Jacob, his oldest, could handle it. The big 12-gauge that the department issued had too much of a kick, the salesman assured him. But it didn't seem to matter; Sarah refused to touch it, and she forbade Jacob to go to the range with his father to learn to use it.

So he purchased the LadySmith that lay beside him now. She had learned to use such a gun long ago, when the PBA offered its program to make the wives more comfortable with the accoutrements of their husbands' jobs. She would be rusty with it, but at least she would be safe with it. If his years of police work had taught Mike Cohen anything, it was that you had to be trained with anything you used.

The argument about the guns crystallized what had fallen apart in their marriage. Mike Cohen had learned at the hospital that night that Sarah thought he had gone crazy. That she had never dug out and loaded the gun. Had never gone to her sister's house with the children.

He still shuddered, thinking of it. His first instinct had been to race to his home—and it was so close—like a wounded, frightened animal running to its den with a terrible predator's breath hot behind it.

If he had followed that instinct, Sarah and the kids would have been home. Vulnerable. Helpless. The gun would still have been uselessly locked in the wall safe, and his department Glock 9 mm still locked in the security box in the bedroom. Neither could have been reached in time to stop the monster.

The beast would have killed him first. Then the kidnap victim. Then Sarah and the children, with no kind Samaritan with a gun to stop him this time.

He felt a great sadness in his chest. It wasn't the stubborn machismo of a man whose pride had been wounded because his wife had dared to defy his will.

It was a sense of deep failure between partners. One had made a request that was overwhelmingly important, and the other had rejected it out of hand, almost in contempt.

She thought he'd gone mad. Paranoid. Nothing since could change her mind. Not the rabbi, not the department psychologist. Even the doctor, who told her, "Mrs. Cohen, most of the cops in this city carry guns off duty and have them loaded at home. Almost all of them, in fact. Your husband was the exception before the shooting, not the rule."

"I didn't marry those other cops," his wife snapped back. "I married Michael. I married a kind, good man who despised violence and guns. Now he brings icons of death, deadly weapons, into my house. And he expects me to wield them!"

The doctor sighed. "Your husband never needed his gun before except as a badge of office," he tried to explain gently. "After he was shot, he felt that if he'd had his backup gun with him he could have protected himself and others better. He felt helpless. He felt as if he had failed. You can't blame him for not wanting to feel that way again. He wants you to be protected and he wants to be able to protect others."

But Sarah shook her head stubbornly. "All those years, nothing bad happened to us. Not even that night when Mike went crazy, when he got this paranoid delusion that the Devil worshipers were after us, no evil came to our house."

"It wasn't paranoid, Mrs. Cohen," the doctor answered. "They *were* after him. They shot him, almost killed him. I think his reaction is normal, a predictable compensation for a past feeling of helplessness."

Sarah Cohen's mouth tightened. "He wasn't helpless before, was he? When he killed the man in the check-cashing robbery. When he killed the man in the Mart robbery."

There was a long pause before the psychologist said, "Is that the real problem, Mrs. Cohen? That Michael killed two men before the night he was wounded?"

After another long moment she answered tautly, "That was the beginning. When my husband became a killer was the beginning of the end, the beginning of him changing."

Those words still haunting him, Cohen shook his head angrily, trying to clear the memory away. He was pulling up to his familiar house. The house that was no longer home.

His son, Jacob, met him at the door and threw his arms around him. They hugged for a long, wordless moment, and then Jacob said very softly, "I was hoping you'd have your suitcase the next time you came back."

Cohen fought back tears. "Maybe next time. Your mother home?"

The boy shook his head. "She said she'd be home late."

Cohen sighed. "Okay," he said, "tell you what. I'm going to leave something for her. Tell her it'll be in the safe."

Mike Cohen went to the master bedroom. So familiar, and now so strangely desolate. He pulled the landscape picture away from the wall safe and spun the dial.

His son home alone, unprotected. He didn't like it at all. The gun that used to dwell in this safe was now on his ankle. He wondered if she had thrown out the cartridges.

There was a neoprene Bianchi Speed Strip in his trouser pocket that held five of the old MPD-issue duty loads, Federal +P lead hollowpoint .38 Specials. He peeled them off the strip and dropped them into the gray box alongside the gleaming new revolver and put it all into the back of the safe. He was starting to close the door when he caught sight of some legal papers.

Reflexively he picked them up and glanced at them.

The top sheet was titled Petition for Divorce.

Something seemed to fill his throat and chest, and his eyes were burning, and this time Sergeant Mike Cohen couldn't stop the tears.

4

John Kearn had ushered the other men out of his office. Now, alone behind a locked door, Miami's chief of police paced the floor like a caged tiger.

The chief of detectives said that multiple rounds had been fired from three weapons: a .45 ACP, probably a Colt pistol; a .223 rifle, with extractor marks consistent with the Ruger Mini-14; and a 12-gauge shotgun, extraction marks consistent with any number of pump guns but most similar to the Mossberg Model 500. The van, with a Silvertip fired from a Glock and consistent with Officer Tyray Borden's weapon embedded in the bodywork, had been found abandoned. There were abundant bloodstains, already typed and filed, enough to indicate a severe and possibly fatal wound in the body of the man who had shed it. There were no suspects.

Kearn hoped the bastard was dead.

The chief of patrol wasn't much more help. His people had found the van. All officers, not just citywide but statewide and in contiguous states, had been issued IdentiKit sketches of the suspects based on the indistinct descriptions of the few eyewitnesses. He had instructed the roll-call sergeants to remind all officers to wear their vests; Borden's had at least kept him alive long enough to shoot one of his tormentors.

The commander of the Organized Crime Unit was putting all the people he could spare onto checking out known paramilitary groups. The witnesses had described at least a couple of the suspects as wearing military-style clothing, and headgear to cover the shaved scalp that was the trademark of a neo-Nazi skinhead. So far, though, they'd come up with nothing.

The head of the Metro Dade County Homicide Unit was coordinating the investigation of the murder of the Florida Highway Patrolman only a few hours after the two Miami cops had been gunned down. The weapons weren't consistent—this cop-killing had been done with a 9 mm pistol—but bloodstains near the scene appeared upon early lab testing to match those found in the van. There was the matter of a half-dug grave near the trooper's body, too. Metro theorized that the gunman that witnesses had seen fall in the Miami shooting was dead, and that the trooper had been ambushed after somehow stumbling upon the others while they were burying the body. But it was all speculation.

Kearn was aware that his hands were clenching and unclenching. He had been chief of police in Miami for more than a year now. Thus far, only two Stake-out officers, Frank Cross and Mike Cohen, had been shot in the line of duty. Kearn had been so up to his butt in work that he hadn't gone to visit the first wounded officer in the hospital, a cardinal sin that still shamed him.

And now two of his people were dead. A field-training officer and a rookie. He hadn't even known either of them. He had learned real quick that he commanded too many cops to be on a first-name basis with all of them. Perhaps it was just as well. If the deaths of two of his people hurt this much when he didn't even know them, what would it be like when it was cops he knew?

It was a rhetorical question. As a young patrolman and union representative in New York City, Kearn had known the cold, empty feeling when one of your brothers was killed in the line of duty. He well remembered the chilling communal ritual of the "inspector's funeral" that was always given a cop who had fallen while wearing the badge.

Other officers were gunned down as Kearn moved up the career ladder to bigger and bigger departments until thirteen months ago, when he had been sworn in as the leader of the City of Miami Police Department. Each time it felt different.

Losing a fellow officer was like losing a brother. For a chief to lose a patrolman, he realized now, felt the way it must feel for a parent to lose a child. Even a child you didn't know.

He found himself standing by his desk, his fingers drumming the mahogany surface. At least there had been some good news today, he thought as he glanced at the topmost letter. It had arrived today from Washington, D.C.

The letter was dated two days previous, and bore the letterhead, U.S. Department Of Justice/Civil Rights Division/Washington, D.C. 20530. It was addressed to the Miami city attorney.

> The civil-rights division recently completed its review of the investigative report submitted by the Federal Bureau of Investigation concerning allegations that officers of your department were involved in a criminal violation of federal civil-rights statutes regarding the deprivation of the civil rights of Roseanne Palisi and Cora Duncan.
>
> After a careful review of that report, we concluded that this matter should be closed. Accordingly, based upon the information currently available to us, this department has no intention of taking any further action, and we closed our file on February 26 of this year.
>
> Thank you for your interest and cooperation.

It was signed both by the acting assistant attorney general for the civil-rights division and the chief of the criminal section.

Lawsuits and complaints about police brutality to the FBI and the Department of Justice were, of course, part of the job. Kearn himself was personally named in all the lawsuits. If one of his people had shot Ted Bundy as he stood with his hands around the throat of a victim, the department would have been sued for depriving the infamous strangler of his rights to life, liberty and the pursuit of innocent victims. Kearn could visualize the lawsuit in his mind: *Joe Scumbag, Sr., executor and next friend of the late Joe Scumbag, Jr., versus the City of Miami Police Department, Chief of Police John Kearn, and Officers John Doe and Richard Roe.*

He snorted derisively. The city attorney, over his objections, had settled out of court with the families of two teenage kids who had been shot by one of the stakeout teams. One boy had been armed with a realistic toy pistol, the other with a very small but very real automatic. When the kids turned on the cops with the guns and the second boy fired a shot, both were gunned down. It was a heartbreaker—one of the officers who had opened fire soon left the job on a stress pension—but the cops had done what they'd had to do.

The letter on his desk concerned a couple of women who had been trying to rob a bank dressed as men when Stakeout Team Two closed on them. When they opened fire on the officers, the cops fired back, fatally wounding both. All Dade County shootings involving police officers were supposed to go before the grand jury, and in this case that body had refused to indict, noting that the officers had fired in clear-cut self-defense. That hadn't stopped the Feds from responding by sending FBI to see if the cops should be charged for violating the rights of the deceased. Well, at least the FBI had done the right thing. Of course, that didn't mean the lawsuit wouldn't keep bopping right along. On this one, at least, the city attorney stood fast and swore he'd take the case to trial.

Kearn shook his head. Back to work. He had to call his captain in charge of the Support Services Unit to see how plans were progressing for the funerals of the two officers. A police funeral was like a huge parade, and very difficult to coordinate.

The buzzer went off on his intercom, and Kearn pressed down the toggle switch and said, "Yes?"

"Chief of Detectives Litton is on his way up, sir," his indispensable secretary, Charlene, said crisply. "I think you ought to see him." That phrase was her way of warning him something heavy was coming down that he'd better get ready for.

"What's he got, Charlene?"

"A tape cassette was just dropped off at one of the radio stations. Some wacko group taking credit for shooting Rodriguez and Borden."

Again Chief John Kearn found himself clenching his fists.

FRANK CROSS DROVE the unmarked, dull red Chevy Caprice as his partner, Dan Harrington, slouched against the right front door, the back of his balding scalp leaning on the headrest. Harrington felt awful. His head was pounding from the hangover, his stomach was all acid and it was as if he was covered with itchy grease. Maybe he should have showered before coming to work. To hell with it, he thought. We're out by ourselves, supposed to look like a couple of scumbags in a private car anyway. No supervisors are here to take a sniff, and Frankie Boy ain't got the balls to turn me in.

Dan Harrington wished he had a drink. At least his stupid-ass, chicken-shit partner was keeping his mouth shut and not bugging him. The Glock .45 on his hip dug into his side the way he was slouching—he was gaining too much weight, too fast—and he shifted position to relieve the discomfort.

Finally Cross broke the long silence.

"Dan," he said in a flat monotone as if he'd been rehearsing what he was going to say, "we need to talk."

Harrington snorted and snuffled. "Yeah? What about?"

"It's been a while since the thing at the hotel. We never really did sit down and talk about—"

Harrington cut him off with an angry growl. "I been over it with Yount and those other piss-ants from Professional Standards. Bastards snuck in there like *ninjas,* coldcocked me from behind. Time I woke up, you were already out of it. Look, they were gonna kill your miserable little ass, if I hadn't killed them first! I'd think you'd show some damn appreciation."

"Hey, look, don't get me wrong—"

Again Harrington cut him off before Cross could finish. "I said, shove it, okay? Don't blame me 'cause you lost your gun and got shot. I got an excuse. Bastards smashed my head against the wall, damn near killed me. Where the hell were *you?* In there putting the pork to that woman we was supposed to be protectin', that's where!'

It was Cross's turn to raise his voice. "Knock it off, Dan! Leave Monica out of this!"

The older man sneered. "My ass, leave her out of it! You been shacked up with her just about since you been outa the hospital, for Christ's sake! Don't take no mental giant to put it together—you started screwing her before you got in the hospital, and that means you were in there screwing her while I was out doing my job, scouting the perimeter and shit."

The younger officer's voice hardened. "I won't say it again, Dan. Leave Monica out of this. She's the best thing that ever happened to me. Keep your mouth off her, you understand?"

Dan Harrington had spent his life analyzing the odds and never going in on anything that could actually hurt him if he could help it. He'd hurt someone else if he could—so long as it didn't involve danger to him—but where risk was concerned, Dan Harrington moved back. He sensed risk moving in now as he heard the tone of his partner's voice change.

"Okay, fine," he sulked. "You keep your mouth off me, then. Just remember, you try to bad-mouth me, I'll have plenty to say about you and your new girlfriend."

The radio interrupted them. "Signal Zero, clear the air," said the flat voice, and even after all their years as cops both men felt the electrical charge of the words. Under Florida police radio procedure, "Signal Zero" meant an officer was involved in a life-threatening encounter.

"Unit in high-speed pursuit of suspect on motorcycle, armed with a long gun. Shots have been exchanged." The dispatcher's flat, unemotional voice gave the call signal of the pursuing unit and the location of the pursuit at that moment.

"Holy shit," blurted Harrington, "that's right up the street! They're coming crossways of where we are right now!'

What they'd been talking about before was gone now, out the window. Both officers braced themselves as Cross, seeing an opening in the traffic, spun the Caprice into a screaming U-turn. Harrington reached down and flipped the toggle switches that activated the emergency lights behind the grille and put the headlights into their wig-wag mode. Alternately flashing high-beam headlamps gave better visibility than most red or blue lights would on a dashboard or in grille mounts. Another switch was turned, and the siren began its mournful wail.

The Stakeout Unit's function today was to serve as "umbrella cars," out and about in different parts of the city, heavily armed and armored and ready to roll to back up the regular uniformed officers in any crisis that even smelled like an ambush setup. They had been notified of the urban terrorist group that called itself the Blizzard and proudly boasted of murdering Borden and Rodriguez. Even cops who hadn't known the fallen officers—and neither Cross nor Harrington had known either one of them—had already committed the names to their memories. To be murdered in the line of duty was to make your name a household word among the other cops in your department for a generation or two.

Cross braced himself behind the steering wheel, his hands in the nine-o'clock and three-o'clock positions the way he'd been trained, as he threaded the unmarked car through the traffic as swiftly as he dared. Beside him Harrington flipped the secret switch on the Benelli entry gun, arming the weapon, and then racked the bolt mechanism to chamber a round of double-O buckshot. The stubby black shotgun had a fourteen-inch barrel and held five shells, counting one in the chamber that was normally carried empty. Harrington plucked another shell from the pocket of his black Hidden Agenda vest and thumbed it into the magazine under the barrel with a positive thunk.

He wanted the gun loaded all the way up. Dan Harrington always figured that a man could never have too much of an edge.

DARRYL BROWNHILL was more scared than he'd ever been in his life. He raced the Honda Gold Wing as fast as he dared, his head huddled under the windscreen, as the sirens screamed behind him.

He'd done it now, for sure!

The plastic film canisters in the left cargo pocket of his BDUs were full of rock cocaine. The money he'd gotten from the day's sales was in the opposite cargo pocket.

His woman had just bonded him out from the Dade County Jail yesterday afternoon. That was why he was pushing rock as hard as he could today, to build up some money to pay the damn lawyer. It would be his second fall, and hard time for sure.

Now, with more than enough crack to fit the requirements for possession-with-intent-to-distribute, they had him cold for the third felony drug bust, which would put him in Raiford State Penitentiary until he was an old, old man. And that wasn't all.

He had his 9 mm pistol.

It was the Detonics Pocket Model, loaded full up with seven hollowpoint 9 mm cartridges. Possession of the concealed loaded gun was in and of itself a felony. Minimum mandatory one year.

In addition to that, he was committing a felony with a firearm on his person, which—as every career criminal in Florida knew—was a minimum mandatory three years.

As if that was not enough, he was a convicted felon in possession of a firearm, which was another separate felony.

He'd be older than Methuselah when he got out!

And besides, they'd take his sled!

On his first drug arrest, they had taken his Ford Explorer. The damn drug laws let the cops confiscate your house if you dealt drugs from there, or your car if you did drugs from that, even before they had convicted your ass! It was, Darryl Brownhill felt, cruelly unfair. That's why he relied on rental cars when he did business lately. Let them confiscate *that!*

But what with his last arrest and the money that his lady had to put up for bond, he hadn't had the capital up front to rent tonight, so he was running his pride and joy, the Honda Gold Wing. And they couldn't take that, damn them! It would be like taking a cowboy's horse. Like taking his soul!

That's why he had to shoot it out when they pulled him over for going through a red light.

That was why, when he'd heard the siren behind him and saw the two-man police car in the mirror, he felt the cold chill up his spine. He pulled over. The two cops got out of the cruiser, hands near their guns. His heart was almost pumping out of his body. He had to do something.

He did.

Before they could close their doors, Brownhill slid the pistol out of his waistband and pivoted to his right, extending his arm, already pulling the trigger. He fired one shot at each, saw them duck back, the one on the right diving prone and the other crouching down by the car door, both going for their own guns.

Brownhill thrust the gun into the open pocket of his leather jacket and grabbed the controls of the bike, peeling out at full speed as the popping sound of their gunfire began behind him. He felt something pluck at his leather jacket, and a bullet smashed a neat round hole through his windscreen, spreading a little spiderweb of cracks around it. Something hit his helmet with the force of a thrown rock.

Then the wind was in his face and the sounds of danger were lost behind him as he accelerated. But now the sounds were back, the persistent wails and yelps of the sirens. He glanced in the rearview mirror. There were two police cars behind him all of a sudden. And then three!

Up ahead of him at the intersection, he could see at least two sets of flashing police lights amid the oncoming traffic. A dull red Chevy was coming on fast along with them, police lights flashing from behind its grille, and its headlights wig-wagging back and forth.

Darryl Brownhill threw his weight into a hard left turn against the traffic. A Mack truck loomed over him enormously for an instant, and then he was past, accelerating again, and behind him was the crazy sound of angry drivers' horns and police sirens and crashing fenders and squealing tires.

But he had gained some distance ahead of them.

There was another intersection up ahead. If he could cut right this time, he'd be ahead of the ones who had come behind him and behind the ones who had been coming in from the front. He had them beat on both speed and maneuverability. There was light at the end of the tunnel.

A big pickup truck was moving out in front of him. He leaned sideways to swing right, and saw that he'd clear just behind it at high speed.

At the last second he saw the red flag far behind the rear of the truck.

At the last microsecond he saw the long steel rods that hung out the back of the truck, between the body of the pickup bed and the red flags.

Darryl Brownhill had time to think, *Nooo!*

He didn't have time to say it.

The steel rod was already at his throat at almost eighty miles per hour.

THREE CARS BEHIND in the pursuit, Frank Cross had his eyes glued on the fleeing motorcyclist when the pursuit ended abruptly.

He had seen the pictures in training, of course, pictures of unfortunate citizens decapitated in a number of ways. But he'd never been there to witness something like this.

The motorcycle went behind the pickup truck that Cross had thought it would crash into a moment before. Almost in slow motion the green-helmeted head of the motorcyclist separated from the body, spinning in midair, as the trunk and the rest of the body on the still-upright motorcycle sailed right along like the headless horseman.

The spinning head didn't go very far at all. Cross saw it bounce to the sidewalk.

As soon as it happened, Cross could see what had done it—the long metal rods that hung off the back of the truck with the red flag far out on the end. At that same moment a geyser of blood rose from the severed neck, six or eight feet above the body, jetting out behind the still-speeding motorcycle like a fountain. The red liquid column seemed as thick as a man's arm and it turned to spray at the top of the fountain.

Frank Cross stood on the brakes. He saw the brake lights of the police cars in front of him go on at the same time.

Far ahead the motorcycle seemed to wobble. Seen from the rear, it looked like a child's spinning top that was running out of momentum. The bike went down, and the headless body on top of it went tumbling away. Both seemed to skid forward in very slow motion for a very long time before they came to a stop.

By then the red Chevy and the other police cars had come to a halt. Dan Harrington was out of the car, running forward, the Benelli automatic shotgun in his hand. That's Dan, thought Cross. I bet he's gonna cuff the headless body and take credit for the arrest.

Other cruisers pulled in behind the red Stakeout Chevy. Cops were running past Cross, all with Glocks in their hands. He didn't wonder why. What he did wonder was why they were all zoning in on the one bad guy they knew couldn't hurt them anymore.

If this was an ambush by those weirdos who made the tape, the bike would be just the bait. The killers would come in from behind. Cross faced that way, his Smith & Wesson 4506 out and in his hands, low ready, finger off the trigger but otherwise off safe and ready to fire. He was waiting for the backup cop-killers.

But all he saw were more cops.

FIFTEEN MINUTES LATER police vehicles and fire-rescue units were parked a block either way from the scene. The downed motorcyle and the headless corpse who'd ridden it were both seventy yards from where the pickup truck with the steel rods had come to a stop. They were even farther from the helmeted head of Darryl Brownhill. There were literally dozens of flashing emergency lights, and the scene flickered with an eerie glow that only cops, fire fighters and paramedics ever become used to.

Lieutenant Ken Bartlett and Sergeant Mike Cohen were on the scene with Cross and Harrington when Bruce Yount, the man from Professional Standards, came waddling up.

"Hey, Bruce," Harrington blurted. "Look like he's one of them Blizzard guys? It all fits. Male Caucasian, opens fire on cops...whaddaya think?"

The overweight detective from the internal-affairs unit did nothing to hide his disdain. "Well, jeez, Harrington," he said, "first I have to congratulate you. I got here and saw you and figured our headless friend would probably have your handcuffs on him by the time I got to the body. Admirable restraint on your part." His voice was dripping sarcasm.

"But, to answer your question, no. No, I don't think you got one of them Blizzard guys. See, what they told us, the Blizzard is some half-assed white-supremacy organization, right? Well, I just took a look inside the face shield on that helmet over there, the one with the guy's head in it. Helluva good helmet. Kept everything pretty much intact.

"And you know what, Harrington? I never did see no white-supremacist group that was so hard up for volunteers that they recruited an albino black man like this dead guy here."

A few feet away a reporter from the *Miami Crier* newspaper was writing it all down in his notebook.

5

A man named Oliver Teasdale wrote a regular column for the city's major newspaper, the *Miami Crier.* The topic was the criminal-justice system. Teasdale despised the new chief of police, cops in general and the Stakeout Unit in particular. Since its inception, Stakeout had been the primary target for Teasdale's vicious, barbed commentary.

The latest column was no different.

Miami Justice
Stakeout Squad Vengeance Goes Awry
by Oliver Teasdale

More than a year ago, fledgling Miami Police Chief John Kearn introduced his deadly Stakeout Squad, a score of men and black widows empowered to ambush and kill Miami citizens suspected of the crime of armed robbery.

Kearn said it was fighting fire with fire. His critics say it's more like fighting evil with greater evil.

In this past year, the Stakeout cops have filled enough coffins to bring a small graveyard to full occupancy. Admittedly some of the people they shot probably deserved it, though it's difficult to explain that to the mother of a fourteen-year-old boy put in the ground by Stakeout bullets because he was holding a toy gun they didn't dare just take away from him.

Chief Kearn said at first that his legal ambushers would carry just regular guns. The next thing we knew, they were blazing away with guns regular cops are forbidden to possess, including their trademark Dirty Harry signature-model .45 automatics.

Chief Kearn said the job description of his ambushers was to interdict deadly armed robberies in progress. Why, then, a few months ago, did the Stakeout Squad's bullets chop down several people whose only known crime was practicing an alternative religion?

The public was silent. They felt it was politically correct, perhaps, to kill people for practicing unpopular religious beliefs. This may explain why the two officers involved in those multiple killings are still on the police force—indeed, still serve on the Stakeout Squad.

This past week three police officers—two Miami cops and a state highway patrolman—met savage, cold-blooded death in the line of duty. We all mourn for them. A bizarre right-wing hate group that calls itself the Blizzard claims credit for the murders. The Blizzard promises a white storm that will cleanse America's melting pot of all that has made it great, and cover it instead with white supremacy.

And naturally the Stakeout Squad swings into action.

Assisted by other Miami officers, the Stakeout Squad hounded to death a man they thought was one of the Blizzard killers. He died horribly, decapitated as he fled an express train of police cars that were chasing him and firing at him.

At the scene one overzealous Stakeout cop—his sawed-off automatic shotgun still clutched eagerly in his hand—said aloud in the presence of a *Crier* reporter, "We got him, Sarge! We got one of them Blizzard guys!"

The policeman he was talking to—a *good* cop—had to remind him that white-supremacist groups did not usually recruit albino African-Americans like the deceased Darryl Brownhill into their ranks.

He did not mention that the officers Brownhill allegedly shot at were white, and that the Blizzard has made it clear that their targets are men and women of color who happen to be police officers.

Is this what the city has come to? That when self-declared white supremacists declare war on black and brown cops, the deadly Stakeout Squad declares retaliatory war on African-

Americans who allegedly have guns when they come into contact with Caucasian police officers?

Perhaps the inmates are running the asylum. Perhaps those inmates come from the ward for the homicidally insane.

Perhaps Police Chief John Kearn should dismantle his Stakeout Squad or be replaced by a new police chief who can, like Dr. Frankenstein, attempt to destroy the monster that has been created.

Team Two remained silent until the *Crier* column passed all the way around the big corner booth at the Denny's restaurant where they sometimes met for breakfast before shift. Their shifts varied, and for that reason the twenty-four-hour Denny's was their breakfast haunt of choice.

Tom West shook his head sadly. "Hey, look. I'm the only black guy sitting here. If this fool had just asked me, had just asked any of us, he would've known that this ain't a racial thing. This is a scumbag thing, that's what it is."

Stan Baranck nodded agreement. "I like the part about 'guns regular cops are forbidden to possess.' Hell, every cop on the job has more bullets in his gun than we've got in our .45s. SWAT had .45s before we did. SWAT's got those submachine guns, too, and I haven't seen one of those in *our* armory yet."

Frank Cross said, "Look, I have to stand up for Dan on this. I didn't have a tape recorder going or anything, but I was right there. He didn't say 'Hey, Sarge, we got 'em!' He just asked if it was one of the Blizzard guys. Hell, we never saw his face! He had the helmet on with the face shield. The patrol cops who stopped him had a look through the Lexan face shield, though. They were the guys who broadcast that it was a male Caucasian who shot at them. That was all we had to go on. We didn't know it wasn't a white guy running the Gold Wing. Christ, we didn't even know it was two white cops the son of a bitch had shot at!"

Melinda Hoffritz put a gentle, calming hand on Cross's clenching fist. "Chill out, Frank," she said softly. "Look, we all take this Teasdale character too seriously. I mean, he hasn't got a clue! That bit about the .45 being the Dirty Harry gun? My God, every kid in this country has to know Dirty Harry carried a .44 Magnum, not a .45 automatic. It shows you the level of the guy's research. Nobody who means anything takes Ollie Teasdale seriously. We're getting worked up over nothing."

Mike Cohen flashed a humorless smile. It was the only kind of smile he ever wore these days. "We're all missing something here. Listen, people. I was there when Dan was talking and that little twerp reporter was writing it all down in his notes. So was Ken Bartlett. We had just walked up. The guy Dan was talking to was Bruce Yount."

Hoffritz cut in. "That SOB from I.A.?" Even though Miami Police called the unit Professional Standards, cops throughout America thought of such detectives as belonging to I.A.—Internal Affairs.

"The very same," Cohen answered. "And what jumped right out at me from that column was Teasdale describing the guy Dan was talking to as a 'good' cop. That tell you anything?"

"God*damn,*" said Bob Carmody. "You think Yount's been working with Teasdale? Hell, both of them hate our guts."

"Wouldn't surprise me at all," the sergeant answered. "Listen, guys, from now on, nobody talks to Yount without me or the lieutenant there."

"Or our PBA representative," Baranck chimed in.

"No, not even that," Cohen answered. "Listen, you have *Garrity,* but your union rep doesn't. Regarding anything you say to the guy from PBA, unless he's the damn PBA lawyer and has the attorney-client privilege, Yount can make your PBA guy spill his guts or lose his job if he refuses. It isn't fair to you *or* your PBA rep. I'm telling you, I don't want any of you to say shit to Bruce Yount or anybody else from Professional Standards until either Ken Bartlett or I get there. These people are out to hang every one of our asses individually—'jointly and severally,' as the lawyers say—and they're out to kill the Stakeout Unit and deep-six John Kearn. We all clear on that?"

Cohen looked around the table. Everyone present was nodding solemnly because they all understood what the distinction meant, and it was significant. The *Garrity* rule evolved from a United States Supreme Court decision that said any police officer forced to make a statement against his best interests by order of his superiors was acting under duress, and that therefore the police supervisors had to tell the officer that he would lose his job if he did not answer. In a criminal trial proceeding in the United States, such a statement may not be used against the officer who speaks.

"Okay," Cohen continued. "Anybody got any idea where Dan Harrington is right now?"

They looked around the table at each other.

"Damned if I know, Sarge," Baranck said finally. "You know Dan. He never shows up for a drink after work, and doesn't show up to have breakfast with us half the time."

Some of the officers couldn't help looking at Harrington's partner, Frank Cross.

"Don't look at me," Cross said quickly. "I don't speak for Dan. We don't see each other except at work." He looked at the sergeant and added, "I haven't seen him there much lately, either."

Cohen smiled his grim, mirthless smile. "I hear you, Frank. I think Dan may have a little burnout going. I'm gonna have to talk to him. Hey, I can't blame him. I got some burnout going, myself. The important thing is, we have to get through this bullshit in the paper and get the job done."

Bob Carmody, the youngest, spoke up sharply. "How the hell do we get through it, Sarge? Look at this crap in the paper! This wasn't even a Stakeout operation! It was patrol cops all the way, from the first contact and shooting to the end of it! Frank told us himself, he was three cars behind it when the guy got his head chopped off, and he and Dan were the only Stakeout guys there! This Teasdale punk made it sound like it was all our deal!"

"Well, shit, Bob," said West, "that's the same guy says you and Melinda shouldn't have shot those nice alternative-religion satanist folks, just 'cause they were trying to kill *you* at the time. Take it from whence it comes, you know?"

The sergeant answered, "Son, it's like this. A guy sells his soul to the Devil. The deal is, he gets all he wants on Earth, and when it's time for him to die, he gets an air-conditioned condo in Hell.

"Well, time goes on, and the guy croaks and he finds himself in the pit up to his ass in hot sulfur and little demons sticking him in the ass with pitchforks and all that. And he says, 'Hey, call your boss! We had a deal goin' here.'

"So the demons call the Devil, and the Devil comes down, and the guy says, 'Hey, Satan, what's *this* shit? I was supposed to get an air-conditioned condo instead of this pit with the sulfur and the pitchforks!'

"And the Devil says, 'So I lied. Who in Hell ever told you life was gonna be fair?'"

No one around the table laughed.

After a moment Tom West said, "You know, all of us are even stupider than that guy in Hell."

The others looked at him.

West grinned and explained, "Hey, nobody ever even promised us the air-conditioned condo."

IN THE MISTS of the darkness, something was coming toward Frank Cross.

Behind him there were children screaming.

He knew they were counting on him to protect them.

He picked up the gun. It was like no weapon Cross had ever held. Huge and heavy. He groped for the safety catches. There seemed to be glowing diodes. He pressed at them desperately, and miraculously an LED readout appeared that said, Fire Mode.

The thing came out of the fog. It was huge, slimy yet hard under its slithery surface.

He aimed the weapon, fired. There was a vivid flash of heat in his face, and a recoil that jolted him. A huge hole exploded in the head of the creature. A red-and-green fountain of bloody slime sprayed from the entry wound.

The thing tottered for a moment, and Cross thought it was going to fall down and die. But then it stabilized itself. It came toward him again.

He yelled at the kids, "Run!"

Then he fired the weapon until it was empty.

At last the thing seemed to buckle, stumble, fall back into the mist. But shapes took form in the mist above its corpse.

More of the same monsters. Coming forward.

And his gun was empty.

He threw the weapon down and reached reflexively for his right hip. He felt the reassuring weight of a Smith & Wesson .45 automatic coming into his hand. He aimed at the creatures advancing on him and fired.

But instead of a .45's throaty boom, the gun only made little *poof* sounds. And the creatures coming toward him were not at all deterred.

He turned and ran. He tried to scream to the children, Run, kids! Run!

But the words would not come out.

His gun, the .45, was gone.

He couldn't breathe anymore.

The things from the mist were almost on top of him.

Cross fell. The ground was invisible under the fog. It felt hot and smooth.

Suddenly he couldn't move.

From a corner of his eye, he saw someone moving in from the side. The man was handsome, dark haired, tall, muscular.

The man was his twin.

There was a gun of some sort in his hand. The twin man was firing. Giant fireballs appeared at the muzzle of his gun.

His gun worked! Cross could feel the concussions of the impact as the bullets hit the creatures coming in behind him. He could feel the hot, syrupy blood spatter onto him as their wounds exploded, as the creatures fell back, dying.

He wanted to shout to the children that it was all right now. That they could stop running.

But he couldn't speak. He couldn't move.

He was paralyzed.

FRANK CROSS AWOKE in a cold sweat. He tried to rise.

He couldn't. He was paralyzed.

He lay in the darkness, helpless, immobile. A soft, warm hand touched his shoulder. Help me, he thought. Help me. But the thoughts had no sound, no voice. Help me!

Suddenly the words had a voice. His own.

The warm hand became more aggressive, shoving against his shoulder, shaking him. "Frank," came a voice. "Frank!"

Frank Cross shot bolt upright, pivoting as he turned, one powerful arm striking away the hand on his shoulder.

"Frank!"

He was awake now.

He sat for a long moment, nude, on the edge of the bed. After a moment his right hand snaked down, touching the Smith & Wesson .45 automatic next to the bed. A soft and desperate voice from behind him said, "Frank, no. It's all right now. You're awake. We're safe. You don't need the gun."

He turned, as if in slow motion.

The woman who had spoken was almost unspeakably beautiful. Her black hair, tousled from sleep, fell across her green eyes. She shook her head to sweep it away. She put her soft, warm hand back on his hard shoulder.

Jesus, thought Frank Cross. *Jesus Christ. I thought this was behind me.*

He stood up.

"I have to go to the bathroom," he said.

DR. MONICA WOLLMAN, alone in the bed, dropped her beautiful face into her hands. She was crying for the man she loved.

Yes, she could say it now. The man she loved. She was in her midthirties, with two teenage daughters asleep in the lower floor of the rented house. Divorced, disillusioned and disaffected... and in love with a younger man.

He had been like the knight in shining armor that she had learned so long ago was only a myth. She and her daughters had been threatened with death or worse. Frank Cross was one of the Stakeout Squad cops assigned to protect her.

She hadn't really thought those creatures—no, even now she couldn't call them people—would have come for her girls. But they had.

This man had stood in their way. Had fought them to the death. For her, for her kids. Had been shot down and left for dead. Each night when they slept together, she touched the marks on his chest, the scars from where the bullets smashing into his soft, bulletproof vest had gouged his flesh away with their residual force.

God forgive her, she had made love to him before then. It had pleased her. He was young and strong and almost unnaturally handsome, and taking him with the children asleep in the other guarded room had been like drinking free champagne. A purely physical satisfaction, a defiant way of taking something positive for herself out of the grimness.

The horror of that night was gone. The Stakeout Squad, in the end, had exterminated it. She had no leftover fears.

Except the ones she felt for Frank.

As they grew to know one another afterward, as he shared with her things he had shared with no other living human being, she learned of the terrors that had seared him. Of the time when three policemen had walked into a place to arrest a bad guy and only one, Frank, walked back out. He suffered a gunshot wound so trivial he didn't consider it getting shot. But one of the officers was dead, and the other could not move and could not speak forever after.

She knew the nightmares haunted Frank.

Even before they'd met, he had redeemed himself in a savage death duel between the Stakeout Squad and some of the most vicious gunmen who had ever stalked Miami.

Frank Cross and his brother and sister cops had survived. Most of the others had not. Near the end of it, as if he wanted to die in a blaze of glory, Frank walked into the very jaws of death—into the criminal gunfire—with his own pistol bucking in his hand.

He won. The dragon lost.

She had tried, oh God, she had tried to tell him that the dragon had been slain and it was over. But he had so much to recover from.

The nightmares had stopped. At least, *those* nightmares, the ones where he was back in the tenement and his brother officers were down and bloody around him and he was hiding instead of fighting, firing his pistol blindly and helplessly over his shoulder.

But the other nightmares had come.

Monica Wollman had discussed it with others she knew who had earned the title "Doctor," and had earned it in ways more relevant to what Frank needed.

"Sleep paralysis," one intoned solemnly. "The patient awakens from a terrifying nightmare unable to move. He blames the nightmare. Actually, it's a very subtle and totally explainable phenomenon that occurs occasionally in deep R.E.M. sleep."

Yeah. Great. That helped a lot....

Another said, "My dear, tell your boyfriend it's just a simple mammalian response. Since the dawn of time, mammals have had the inbred instinct to freeze motionless when awakened from sleep. It kept early man from being spotted through sudden movement, and therefore devoured, by the saber-toothed tiger. Today it doubtless helps a rabbit awakened by the sniffing of a fox keep from moving suddenly and letting the fox know where he is."

Great, Monica thought. Tell that to a man whose job is dealing with saber-toothed tigers at the height of their power and alertness.

She also talked with the doctors about that dream where the troubled cop was shooting at the bad guy, or the bad *thing,* and the gun didn't work. They all said the same thing. The police psychologist from San Francisco said it best.

"Let me guess. The gun fires, and the bullets hit the body, but the amorphous opponent just doesn't go down—am I right? Like that thing on the TV comedy show where the opposing knight has all his arms and legs chopped off, and he still keeps fighting the good knight?

"Or the cop is firing at the bad guy and his gun jams. Or it misfires—he pulls the trigger, but the gun won't go off. Or the impotent-bullet dream.

"Shrinks who don't know cops have fun with that one. It's the nightmare where the cop keeps firing into the guy and the bullets bounce off or they just make little pinpricks and whatever goblin is in his nightmare still keeps coming at him.

"Don't worry about it, Monica! For heaven's sake, whatever policeman you're trying to help through this has to know that the failure of the safety device is the occupational nightmare of any professional!

"The pilot's symbol of his job is his plane. He will spend his career with recurring nightmares of being at the controls in the cabin and the plane is going out of control. He will have nightmares about plane crashes until the day he gives up his pilot's wings.

"The symbol of the policeman's job is his gun. He will spend his career, if he takes his job seriously and actually works out where it's dangerous, having nightmares about his gun jamming, or misfiring, or hitting the bad guy without effect.

"It's really that simple, Monica. The icon, whatever it may be, of the job-doer's ego investment will fail him in his dreams, or I should say, in his nightmares. I would have to assume that whatever cop on whose behalf you're asking me this learned that at the police academy.

"Or at least, I would *hope* he did...."

That input hadn't been much help after the fact, either. None of it helped, the interpretations, playing around with symbolism, amounting to no more than explanations of tectonic movements to a devastated earthquake victim.

Monica threw off the covers and stood up. She was unashamed of her nakedness. She was also largely unaware of her beauty, and it still warmed her to know that someone like Frank Cross, the kind of guy who should have been a male model on the cover of *Gentlemen's Quarterly,* would fall hopelessly in love with her.

She went to the bathroom. She found him standing over the toilet, as if he wanted to throw up but couldn't.

She said the first thing that came into her mind. She spoke it in a whisper.

"I love you, Frank."

He looked at her, his head hung low, like a wounded buffalo. The dark hair hung in his eyes, and he didn't try to brush it away. "Monica, I'm sorry. I—"

She was next to him then, pulling him close. They were both naked.

"Shh. Don't talk. It's over."

He hugged her, fiercely, desperately. "I don't think it'll ever be over. You shouldn't be having to go through this with me."

She hugged him tighter. "Listen to you. The operative phrase isn't 'go through this.' The operative term is 'with me.' Frank, you've paid your dues. You've been there and back!"

"Not yet. I haven't been all the way yet."

"Jesus," she moaned, "what's left? To die? Frank, I want you to live! To *live!* With *me!*"

"Blizzard," he said stolidly. "Blizzard is left. They're killing cops. We have to stop them."

The tears came into her eyes, and Monica bit her lip. She forced herself to calm down, and after a moment she said, "Then when the Blizzard thing is done? When these bastards are put away like the others, can you give it up then?"

He lifted up, pulling his head away from hers. He looked down. "Monica," he asked innocently, "Stakeout's the best job I've had since I've been on the department. Why should I give it up? And, hey, why are you crying?"

"Because," she wept, "you just asked me the same question twice, you big lug! Why should you give it up? Why am I crying?

"Frank, you do the most dangerous job there is on the department! You know how it's messed up your life! You fought back, and you came out from under it! What are you going to do, wait until you get shot in the head?"

Cross hung his head. "You don't know what it's like to walk into someplace with two role models you want to impress, and suddenly some asshole is trying to kill you. You see one of your role models fall, shot down like a dog. You duck instinctively. You don't realize you've ducked behind your other role model. He takes the bullet that ruins him for life.

"If you had stayed where you were, you would have stopped that bullet instead of him. He'd be alive, and you would have been the hero, then!"

Monica shook her head in frustration. "For God's sake, Frank, what kind of role model would let his student take a bullet for him? Was he a hero for winding up a vegetable? No? Then what makes you think you would have been?

"Dammit, you were the rookie when that happened! You were the student! They should have done it right, taken that bastard down right, instead of getting themselves shot. Instead of letting a brave young man get caught up in something he wasn't ready for, almost get him killed along with them for their own stupidity, and make that kid spend the rest of his life on a guilt trip for not somehow magically knowing better than his senior officers!"

He started to speak, and she reached a fingertip tenderly to his lips to shut him up.

"No. Let me finish. Frank, you've got a thousand-some cops on Miami Police Department. Most of them haven't been shot. Most of them haven't killed anybody. Most of them haven't had a brother officer shot out from beside them. You've had all of that happen to you, and you've gotten through it and you've come through it okay!

"It's going to happen to some more of them, though. You know it and I know it.

"Some of them will have a brother cop die in their arms, blame themselves and think they're the only person it ever happened to. Some of them are going to have to kill somebody, and they'll go through all the recriminations and all the tortures of the damned, because there's nobody to tell them how much worse it would have been if they hadn't pulled the trigger, if they'd hesitated instead and let a little kid get killed, or let some cop's wife be a widow and his kids be orphans because they hadn't thought it out all the way to the third dimension. If they didn't know what you could tell them.

"No, damn it, Frank, don't make me stop! You can keep cops from getting killed. I teach classes, Frank, I do seminars, I write books and articles.

"How many people do you protect each night on tour? One? Two? Three? Talk to me about protecting thousands, Frank, hundreds of thousands. Talk to me about telling people where you've been and what you've had to do. About going through what you've gone through and coming back out alive. Coming out still a man, maybe a better man than before. Coming out a man, a husband, a father..."

She was crying too hard to talk anymore.

Frank Cross hugged her tight. It took a moment for what she had said to sink in. Husband? Father?

"Monica," he whispered. "Monica...are you serious?"

She hugged him even more fiercely than before. "Dammit," she blurted, "why do you think I leased this house and canceled my book tour? The girls feel safe with you, Frank. After what they went through, what other man would they ever feel that way about? And me, Frank, me! I was a strong woman before. But you taught me a different strength. A new strength I have for myself... and a strength of yours that I appreciate in you."

She looked up at him, rubbing the tears out of the stunning green eyes. "You have so much that you can do for other people like you did for me and the girls, Frank. Other victims. Other potential victims. Other cops. Please. Please! Get this thing done that you have to do, and then—let's put it behind us. Your identity isn't about the Stakeout Squad. Your identity is about finding strength where you thought there was weakness and helping other people do the same. Please, Frank. Please! I love you, Frank."

He held her. Tightly, wordlessly.

They stood like that for a long moment.

Cross lifted his head. He saw the two of them reflected in the mirror, the slim, nude woman in the arms of the naked bodybuilder. He realized that the mirror didn't always show the truth. He knew the smaller one was the stronger one.

He reached down and lifted her up off the tile floor, into his arms, holding her like a child. She nestled her head against his chest as he carried her back into the bedroom.

As they reached the bed, he glanced down and saw the gun. He remembered a time when, after his first shooting, he wouldn't get up from his own bed to walk to the bathroom without putting the pistol in his hand.

But that was behind him. He realized now just how far behind him it was.

The pistol would stay. Whatever happened with him and Monica, he didn't see himself ever being where he couldn't reach a gun in an emergency. He imagined that men who had been burned felt the same way about fire extinguishers.

But the gun was just a tool now, an optional tool, one he didn't think would haunt his sleep anymore.

His mind flashed back to the Mart. Back to the hotel room.

Men who had tried to murder him, and those he had been sworn to protect.

He had fulfilled the oath. The innocent were alive. The violators of the innocent were dead.

He stepped over the lifeless metal thing that was his pistol and set the woman gently down on the bed. Monica looked up at him.

He asked, "Will you really marry me?"

She smiled back. "I was hoping you'd ask me eventually," she murmured.

She drew him down to her.

THE SURVIVING MEMBERS of the Blizzard sat in the deep-pile-carpeted living room of Ian Altman's fabulous house. Altman spread himself over his oversize recliner, his .357 Magnum in easy reach as he spoke in his nasal whine.

"We have done well, my brothers. We have done very well. But there is much more to do. The butchering of the pigs has just begun.

"But we don't have enough to do what we want to do, the way we wanted to do it. Four of you went out, and three of you came back. This is a twenty-five percent casualty rate. It is too high for a dedicated elite force such as ourselves. We do not have the redundancy built into our forces, at least not yet, to sustain such losses."

Unseen by Altman, Wallace Crowther rolled his eyes in disbelief. Who was this idiot kidding? They were a bunch of losers on a mission doomed to end in failure—that was all.

But what the hell? They had been like that before they'd met Ian Altman. This way at least they'd all go with some style. With a blaze of glory.

Crowther forced himself not to laugh but to listen to what the fat man was saying.

"We need to alter our strategy," Altman intoned pompously, not noticing that Crowther was the only one of his minions who wasn't listening raptly. "We need to fight the way our white forefathers, the first revolutionaries, did. Remember when King George of England, the ZOG of his time, enlisted the subhuman Indians to fight against the white American settlers? The patriots fought both the redcoats and the redskins the way we must fight the bluebacked ZOG dogs now.

"With guerrilla warfare. Not charging in against their strength, trading casualty for casualty. No, we must stay in the forest—the urban forest now—and pick and choose our targets.

"We must shoot them at long range, the way the colonists of the Revolution did, picking them off with hunting rifles. One at a time. A war of attrition. This is what we must do. Wally has been plotting the targets. Wally?"

The rich psycho turned toward him, and Wallace Crowther was glad he had picked this moment to pay attention. "Yes, sir," he answered crisply. "I've got a few places all laid out. There's a Circle Q minimarket on the edge of town where five nights out of the week the cops drop in for coffee like it's clockwork. The ones who'll be working the sector this week, if they stay with the pattern I've been observing, are both niggers. They'll be lit up inside the place. Easy pickin's."

A smile spread into Ian Altman's bulbous cheeks. "Ah," he proclaimed. "Good. They'll be the next targets. Don't use your light rifle for this. Use the Mausers. You won't need guns that can shoot fast. You'll need guns with telescope sights. Very powerful guns, to shoot through the glass. Make sure you have multiple cars. This time take things you can use for body bags. Buy new shovels. I don't expect us to have to bury our dead, but we have to learn from the history of *our* revolution. We have to be prepared. By the same token, have a backup car. I want one vehicle with a driver and a shooter and a second vehicle with a backup shooter, just in case."

Crowther forced himself to smile a false smile of agreement, to hide the contempt that rose in him like vomit to the throat. Who the hell are you to tell us, the real fighters, how to do it? he thought. Your humongous fat ass never leaves your house. You're a recluse. You send us out to do the dangerous stuff for you, so you can sit here wallowing in your candy and your money. We're just so many little toy army men to you. You couldn't care less if we get killed to fulfill your fantasies.

For a moment Crowther indulged his own fantasy. He pictured himself waiting until the others had gone to bed. Going into the bedroom where the huge Altman sprawled himself out on the king-size bed that they had to come in every morning and help him out of. He pictured himself aiming his .38 at Altman's head and watching the piggy eyes get as wide as they could get in their rolls of fat as he stared at the gun muzzle in horror.

Then he imagined pulling the trigger, pumping five fast shots into that ugly porcine face. It would have to be head shots, Crowther thought. A man that fat was protected from a belly shot by his layers of flab as surely as if he was wearing a bulletproof vest—certainly if you only shot him with a .38.

But Crowther choked that all down. Instead, he said with a straight face and a steady voice, "It will be done, sir. I'll see to it. Long live the patriots of the Blizzard!"

The fat man smiled and leaned backward in smug satisfaction. He pointed to the television set, a giant-screen model that filled an entire wall. "Turn on the news," he said imperiously. "They should be talking about us by now."

Tony Mann pressed the remote-control button. A gorgeous brunette woman was speaking earnestly into the camera. She was saying, "After hearing the audio tape you yourselves just heard, the mayor had this response."

The screen cut to the familiar face of the current mayor. His eyes were furrowed with anger. "I have ordered all members of the Miami Police Department to wear their bulletproof vests," he said self-importantly. "The SWAT team and the Stakeout Unit are on full-time alert to back up patrol officers until this threat to Miami's finest has been resolved."

Crowther rolled his eyes again. This guy's an even bigger asshole than our own fearless leader. Go right on TV and tell whoever's gonna kill your guys that they've got bulletproof torsos now, so you gotta shoot for the head. Give 'em the consumer's guide to killing your own people. And let 'em know just what you got in store for 'em. Tell 'em just exactly what your best shot's gonna be. SWAT and Stakeout.

Crowther shook his head. Up against people led by an asshole like this, he and his buddies might just come out of all this alive.

If they didn't, what the hell. They were going to die like everybody else anyway, weren't they? The only difference was if it was sooner or later. And if your life sucked so much you didn't care if you lived or died, what did it all matter anyhow?

ROBERT KINCAID and Marla Waters carefully locked the doors of the white Miami Police Department patrol car in the parking lot of the Circle Q. They looked around them. After all, something out there was hunting cops of color, and both of them were African-American. But the suburban Miami street looked clear. Nothing but the usual parked cars, and nothing out of the ordinary in the parking lot or inside the glass windows of the minimarket.

They strode inside, relaxed and made their way to the beverage counter. They each pulled a twelve-ounce plastic cup from the steel tube. Kincaid nodded to his partner, and she went first, holding the cup under the nozzle as she pressed down the lever for coffee.

Behind them the window exploded in a shower of glass.

The first bullet caught Marla Waters in the base of the skull. It weighed 139 grains and, even after smashing through the heavy window, it entered the medulla of her brain at a residual velocity of well over two thousand feet per second, its soft nose mushrooming as it went, widening the cone of damage in its wake.

The bullet exploded from her mouth, spraying teeth and blood and bits of flesh in a scatter pattern as it smashed into the stainless-steel coffee urn.

The instant corpse of Marla Waters dropped straight down, crumpling in an ungainly pile of disjointed flesh held inside a blue uniform.

Beside her, Robert Kincaid pivoted toward the doorway and the window. He had heard the glass break and seen Waters's head virtually explode, and an instant later had heard the loud boom of a high-powered rifle's report. Even as his hand flashed to the Glock in his holster and his thumb released the safety strap, there was time for him to wonder at the incongruity of the shot coming after the impact. No one had taught him at the academy about the speed of sound and how you would hear and feel the bullet hit before you heard the shot itself, because most bullets and certainly all high-powered rifle bullets traveled faster than Mach 1.

Kincaid had been a street cop for more than five years, and his experience had cultivated in him a quick reaction time. But not quick enough. His 9 mm was just coming up out of its holster when the glass in front of him exploded in another crystalline shower. Something like an invisible iron fist smashed into his face, driving his head backward even as his body buckled underneath him.

The bullet had caught him just above the left eyebrow—his head had been centered in the killer's cross hairs as he turned, just when the killer was pressing the trigger—and the bullet shattered the skull, coursing through the left hemisphere of his upper brain and blasting a two-inch hole in the back of his skull as it exited, sucking a jet stream of bloody brain matter in its wake.

The pistol fell, unfired, from Officer Kincaid's nerveless fingers as his body collapsed to the floor. His limbs convulsed violently for a few seconds, and then everything left of Kincaid became still.

He had been dead since the moment of the shot. It had just taken his body a few seconds to realize it.

There was only one employee behind the counter of the Circle Q this late. Shabazz Kareem looked on in horror as the shots from outside smashed the glass of the storefront and exploded the heads of the two cops, who collapsed on his freshly washed floors, pools of dark blood quickly spreading out from what was left of their heads. He saw the male officer twitch and jerk and then become still.

Numbed by the horror of it, Kareem stood frozen for a few moments. Like a zombie he moved out from behind the counter and toward the fallen cops. He looked down at them, his guts cramping with the unspeakable horror of what he had just seen.

Then he looked up, toward the windows and the door, toward the outside, toward where the two giant splashes of glass spiderwebbing in the windows surrounded the bullet holes in the window.

He looked up in time to see the third bullet hole appear.

It was as if time had been slowed by some unearthly force. The hole appeared in the window, first round, then the cracks emanating out from it, the glass frosting over and pulling itself inward toward him. Then Shabazz Kareem felt the impact in his chest, a force like nothing he had ever experienced before, something that seemed to empty his lungs and suck his heart dry even as it slammed him backward and made the inside of the store spin crazily in his eyes.

The floor came up from behind him and slammed into his back. He was staring at the ceiling, which had become very blurry. He saw his own dark brown hands come up before his eyes, and they were covered with rich red blood.

They've killed me, too, he realized.

It was his last conscious thought before the darkness swallowed him forever.

WALLACE CROWTHER pulled his 7 mm Mauser rifle back inside the front seat, leaving its muzzle down on the floor next to the open right front window he'd fired from and the butt of the stock resting against the seat. He threw the stolen Buick into gear and floored the accelerator. Behind him he heard Tony Mann grunt as the G-force threw him back against the seat.

"Get the gun back in the car, out of sight," Crowther yelled as he raced the stolen car toward the intersection, putting the Circle Q behind him as fast as he could.

"Don't worry, it's down," Mann barked back, locking the safety on his identical 7 mm.

They were through the intersection. Another intersection coming up. Crowther cut left, then right and then right again to put them on the interstate running north. In little more than a minute, the death scene was almost a mile behind them and receding fast. He didn't even hear any sirens yet.

From behind him, Mann said, "Wally, I gotta know. Why'd you shoot that stupid clerk?"

Behind the wheel, his face lit in the eerie green glow of the dashboard instrument lights, Crowther grinned. God, he loved it when people asked him stupid questions.

"Why the hell not," he said teasingly.

"He wasn't no cop, was he?"

"Shit, he didn't have to be no cop, Tony! He was a nigger, wasn't he?"

Stupid questions. Crowther glanced in the rear-view mirror. Good—he recognized the distinctive headlights of Dewey Huxley's stolen car behind them. The backup man was right there. One more exit, and they could dump these stolen shitbox cars and get into the better car Wally had stolen for them earlier to take them home from the mission in style. It was waiting in the mall. They'd just have to remember to circle the area before they went in on it, make sure nobody had spotted it and alerted the ZOG dogs and staked it out.

Behind him Tony Mann interrupted his thought pattern again.

"I don't get it," said Mann, sounding peeved. "I thought the whole deal was, we kill cops."

Crowther shook his head in frustration. This was the man who just a few days ago made it clear that he was there to kill cops while the rest of them were there to kill coloreds.

Well, hell, what did you say to a guy like that? Especially when he was behind you with a gun and you had both your hands tied up on the steering wheel? You didn't want to piss him off.

"I dunno, Tony," Crowther said after a while, being as diplomatic as he could. "I guess maybe one or the other of us just ain't clear on the concept."

6

Melinda Hoffritz had gotten home at dawn, with several hours of welcome overtime on top of the twelve-hour shift she'd been assigned in the umbrella car. Half-day shifts represented an emergency footing for MPD. In the past that scheduling was used only during the riots and Hurricane Andrew.

Yet she was still awake, the adrenaline almost a bittersweet chemical taste in her mouth. Her new beau had the day off, and she was scheduled to meet him for breakfast.

She'd be running again today, 3:00 p.m. to 3:00 a.m., in response to the cop-killings. It didn't leave much time for sleep. What the hell, she thought. She was young. Besides, if things worked out, there might be a little sleep time.

It was a short walk from the front door of her small apartment to the bedroom. She lived alone.

She slid off the Hidden Agenda vest, its pockets heavy with extra shotgun shells, and tossed it onto a chair. The lightweight, loose black turtleneck was peeled away next, and then she undid the straps of her Second Chance bulletproof vest.

It felt good. The ripping sound of the Velcro had become like a signal to her, the final proof that her tour of police duty was over. The air-conditioning hit her sweat-soaked skin underneath like a refreshing sea breeze.

Hoffritz took a moment to pull the ballistic Kevlar panels out of the cotton carrier and set them aside before she tossed the carrier into the hamper. She pulled off the drenched open-weave T-shirt under it and threw it into the same place. She had half a dozen spare carriers, the strap type and the spandex T-shirt-style they called the Deep Cover; she'd let the ballistic panels air dry and reassemble the vest tomorrow. The panels themselves hadn't been permeated with sweat yet, and besides, you had to wash them in Woolite and let them dry indoors. They wouldn't be dry by afternoon if she washed them.

She reached down by the bed and lifted the coverlet, exposing the large steel box that was bolted to the floor. Her strong, slender fingers deftly punched the combination into the row of buttons, and she lifted the lid. Inside the lockbox was one of the three firearms she possessed, the department-issue Glock 17, fully loaded.

Hoffritz slipped her Colt Gold Cup .45 automatic from her Bruce Nelson inside-the-waistband holster and slid it into the lockbox, still fully loaded and on safe, next to the Glock. She stripped off her jeans and tossed them on the bed; she'd remove the gun belt, holster, spare magazine pouches and clipped-on badge later. She kicked her panties toward the hamper.

Now she was naked except for a black nylon Jerry Aherne holster strapped to her left ankle. It held a scaled-down version of her service pistol, a Colt Mustang loaded with .380 Silvertip hollowpoints. She flipped the holster onto the bed and put the pistol in with the others, locking the lid.

Before Stakeout duty, even after the incident on patrol where she'd had to shoot two men, she had never carried a second gun for backup and only occasionally packed her Glock off duty. But her exposure to violence changed her slowly. First she began carrying the cocked-and-locked Colt automatic all the time. Then, after Frank Cross was shot and disarmed, she went out and bought a second gun for backup. So did most of the other Stakeout cops who didn't already own a weapon suitable for the purpose.

She strode toward the shower, feeling her second wind. Today would be good, she thought as she stepped into the glass-sided stall and treated herself to a tingling cascade of the hottest water she could stand.

Ben Warren was the reason the day would be good. He worked for the state attorney's office as an assistant prosecutor: thirty-two, great looking, athletic build, divorced with no kids and absolutely smitten with her, it seemed.

She had reluctantly accepted the first date, a Miami Heat game. Sports had never excited her, and that night's game was no exception, but Warren was bright and attentive and caring. They talked throughout the game and necked a little after the quiet dinner later.

They had met when she was in Dade County Court to testify against a robber she and her team had arrested during an attempted holdup at an automatic teller. She was used to being hit on but was very selective. Ben Warren was different. He seemed sincere. She had tentatively accepted his offer of the first date and now she was glad she had.

Their second evening was even better. A popular, controversial movie and a fine late dinner on Biscayne Bay. They became more physically involved afterward, but nothing heavy.

Today, she sensed, was the day.

It was about time, she mused, rubbing the herbal shampoo into her naturally light blond hair. How many months had it been since she'd had sex? She couldn't remember. Maybe over a year, since she'd joined Stakeout. All policewomen had the same problem with men, and Hoffritz had it fourfold.

First, any female officer had to avoid dating other cops. It trashed your reputation if you slept with a brother officer, and confirmed the collective fears of all the married ones' wives. She knew policewomen who'd had affairs with cops, and except for a couple of them who wound up marrying, most came to regret it. She felt it was a lesson she didn't have to relearn.

Second, Melinda Hoffritz had come to realize that people considered her drop-dead beautiful. She hadn't figured it out; after all, she had a crooked tooth and everything. But you couldn't argue with people about their perceptions. There was that magazine that wanted her to pose nude, an offer she had turned down less than diplomatically. Her older sister had been a highly paid model and had made a second fortune in a career of multiple planned marriages followed by judiciously settled divorces. She'd always told Melinda that it was the cop, not the model, who was the real beauty of the family and that Melinda was wasting herself on police work. All Melinda knew was, when you had looks, it was awfully hard to gauge men's sincerity and you had to become a very selective judge of character.

Third, most men couldn't cope with a woman who was a cop. Law enforcement was one of those macho professions that people grew up believing only a six-foot-tall man could perform. Six-foot-tall men who did other things for a living seemed to eventually become very insecure in the presence of a woman who carried a gun, got into fights and took people's freedom away. Only an unusually strong man could handle it, and Hoffritz had learned the hard way that there weren't many of that kind around...except for the cops—who she had declared off-limits.

Finally, of course, there were the killings.

After that first incident on patrol—the gunmen's bullets raging at her in a firestorm and doing exactly as she had been trained, dropping each of them with a coolly placed shot—things had changed.

It was strange, she reflected. It wasn't just shootings. She knew female officers who had been shot at, who had shot back, who even wounded people. Within a few weeks of the incident, they were back to being treated like normal people.

But when you had to shoot someone in the line of duty and that person died, Hoffritz had discovered through bitter experience, things changed. You weren't just a cop who had good war stories.

You had become one of those who killed.

Her first day back on the job after the shooting when she was still a patrol officer, some of the guys and one of the other females had met her after work with two bottles of medium-priced champagne. Pasted over each bottle's label was the picture from the front page of the *Miami Crier* of one of the men she had killed.

She just bit her lip, took the bottles and left. She never opened them and eventually took them from the back of her cupboard, emptied them down the sink and threw them away. She couldn't understand why ending someone's life would be cause for celebrating. One of your own surviving, sure. Party hearty. But why did so many of them celebrate the killing, not the surviving? Did the constant proximity to death that accompanied police work somehow blur the distinction? It didn't for her. Why did it for so many others?

And when men who weren't cops found out that you had shot men to death—men, not just one dead man—well, it was as if they had discovered that you were the black widow incarnate. They couldn't look you in the eye anymore, and their potency suddenly dwindled when they were around you. It was as if having taken life, you had become bigger than life and thereby terrifying.

She shook her head in the stinging shower of hot water, trying to clear away the depressing thoughts.

As she washed between her legs, she felt a powerful throbbing. God, she thought, it's been too long.

She tried to picture herself with Ben Warren later.

Instead, she visualized the face of Bob Carmody.

Carmody was a year or two younger than she, fresh-faced, blond. Everyone said they looked like a natural couple. They worked together great. He was shy, sincere, smart, caring. He had tentatively asked her out a few times, and she had gently turned him down, explaining that she didn't date cops. He accepted that, and they were good friends. They saw each other socially sometimes, and he was trying to get her into his hobby, competition handgun shooting.

More important, he understood. He had shot people, too. They had shot criminals together. During one terrible night, that the police psychologists said should have scarred them for life, they had almost died together but had prevailed. They had seen each other naked that night, and what she saw then in his eyes was concern, not lust. That meant something.

But she couldn't violate her own rule. She stopped touching herself and forced herself to think about Ben Warren. Today was going to be the day, dammit, and she had to focus on that.

THE OBSCENE BUDDHA SHAPE that was Ian Altman sprawled on the oversize recliner, his Magnum near his right hand and the newspaper waving in his left. His obedient soldiers of the Blizzard sat around him as he cursed the Miami Police Stakeout Squad.

He squeaked, "Did you see this column by Oliver Teasdale? The pigs have got their killer elite, the Stakeout Squad, after us now! You know what this means?"

None of them answered. Wallace Crowther was thinking, No, asshole, we got no idea at all what you're talkin' about. Why don't you tell us what it means?

As if in answer, Altman shrieked, "I'll tell you what it means! It means they're taking us seriously! It means we've hurt 'em bad! It means they gotta play dirty!"

Dewey Huxley frowned in puzzlement. Crowther winced inside. He knew his burned-out compatriot was about to say something stupid that would piss off the fat man with the money.

He was right. "I don't get it," Huxley told Altman. "We're sniping them, and they're fighting back. Shit, we knew that was gonna happen. How are they fighting dirty?"

Altman's jowls seemed to turn red with anger and quiver. "Don't you know anything? Here, read this guy Teasdale!" He threw the paper at Huxley, who ducked reflexively.

Altman ranted, "These are baby-killing cops! They shoot people for practicing religions they don't like! Can't you see? They're evil! We're the good guys, and they're the bad guys!"

Terrific, thought Crowther. We shoot people for being a different color, and we're the good guys. They shoot people for being a different religion, and they're the bad guys. What's wrong with this picture? But he kept his silence.

Not Huxley. "Wait a minute, man," he told Altman. "I remember what they're talking about there. That was the deal a few months ago, the Devil-worshiper church that caught fire and all them assholes got shot or burned up? Those guys were raping little girls and chopping 'em up. *We* woulda shot their asses for that."

Ian Altman gestured violently, impatiently. The effort seemed to make him short of breath. "If *we* had killed them," he wheezed, "that would have been fine. We are racially pure. We are just. We have the moral imperative. The problem is when mongrel pig bastards do it, it's like that war in the desert where one side's sand niggers were killing the other side's sand niggers. When a good white man kills a subhuman, *that's* a victory. Don't you see?"

Tony Mann moved to head off their leader's growing anger. "I think he sees now, Ian," he said in a calming tone of voice. "I guess what it is, if you aren't the right color—if you're black or if you're blue—if you haven't got the right to live, you haven't got the right to do nothin', see? So even if what you do would be right if we did it, it isn't right if you do it. Dig it, Dewey?"

By now the truth was getting through to Huxley; if he didn't agree with Altman's ravings, he'd be in trouble. He could wind up with Ted, buried in a swamp. "Uh, yeah, man. I gotcha now. I understand, Ian. It just took me a minute, is all."

Altman settled back in his chair, a smug leer of satisfaction spreading over his flabby face. "All right, then," he said, and everyone breathed a sigh of relief.

Crowther had to cover his mouth with his hand to hide his sneer of contempt. Jesus Christ, he thought. It's like a bunch of crazy little boys. They're acting out this weird fantasy like it was real, and with us pulling the triggers for Ian, it *is* real.

Crowther wondered for the hundredth time if there would be any safe way to kill the fat man, steal his money and get the hell out of town.

Then Altman said, "So, here's how it's going to be. They play dirty with us, we play dirty with them.

They're gonna send their hunter-killers after us? We'll just up the stakes.

"Forget just shooting cops on patrol. Let's take it to the pigs' homes, man! Bring it home to them, you dig?" He cackled at his own joke.

It was Tony Mann's turn to look puzzled. "I don't get it, Ian."

Altman turned red again. "Christ, are you *all* idiots? Look, every one of us had some cop take shit home to our families that made them suffer, right? Every one of us here had his life ruined by some cop brought us home in handcuffs, right? Well, why should these ZOG dogs be immune? It's time we went after them *and* their fuckin' families. Give 'em a taste of what they done to us!"

Totally nuts, thought Crowther in disbelief. If it wasn't for Ian's money, and this house to hide in, any bunch of assholes as nuts as this would have been busted days ago. It's only a matter of time. I oughta get the hell outa here, now.

It was then that Huxley smiled and said, "Hey, Ian, I got just the guy. You up for doing a gook instead of a nigger or a spic for a change?"

PHAM TRANG STOOD in front of the mirror in his bedroom, adjusting his Miami Police uniform until it was perfect.

Most Miami cops dressed at work, in the locker room. The Crime Prevention Unit had an exemption. Working a specialty assignment, they were not required to attend the daily roll-call briefings. Because the public schools started at the same time in the morning as the police department day shift, an officer who left from home could be teaching a DARE program to the big kids or a Patch the Pony program to the little ones during first period and make more efficient use of the day.

Trang was, of course, aware of the wave of police killings and the mandatory order to wear the bulletproof vest under the uniform shirt until further notice. But looking in the mirror at the way the tailored uniform perfectly fit his trim body, he rationalized his decision to leave the bulky protective garment in the closet.

He wasn't going out on patrol, into the environment where the murdered officers had been shot. He was going into schools. No terrorist group in America had yet been crazy enough to blow any hope of public support by shooting into schools.

It wasn't just that the vest was hot. His uniform shirt was scrupulously tailored to accentuate his lean, mean body, and with a vest on under it, he'd look as if he was wearing a parachute in back and a reserve chute in the front.

That would appear sloppy. And what if the kids figured out it was a bulletproof vest under his shirt? Wouldn't they be scared? Shouldn't a cop project an image of being unafraid? Did the department want to frighten little kids into thinking even cops weren't safe in Miami unless they wore a bulletproof vest?

Besides, his job for today was teaching in the elementary schools. It was unlikely that he'd even see a supervisor all day. If you violated a rule the bosses didn't notice, was a rule violated? If a tree falls in a forest where there's no one to hear, does it make a sound as it crashes to the floor of the woods?

He was satisfied. He glanced down to make sure that his Glock was properly snapped into the holster. He couldn't remember the last time he'd drawn his gun. But, he knew, kids stared at the gun more than anything else, more than even the badge, when you stood before them in uniform. The teachers all had them draw pictures of Officer Friendly to send to the police station, sort of like thank-you cards. It wouldn't do for a sergeant to see a bunch of childish drawings come in depicting a gun that wasn't snapped into the holster right.

He was satisfied. Pham Trang turned and walked toward the living room and the front door.

Life was good.

In his most-distant memories, Pham Trang could remember the airlift that took him and a couple of the other small children in his family out of Vietnam during the fall of Saigon. The parents never made it. He remembered the lost and lonely helplessness of being a foster child, even in the most well-intentioned and caring homes.

It took him a while to adapt. When he got his U.S. citizenship as a preadolescent, he felt more relief than pride. The bigotry? Sure, that was always there, but at least in the States they didn't murder you for not having politically correct beliefs the way they did in the old country.

Still, Pham Trang was conservative by nature. Only five years ago he married, bought this small house in the suburbs and fathered his first child. They named her Su, because it would sound like Sue, anglicized. He learned early on in the melting pot of America to emulate the adaptations the earlier immigrants had learned. A foreign-sounding surname meant nothing so long as you had an Anglo-sounding first name. If your first name was as ethnic as his own, he learned, you were treated like an alien no matter what the color of your skin or the shape of your facial features.

Su was four. She was proud of her daddy in uniform. He was going to take her with him in the unmarked department car—it was the most trivial of regulation violations—and drop her off at the Montessori preschool on his way to the first stop of the day. There he would solemnly give the children handouts and tell them the story of Patch, the one-eyed pony. Patch the Pony would neigh to the kids, as cute as any living Shetland save for the ominous black patch over the eye he had presumably lost to grown-up humans he trusted. Patch's message was, Nay, Nay, From Strangers Stay Away. All Pham Trang's Patch books and props were in the car, ready to go.

His wife kissed him and Su goodbye and walked back into the kitchen. Trang took his beaming, beautiful daughter by the hand and opened the front door.

He took half a step before he saw what was across the street.

Blue car. Two men. Soldier hats. Rifles. Pointed at him.

Pointed at *Su!*

Instinct took over.

Pham Trang shoved his little daughter roughly aside, coming into the space she had occupied as he thrust her little body back into the safety of the doorjamb just as orange fire flashed from the muzzle of one of the rifles. He heard no sound and felt no pain. He was only aware of a crushing, numbing impact to the left knee as it buckled away from him.

His hand fell reflexively to the crackle-finished polymer butt of his service pistol. He broke it free of the leather holster and was bringing it up when the second rifle, the one in the back seat, bloomed roaring flames.

Again no pain. Only an unbelievably brutal impact into his chest that took his breath away, an awareness that he could no longer feel his lower body and the sounds of screaming behind him, impossibly distant.

He fell back. He knew his hands were weakening. Still he managed to point his lightweight automatic toward the car and pull the trigger, once, twice, three times. He saw glass break and a circle of paint puff away from between the front and back car doors. Suddenly the tires squealed, and the men inside ducked as the car roared away.

The gun now seemed enormously heavy in his hand. Pham Trang couldn't feel his fingers. He lay on his back in the doorway of the house, the car across the street gone now, his eyes trying to focus on the fountain of blood that squirted from the hole in the center of his chest.

He realized he was going to die.

Now his wife was over him, looking at him in horror, little Su clutching her skirt, eyes wide. Pham Trang raised his right hand with enormous effort, and his wife understood: take the gun, protect our child.

He felt her take the pistol from his palm, and spent by the effort, his arm thudded numb and useless to the floor beside him.

The spurts of crimson from his chest weren't rising as high now. He felt light-headed, tingly. Soundlessly he mouthed the words "I love you" to the two people who hovered above him, the two people he loved more than anything. He realized he had protected them.

It was his last awareness on Earth before the darkness became complete.

7

The church was packed, beyond standing-room-only and overflowing out into the street. They had rigged up speakers so the crowd outside could hear Chief John Kearn's eulogy for the murdered policeman Umberto Rodriguez.

Kearn was wearing his dress uniform: gold braid on the shoulders, gold eagles on the collars. There was no gun belt. His 9 mm Glock rested in its usual holster underneath the administrative uniform jacket, which looked like a blue tunic. His uniform cap—nearly new, almost never worn in the more than a year that he had commanded the department—had been respectfully tucked under his arm until he took the pulpit to speak. Beneath him, in a mahogany casket, was the lifeless body of one of his officers, dressed in a similar uniform but without a holster.

He wondered for a moment why, in something as ritualized as a police funeral, they didn't bury a cop with his gun or at least his holster. Didn't other cultures send warriors to their graves armed for the battles of the afterlife? Grimly he realized the answer: in this town they'd dig up a corpse to steal a gun. The ritual had to be modified.

Chief Kearn began to speak.

"It is nothing new that brings us together to mourn these honored dead," he began. "Patrolman Umberto Rodriguez and Patrolman Tyray Borden were not the first two law-enforcement officers to be murdered side by side in this city. It happened a few years ago to a pair of courageous Metro Dade officers. A few years before that, it happened to a pair of FBI agents in our city.

"Nor were they the last to be murdered in tandem. In recent hours officers Marla Waters and Robert Kincaid made the ultimate sacrifice to the people of this community. Many of us will, later today, be at the same solemn ceremony to bid Officer Borden goodbye, and in a few days we shall do the same for officers Kincaid and Waters. And we shall pay identical respects to Florida Highway Patrolman William Eustiss, killed in the line of duty the same night as Umberto and Tyray.

"I hope everyone listening to me knows what it means to be a sworn officer, as these fine people were. To be a sworn police officer means that you have sworn an oath that you will protect the public you serve, up to and including giving your life as you stand like a shield between those innocent persons and the most terrifying evils a police officer exists to protect his or her society from.

"There are times when you can accept the death of a police officer as fate. The building caught fire by an act of God, and the cop gave his life to save that of another. The child was drowning in the river, and the law officer exhausted himself rescuing the child and could no longer stay afloat and drowned, himself. The brakes failed on the bus that was rushing toward the child, and the officer pushed the child out of the way and was run over instead.

"Those are cases where you can wipe your tears and say your prayers and go on with your life, knowing you could have done nothing to change what happened.

"But the tragedy that brings us here today is different.

"I came to this city a little more than a year ago, replacing a police chief who had honorably retired. I was told that it would be the greatest challenge of my career. So far, that has proved true.

"I found a city torn by violence and riven by hate. A city where the patterns of crime were sometimes random and sometimes specific. A city where I saw attacks of white on black and black on white, of black on Hispanic and Hispanic on African-American, and all other combinations imaginable.

"I command a multiethnic police force. I am enormously proud of the men and women I am privileged to lead. All of us are one color—blue.

"A sick and twisted group has taken credit for the murders of the brave officers we have come together to mourn. If we take that group's statements at face value, they have committed these heinous murders out of a bizarre motivation of hatred that no sane and normal person can accept.

"I call upon the people of this city, as I have called upon my police officers, to stand together in the face of this awful and deadly sickness. To stand together to stop the horror, to stop the killing. To close together as one people who say 'No more.'

"When I was a young police officer in the city of New York, we learned the lessons of Foster and Laurie and Piagentini and Jones. They were two pairs of young police officers assassinated by murderers motivated by racial hatred. Each pair consisted of one white patrolman and one black. Each pair was ruthlessly and barbarically murdered for reasons of nothing more than racial hatred.

"The killers in that case happened to be African-American. The obscene and unnatural alliance they had formed was called the BLA, the Black Liberation Army. It was subsequently stamped out by a society that refused to tolerate racist murder in the name of racial pride.

"What we have here is the opposite—people of color who happened to be police officers, murdered partly because they were not white and partly because they wore the shield of the protector. The people who take 'credit,' if that is the word, for these cowardly murders, claim to be Caucasian. But it makes little difference. Their actions are profoundly aberrant and immoral, and a free society cannot tolerate such behavior.

"In the past, I know, people of this city have risen up in anger when they felt that someone like them had been wrongfully slain by someone unlike them—someone who had gotten away with a crime or was likely to, at least in the public perception. But the reality of the situation was not always what that angry public perceived it to be.

"That requires no editorial on a day so solemn as this. But it does remind us that the acts of one or two or half a dozen mutants are not the acts of any segment of this broad society we call Miami. There must be no anger, no revenge, in the streets.

"I am African-American. I have felt, as many of you have felt, the stinging pain of insults hurled by the majority at those who do not belong to it. But I have never violated the public peace in protest against others who have done so.

"I ask most sincerely that you do the same. I ask that no one but the police take to the street. The police, after all, are required to be there anyway. As an innocent clerk in a Circle Q store learned recently, in his last moment among us, one does not have to be the intended victim of a hate crime to become the victim of that hate crime.

"All of us today, my friends, are victims of the bullets that cut down Umberto Rodriguez and Tyray Borden. I ask that we stop the bleeding, not accelerate it. I ask for peace and patience as our officers and detectives work diligently to root out the cause and stop the horror.

"If we do not—if instead we let anger and fear and similar powerful emotions gain the best of our judgment—then more, many more, of our community's members and servants will die.

"If we do not learn these lessons, then, like Umberto Rodriguez, other brave people will die needlessly.

"Thank you."

There was a long and pregnant pause. Then, spreading like a wave, applause moved through the packed church. Many of the congregation were crying.

The chief waved a hand to show his appreciation, and then he was gone. As he strode toward the end of the church, he glanced at his wristwatch. It was just before 9:00 a.m.

John Kearn was almost at his car when he heard his beeper go off. He had told Charlene to beep him only in the most serious emergency. He felt a sense of foreboding.

He was in the car, huddled over the cellular phone where no one else could hear, as he listened to his secretary tell him that another officer had just been assassinated, this one at his home in front of his wife and little girl.

John Kearn bowed his head. He felt his hands clench as if on an invisible throat. It was the only coping mechanism he had to deal with his lonely grief.

IN A PENTHOUSE SUITE of the Peach Tree Marriott in Atlanta, Georgia, three men sat around a conference table. They were all white and middle-aged, with the look of businessmen or accountants about them, dressed in business suits. One would have had to see their stolid-looking, discreetly armed bodyguards out in the hall to guess otherwise.

A small man, looking owlish in his horn-rimmed glasses, spoke first. He was second in command of the CCC, Champions of the Caucasian Cause, for the southeastern region of the United States.

"It is most emphatically not us," he said in a cultured voice. "We have never heard of the Blizzard. We are as concerned as anyone in the movement about ZOG, but we are not on an active physical footing at this time. CCC's current philosophy is to work within the system for change. We almost elected a governor and a congressman in my region last election. We're not going to do anything to disturb that."

The heavyset man in the next seat sneered and hawked contemptuously as he spit tobacco juice into a plastic cup. The man was the Florida State colonel of ARM, the Aryan Revolutionary Movement, and he said, "Shee-it, I didn't think so. CCC done turned into a bunch of pussies like that David Duke in Louisiana. Wouldn't have the balls to plink a li'l ol'

Explorer Scout with a .22, never mind blow the shit out of half a dozen cops."

The third man shook his dignified silver mane and said, "Gentlemen, please. This is not the time to air internecine disputes. All we want to know, Bull, is whether this Blizzard thing is running under your auspices."

The big man snorted again. "Christ, *no,* Hoss! We been wantin' to do that, we would have offed that uppity nigger what's their chief of police first! An' that greasy little spic mayor right alongside him! Would have done it from the inside out, too! Difference between ARM an' you guys, we done *got* cops in our membership! We done infiltrated our patriots right on into the heart of the beast!"

The silver-haired man sighed. "Very well, then. There's something I need to share with you both. As you know, I'm Southern field commander for the Sons of Liberty Independence Movement. SOLID is the newest of the patriotic organizations, and as you know, we've taken a different tack.

"We believe that the white-rights movement in this country has been balkanized for far too long. Our hope—our great white hope, as it were—is to forge an alliance between all groups who share our beliefs. This is why we've been working with both your organizations, which are presently the strongest such groups in Florida. Along, of course, with our own."

"Yeah," interrupted the big man, "and we hear you done been truckin' with the niggers, too."

The silver-haired man flashed a small, tolerant smile. "Only very selectively. We have created, shall we say, a détente with Force X, the recently established group that believes Malcolm X was right about black and white having to be separate. It gives us a legitimizing leverage on the one hand, and on the other, leaves us free to fight our battles on a single front when we do decide to go mobile with armed revolution. Hitler, as you know, had the right idea—make a deal with Stalin just long enough to keep him off your back, and when you've won your battle on the one side, you then unilaterally end the détente, if you get my meaning."

"Shore do," said the heavy man sarcastically. "Y'all remember how well that shit worked for Hitler?"

The small man with the glasses spoke again. "I think we're losing the point here. CCC has nothing to do with the Blizzard. Neither does ARM. We're waiting to hear from SOLID."

"Very well," said the third man. "As I was getting to, we have reached out to form a powerful alliance of all who think as we do. One group that responded to our messages on the computer net does indeed call itself the Blizzard. They gave us all the rhetoric we've been hearing on the tapes that were sent to the radio stations. 'The great white storm that will blanket over the mongrel filth' and all of that. I arranged a meeting on neutral ground.

"It turned out to be most disappointing. Their 'leader' is a gross whale of a man, totally self-indulgent and totally immature. He simply doesn't have a clue. I get the impression of someone whose social development and awareness of the real world stopped somewhere around age ten. Like a little boy who wants to play war with real guns and real targets but doesn't begin to understand what the war is about."

"So," asked the CCC man, "what did you do with him?"

The third man sighed. "In retrospect, we should have put him in the swamp. Who knew he'd act out like this? I just brushed him off, 'Don't call us, we'll call you.' We attempted to trace him. False name and address, of course. The car he came to the meeting in was rented for cash by someone stupid enough to use his real name and driver's license. A Dewey Huxley from Miami. No known address at this time. Small-time dope dealer and junkie."

"Damn," said the big man from ARM. "Lost him, huh? Too bad."

The man with silver hair smiled again. "Not exactly. The whale is really eager for acceptance, apparently. He contacted SOLID a while ago, promising to deliver a large shipment of stolen handguns. No charge. Sort of like an initiation ritual. Like a left-out loner trying to bribe his way into a fraternity."

The men from CCC and ARM looked at each other. The man with the horn-rims said, "Something does need to be done. The killings have brought down the heat on all of us. Our members in south Florida are being terribly harassed by FBI and BATF agents looking for the Blizzard cop-killers."

"You're right on that," said the big man, spitting into his cup again. "I'm keepin' my ass up here in Jo-ja for a spell, just to stay the hell *outa* south Florida till all this blows over. Sooner this ol' fat boy and his asshole friends are in the ground, sooner we can all get back to business."

"We're agreed, then," said the man from SOLID. "Blizzard said it would be contacting us again this week. We'll take them up on their offer and arrange a meeting. I'll provide three fighters from SOLID. If I can count on the same from each of you gentlemen, our problems will be solved."

FRANK CROSS pulled into the station a few minutes after 9:00 a.m. and signed himself and Harrington off over the radio. There was no need to fill out any reports if there had been no action, and there hadn't been.

The Stakeout Unit umbrella cars were working staggered shifts. For Team Two, Cross and Harrington did 9:00 p.m. to 9:00 a.m. West and Baranck were running 5:00 p.m. to 5:00 a.m. Hoffritz and Carmody were assigned 3:00 p.m. to 3:00 a.m. watch. He wondered how long that schedule would hold. The assassination of the crime-prevention patrolman early in the morning was a deviation from the Blizzard's previous pattern of ambushing cops on late-night patrol.

Frank Cross looked at his partner and shook his head. "Wake up, Dan," he snapped, not caring that his voice was sharp.

Harrington grunted and opened his eyes. They were red and rheumy. His lips were the color of raw liver. There were tiny tremors in his hands.

"Where we at?" Harrington's voice was a mumble.

"For Christ's sake, we're at the station, Dan! I just signed us off!"

The older man's red eyes narrowed. "Don't talk to me in that tone of voice," he growled. "Who the fuck you think you are?"

Cross was stepping out of the car, about to open the rear door to retrieve his gym bag of equipment when he said, "I'll tell you who I am, Dan. I'm the guy who has to rely on you to back him up. You know what? I don't think I can count on that anymore. The more I think about it, the more I wonder if I ever could."

Harrington stormed out of the front seat, coming around the back of the dull red Chevy. His chest was heaving. "You little punk," he barked. "You, of all people, talk like I'm a coward? You? I heard all about you, pal! You panicked in that doorway, punk! You let your partners get shot down!"

They were face-to-face now at the back of the trunk. Cross set his gym bag down on the ground. His own voice was seething with rage.

"Let me tell you something, Dan. I had my doubts about myself. More doubts than I had about you at first. But I've got nothing to prove to myself anymore. I stood up, man!"

He was breathing hard. "I remember the Mart shooting, Dan. I was there, remember? I was out there getting shot at while you were cringing behind cover, shooting some dumb shit when it was safe, while he didn't even have his gun loaded.

"And I was in that hotel room, Dan! I remember calling for you, and you weren't there! I remember knowing I was gonna die, and my partner wasn't there!"

Harrington's hand lashed out, grabbing Cross by the collar. He started to say, "If you tell—"

He never finished. Cross reacted before Harrington could finish his words.

Cross worked out every day of his life. He grabbed his partner's wrist with one powerful hand and, with the other, launched a punch as hard as he had ever thrown.

Cross's fist caught Harrington on the side of the face, and Cross felt the shock wave all the way up his arm. Harrington spun and fell heavily to the pavement.

Harrington swore viciously and went for his gun.

His right hand was just closing over the butt of his Glock 21 when Cross cleared leather, his Smith & Wesson .45 automatic coming off safe with an audible click.

Harrington froze. Frank Cross sighted down the barrel of the big silver-colored pistol. "Do it," he breathed. "Go ahead, you yellow bastard. Go ahead. Somebody should've killed you before for what you did."

Harrington didn't move. He just muttered, "You'll be sorry!"

"No," said Cross. "I won't be sorry at all."

After a long moment Frank Cross picked up his gym bag and backed up slowly to his car, never taking his eyes off his supine partner. He set the bag on the roof, fumbled the car open by feel and threw his equipment inside without turning his back on Harrington. He transferred the pistol to his left hand, started the car and slowly drove away.

He didn't put the gun down until he was out of the parking lot and out of sight of his partner.

There had been no one else in the parking area to see any of it.

BEN WARREN DIDN'T show up at seven. The bacon and scrambled eggs Melinda Hoffritz had cooked for them got overdone, and after a while she threw them out.

At seven-thirty she called his apartment. No answer. She dialed his beeper number and punched in her home phone number after the tone. No response.

After a while she stretched out on the couch and fell into a fitful sleep. At almost nine the doorbell rang.

She was on her feet instantly. She glanced in the mirror as she went past it in the foyer. Her blond hair in the ponytail still looked fresh.

A look through the peephole in the door. It was Ben!

She swung the door open and, as soon as he entered, threw herself into his arms. She was wearing nothing under her loose T-shirt and sweatpants. His body felt hard and good.

When she kissed him, he just stood there. Perhaps she had taken him off guard. She teased his lips with her tongue, but the jaws were closed, and she realized now that his arms still hung by his sides.

She stepped back, puzzled.

His expression was somber. "We need to talk," he said.

IT WAS ONLY a few minutes after nine when Hoffritz closed the door behind him. She bolted the locks and reset the alarm like a zombie on autopilot, then walked slowly into her room and threw herself facedown on the bed.

She couldn't get his words out of her mind.

No sooner was he inside her apartment than he'd said, "I told Judy Wecht at the office that we were going out. She told me some things. Tell me honestly, Melinda. Just how many people have you shot?''

She felt the question like a knife. ''I don't put notches on my gun, Ben. What does—''

He cut her off. ''My God, Melinda! I had no idea. I mean, I've taken police-shooting cases before the grand jury. The average police officer in this city never gets into a shooting! But you...''

She tried to tune him out after that and, when she saw that it was hopeless, walked him to the door without another word.

Was it going to be like this for the rest of her life? She felt cold and terribly alone.

She glanced at the telephone by the bed. She pictured Bob Carmody so vividly that she could touch him, taste him.

She saw her hand pick up the phone, saw her fingers punching in the number. Stakeout Unit Team Two had bonded a long time ago. They knew each other's home phone numbers by heart.

After a couple of rings, his sleepy voice came on the line. ''Carmody.''

''Hey,'' she said softly. ''It's Melinda.''

His voice cleared instantly. ''Melinda! Hi! What's up?'' He sounded cheerful, eager. Someone's happy to hear my voice, she thought.

''Nothing much,'' she answered. ''Sorry I woke you up.''

"Oh, that's okay," he said. "I had to get up and answer the phone anyway."

They both laughed for a long moment. Hoffritz tried not to sound like someone on the edge of tears when she said, "Listen, I was wondering . . . do you, um, feel like going shooting or anything?"

8

Dan Harrington parked his ancient Pontiac in the lot at the Metrozoo, as close to the main gate as he could get.

Locking the car, he checked to make sure he'd have everything he needed. The pager was clipped to the left side of his belt, in front of the spare magazine pouch. The Glock 21 .45 automatic, unbelievably light for its size, was holstered behind his right hip with his Miami Police detective badge clipped to the belt in front of it. All the equipment was covered by his dark Hidden Agenda vest, which looked like something a photographer would wear.

He patted his pockets. There was a half-pint flask of Jim Beam in the cargo pocket, curved to fit perfectly against his thigh. Elsewhere in his BDU pants were a pair of handcuffs and a throw-down gun.

None of those things was standard off-duty wear for cops, but they were all indispensable to Dan Harrington.

The gun in his right hip pocket was a cheap little RG 14 revolver that he'd taken off a street kid years ago and kept for himself. Like the five hypervelocity

Stinger .22 Long Rifle cartridges it was loaded with, he had wiped it clean of fingerprints before inserting it into the plastic sandwich bag in his hip pocket.

You never knew when someone might get your gun away from you, and a second weapon could come in handy then. Miami PD approved backup guns, but nothing like this. The caliber was too small and the quality too poor. Harrington even had to carry it with the hammer resting on an empty chamber for fear that it might go off if he dropped it.

Besides, the department rules and regulations stated that any secondary weapon had to be listed to the officer by make, model and serial number in his personnel file. That would have defeated the officer's other, major purpose.

This gun wasn't so much a backup as a throw-down. If he shot the wrong person by mistake, this gun would be in the dead person's hand by the time the other cops got there.

Harrington took pleasure in always having the equipment on his person to commit the perfect murder and get away with it. It gave him a sense of power that all too often had been lacking from the job lately.

Most cops didn't carry handcuffs on their own time, either. Harrington thought they were stupid. His rise from patrolman to detective was due to the extraordinary number of arrests he had made over the years.

If you put on the cuffs, you made the collar. Someone else did the dangerous, dirty work of chasing the suspect down, and all you had to do was move in and snap on the bracelets, and the other cop's pinch was now yours. But you had to have the cuffs to make it work. You also had to know that some other cop with less smarts than yourself was chasing down some bad guy; that was why Dan Harrington also had a scanner in the front seat of the battered sedan, fitted with the proprietary crystals that descrambled the guarded airwaves of Miami Police Department's dispatch center.

The flask hadn't been standard equipment for Harrington when he started on the job some nineteen years ago, but it was now—that or a few of the tiny airplane-size liquor bottles that seasoned drinkers called "nips."

Alcohol, he had learned, was more than just an effective general analgesic in the physical sense. It cured the pain of the mind, as well. It cured fear. It cured humiliation. It cured the hatred of others. . . and of oneself.

It was early afternoon. He'd be doing a night stakeout starting at four. He had slept in as long as he could, but he could still feel a little bit of a hangover from the fifth of whiskey he'd consumed the night before. Already, though, his body craved more. He felt a sense of vague anxiety, a shortness of breath, that he had come to recognize was his body telling him that he needed a small dose of the cure-all.

Naturally there were no cocktail lounges at the public zoo, but then he had his own.

He found his way to a public men's room. He was the only one there. He locked a stall door behind himself and sat down on the lid without dropping his drawers, then slipped the aluminum flask from the side pocket of the BDU pants.

The amber fluid seared its way down his throat, soothing, clarifying. He felt the anxiety melting away.

He thought about what had brought him here, a man in his midforties, locked in a stall in a public john and sipping whiskey....

DAN HARRINGTON WAS BORN forty-five years before in Okeechobee County, Florida. He was a big baby, and his mother, small and frail, died shortly after his birth.

His father was a big man, with iron hands and a taste for liquor. Big Don Harrington was a field boss on one of the sugarcane plantations near Lake Okeechobee. He supervised up to a hundred migrant workers at a time.

Big Don was a lonely and hate-filled man. His one consolation was his only son. Each night, drinking himself to sleep with quart after quart of Ballantine ale, Big Don would insist that his son sit at his feet to learn the ways of the world.

If Dan, in the course of the lesson, asked a question that would put Big Don on the spot for lack of consistency, then the lesson was reinforced by a workout with the big buckled belt.

"Big Don don't take shit from nobody, least of all you!" The belt swept down viciously, again and again.

"Don't take no shit from the big boss! Don't take no shit from the greasers or the jungle bunnies! Don't take no shit from those goddamn bookified assholes at your school!"

Smack!

At last Danny caught his breath enough to blurt, "I get it, Daddy! I get it! You're smarter than them! You tricked 'em good! You made 'em think you was on their side, when you was really foolin' 'em all along!"

The old man stopped for a moment. The boy's words slowly soaked through into his booze-softened brain. He looked down at his son's face, red and desperate.

At length Big Don grinned slowly and let the belt hang loose in his hand. "You right, boy! I fooled 'em good, didn't I? Why beat 'em with your fist when you can beat 'em with your head, I always say!

"On your feet, boy! Let that be a lesson to you! And quit that blubberin'! You're a Harrington, boy, and Harringtons don't cry! C'mon, have a drink with me! I'll learn you to be a man! Hell, what you need a mom for anyhow? We're better off the way we are."

A grateful Danny dragged himself up to the table and forced down the bitter ale his father poured into a dirty water glass for him.

That was how young Dan Harrington formed the values that had guided him to this day. If he stopped to think about it, every rule he followed in his life had been born in those days.

It doesn't matter if you do something society says is bad, so long as you don't get caught.

Everybody's out to screw you, and the only remedy is to screw them first and worst.

What other people think of you doesn't matter. Other people don't matter, period. All that matters is you and how you see yourself.

The strongest fist rules.

When the fist is not appropriate, the right way to handle things is to get behind the other guy's back and screw him up before he even knows he's been had.

Young Harrington was never much for book learning. He went through high school with one year repeated, graduating at nineteen. Then he did a four-year stint in the Army.

That was hell. You couldn't drink nearly as much as you needed to on base, and you couldn't bully a master sergeant.

It was then that the little nips became his friends. His dad would send them to him, hidden inside boxes of cookies, so long as his son paid for them out of his meager private's wages.

He didn't relate well to the others. The young soldiers talked of their girlfriends and their plans for marriage. Harrington had no need of that. The once or so a week that his loins demanded release, his hand was good enough. His old man had warned him about women, weak creatures that demanded much and gave little and left you alone, one way or another, at the least opportune times.

He was twenty-three when he said goodbye to Fort Dix. He headed home to Lake Okeechobee, bunking with his dad at the old man's ramshackle little house. Big Don got him a job working security for the sugarcane plantation.

Dan Harrington had found himself.

It was so easy to get licensed as private security in Florida that even someone who hated school and exams could pass the test with no effort at all. Soon Dan Harrington, now standing over six feet and weighing more than two hundred pounds, reported to work wearing a tin star that said Security on his pale blue uniform shirt. He didn't bother with a billy club; a massive black flashlight with five D-cell batteries swung from a carrier on his left hip. He called it his "nigger-knocker."

It was balanced on his other hip by a Colt Python .357 Magnum revolver.

The Python had cost him three weeks of his guard salary, but the extravagance was worth it. The gun was the Cadillac of firearms, easy to shoot well, and Dan Harrington had learned that a gun was an equalizer. It followed that the better the gun you had, the more "better than equal" you would be. He carried the massive revolver in a swivel holster that slapped against his leg when he walked, constantly reminding him of the power he wielded over the campesinos, the migrant laborers.

The big Colt Magnum had another advantage. Fully loaded, it gave him another three pounds of sharp-edged steel to hit people with. Its heavy barrel was specially reinforced at the Colt factory, he presumed, for just this reason.

His greatest job satisfaction came in prowling the dark corners of the vast plantation compound searching for young lovers and harassing them. The lives of the migrant-labor families were so miserable that sometimes young love and furtive sexual liaisons were the only human pleasures available.

But in one instance, when he dragged a humiliated girl to her parents to get her into trouble and cause ultimate mortification for the parents, he met with more resistance than he'd counted on. After implying that the girl was maybe making out for money, he demanded the father's name, ostensibly to report him to the company.

What he got instead was a broken nose, a dislocated jaw and mangled testicles. Eventually he managed to crawl away, and the next day when he came back with reinforcements, the family was gone without a trace.

He was more determined than ever to strike first, and when his tenure was over with the company, he started looking around for something in the same vein. His lordly position of power had come to an end when the owner died, followed by Big Don Harrington, who slammed his car against a mangrove tree in the aftermath of a drunken celebration of the demise of the big boss.

And the boss's son, whom the Harringtons subtly blackmailed because of his covert homosexuality, gave Dan his walking papers.

That's when he read in the *Miami Crier* that the Miami Police Department was hiring. The pay and the benefits were a lot better than anything in Okeechobee County. His application was accepted, and he worked his way through the academy, and then in the force, with the same beliefs and attitudes that he'd made his own from childhood.

Still sitting on the lid of the toilet at the zoo, Harrington took another swig and snorted derisively when he thought of his interview with that black preppie, Ken Bartlett, for the Stakeout Unit staffing.

Lieutenant Bartlett clearly wasn't impressed with Harrington's role in the four shoot-outs he'd participated in, pointing out that having other officers actually take down the aggressor, or emptying his weapon blindly, or simply being one of many people fired upon, didn't indicate successful positive action.

But then, Harrington's unerring ability to put the cuffs on someone another cop had captured had given him a phenomenal arrest record.

The lieutenant had finally just sighed and closed the file. "Very well, Harrington," he finished crisply. "I don't have anything else for you today. I'm sure we'll be getting back to you."

And he had, by God, he had gotten back! So few cops had volunteered for Stakeout that they'd had to make do with the applicants they had. Including Detective Dan Harrington.

Harrington knew the black lieutenant had no use for him. He returned the sentiments a hundred percent. He remembered one day early on, right after the formation of the three teams on the squad, when Bartlett had come by the range to see how the new Stakeout cops were doing on shooting.

The lieutenant figured Harrington couldn't hear what was happening behind the firing line, what with the din of the shooting and everybody wearing the protective earmuffs, and he made a disparaging remark about his shooting.

And Harrington heard Carmody defend him. The young officer said, "He doesn't screw up and then give up—if he screws up, he gets right back there and fixes it." Harrington would always remember those exact words with as much gratitude as he had ever felt for anyone.

And then the lieutenant said something about how they couldn't afford to screw up at all because they couldn't fix screwups after an innocent citizen was left dead. God, how Harrington hated the lieutenant, the same way his father, Big Don, had hated the big boss on the sugarcane plantation.

SUDDENLY THE FLASK was empty. Harrington couldn't believe he'd finished half a pint of strong liquor that quickly. He stuffed the empty back in his cargo pocket, then stood up. Lost in his reverie, he hadn't noticed whether anyone had come into the men's room or not. Just in case, he made a show of flushing the toilet and adjusting his belt before he came out.

There was no one there.

He looked in the mirror. His face was red; he couldn't help that. His eyes were bloodshot. He reached into his pocket for a pair of Oakley aviator-style sunglasses. Another problem solved. He sprayed breath freshener in his mouth and went outside.

He glanced down at his watch. It was almost time for his meeting, and he started walking toward the appointed part of the zoo.

That, he thought smugly, was the difference between him and the other people on Team Two of the Stakeout Unit. Except for the sergeant and, of course, the hated lieutenant who commanded all three teams within the unit, all of them were patrolman rank. Only he, Harrington, was a detective.

Did that cut any ice? Hell, no!

In other police departments, detectives were paid considerably more than patrol officers of the uniform division, and Harrington thought that was only proper. In Miami the paychecks were virtually the same for both job descriptions. The only cash advantage a cop got with his "promotion" to detective was the opportunity for more overtime.

That was no good to Harrington at all. He didn't need that much more money. Besides, overtime cut into drinking time. It wasn't as if you could drink after work with your buddies, the way the other Stakeout cops seemed to do all the time. That established a pattern of people who had seen you drinking, who'd come forward at the worst possible time to say, yeah, you were always pie-eyed so nobody should be surprised that you were pie-eyed this time, when you got into trouble.

Besides, they didn't know how to drink. Didn't know what good liquor was for. They'd have a few, then bag it. Just a few didn't do the job. When life was a major headache, you didn't take just one aspirin for it, did you?

He approached the intersection of the walking paths in the zoo, where he'd been told to meet his contact. *This* was what distinguished a detective such as himself from an ordinary, blue-suited, loser cop: the ability to cultivate the right sources and the right conduits of information. Information, after all, went in all directions. Doing good at a job didn't mean just tripping up the enemies of whomever you worked for; it also meant knowing how to undermine the people who were on your side and in the way of your ascent to power.

Stakeout didn't appreciate the skills of a detective in their ranks now. But they would. Oh, yes, Dan Harrington chuckled to himself . . . they would.

He was at the appointed place. He glanced around for the first time at the animal cages.

The creature looked like a wolf at first, but squatter, scraggier. It was brown and its back seemed to be shot through with a silver color. He glanced at the sign.

Hyena.

Dan Harrington felt rage flushing his cheeks. Hyena! What was this, the asshole's idea of a statement? Of a joke?

THE FAT MAN with the sweat stains under the armpits of his dress shirt loosened his stained brown necktie. Even though the air-conditioning on the city-issue Chevy was going full tilt, he was hot and uncomfortable.

His rumpled jacket lay alongside him on the front seat of the unmarked police car. It concealed from casual pedestrians on the sidewalk the fact that he had a Glock 19 semiautomatic pistol holstered at his hip. In front of it, clipped to the belt where it could be seen by anyone who saw the holster, was the gold shield of a City of Miami police detective.

His name was Bruce Yount, and he was assigned to the Professional Standards Unit. Miami's internal-affairs squad consisted of ten to fifteen detectives at any given time, plus three sergeants and a lieutenant. Right now, the unit was at full strength: outcries of corruption, bribery and abuse of police powers had plagued the MPD as never before.

Other cops called Professional Standards guys "headhunters." There was, Yount knew in his heart, some truth to that. Being an I.A. dick was fat duty.

Everyone was afraid of you. Even the big bosses left you alone because they knew that if you were disciplined, you could always argue that you were being railroaded because you were sniffing out a dirty cop that the boss in question was trying to protect.

Overtime was ample, and that was unique among Miami cops these days. For most of the department's history, almost unlimited overtime was the great financial advantage of trading a silvery patrolman's shield for the gold-colored badge of a detective.

Today, though, money was tight. The city was strapped. It was bad enough that the recession of the eighties and nineties had left only Coconut Grove, Bay Point, the Brickell Avenue District and the fancy downtown office buildings as tax-generating neighborhoods. Then in 1992 Hurricane Andrew had laid waste to the community, and a huge number of homes and apartment buildings that had once generated municipal taxes now generated nothing but rats that spawned in the as-yet-unrepaired debris.

Budget cuts had hit the department hard. Overtime became almost nonexistent, except when riots threatened.

Professional Standards was an exception. Rooting out corruption within the department at a time when the police weren't popular with the public or the mayor was something that would always get priority.

All Bruce Yount had to do was tell a supervisor that he was staking out a cop he thought was getting payoffs, and he had the authorization for all the overtime he wanted. Never mind that he spent that time reading his cherished true-crime paperbacks; they paid him by the hour, not by the arrest.

Driving along the Florida Turnpike, he saw one of the billboards with the new ad campaign. It gave a toll-free number for turning in people the citizens thought might be up to something naughty and it read, in bold letters, Remember: Public Safety Is Everyone's Business.

He chuckled. For now the only safety that was his business was his own.

That was why he wore the pistol. A lot of the internal-affairs detectives carried their guns in attaché cases or left them locked in their desk drawers. Yount thought they were idiots.

He was hunting cops. Bad cops at that. All cops had guns, all cops were ready to use those guns and bad cops were ready to use them against anyone who was about to expose them, humiliate them, take their power away and send them to a prison where they'd have to bunk with the child molesters in protective custody or get gang raped or murdered by some of the people they'd sent there back when they were good cops. No, Yount would keep his 9 mm pistol very handy, thank you.

He took the 152nd Street exit and followed 152nd Northwest. Soon he would meet the man who would probably be the biggest find of his career in Professional Standards.

His goal was to make deputy chief before he was fifty. He figured he was on a fast track. Professional Standards knew where all the bodies were buried. A former internal-affairs dick was seen as obviously unblemished, for whom could you trust more than the cops who investigated the other cops?

They were also the darlings of a public, a media and a mayor that hated cops in general and the new City of Miami police chief in particular.

He chuckled. All you needed was a controversial unit that had had some explosive incidents. Get one guy who was worried about winding up in the hot seat and convince him to rat out the others.

This was the history of internal-affairs investigations. Yount had deeply studied the "princes of the city" investigation that had led to the complete revamping of SIU, New York City's elite Special Investigations Unit.

They'd caught one cop dirty. He ratted out all the others, setting them up for tape recordings and pictures so they could be caught in illicit acts. Some, when the arrests came down, committed suicide. Most of the others were ruined, and many were imprisoned.

The one who had sold out the others, the Judas goat, became a highly placed investigator with NYPD's internal-affairs section as a reward.

Bruce Yount had driven ten blocks along 152nd Northwest. Coming up on one side was the Metropolitan Correctional Center, the lockup for criminal suspects arrested on federal charges. It seemed an amusing and ironic background for what he was planning to do.

Opposite the correctional center was his destination. He pulled in, parking the car. Even though it was hot, he slipped on his rumpled brown sport coat. In its pocket was the latest Sony miniature tape recorder. It was virtually silent and was voice actuated, yet it rendered sound with incredible clarity. He turned it on.

Leaving the parking lot, he entered the gates of the Metrozoo. He had told his target to meet him near the hyena cage.

That, too, seemed ironically appropriate.

THE TWO MEN STOOD side by side in the metrozoo. The balder one pointed at the bars that held the nearest exhibit and snarled, "What's *this* shit? Hyena's cage? You trying to make a statement or something? If you are, pal, you better spit it out, say it to my face."

Dan Harrington's face was cherry red, and spittle foamed at the corners of his mouth. It was something that Bruce Yount had long ago learned to handle.

"You seem angry, Dan," he said soothingly. "What is it about the hyenas that upsets you?"

"You damn well *know,*" Harrington spewed. "You saying just 'cause I talk to you, I'm some kind of scavenger, licks up the shit the king-of-the-jungle types leave behind? 'Cause if that's your attitude, mister, you and I ain't got a thing to talk about!"

Yount's voice was slow, soothing. "Dan, Dan, Dan. It isn't like that at all. You're not any kind of a scavenger. Neither am I. You're thinking of jackals, not hyenas."

He gestured at the powerful animals behind the bars. Their muscles rippled under sleek, short coats of silver-backed fur.

"My first year doing what I do now, some dirty cop I was investigating called me a hyena," Yount continued. "It sort of piqued my interest, you know? I went to the library and looked them up. Hyenas are a lot like wolves. They work in a pack. They're incredibly loyal to each other. Work together like a smooth, organized team.

"They don't lick up scraps from lions. The doctors who've studied them say they're so strong, they back the lions down off their own kills!"

Yount pointed toward the floor of the hyenas' cage and went on, "Take a look at their droppings. See how white they are? A lion kills a gazelle or something, it eats the choice parts, leaves the skin and the skeleton and everything else. Not the hyena. You know why a hyena's droppings are white?

"I'll tell you why, Dan. Because it gobbles up everything in its path and doesn't leave a thing behind. It eats the bones, Dan. Might leave a tattered scrap of hide just to show he's been there. A hyena's jaws are stronger, pound for pound, than a lion's. Stronger than a great white shark's, for that matter.

"Remember, Dan, I said a hyena's like a wolf? It's loyal to its own kind, and they work together, organized? It's just a wolf that's a helluva lot stronger, that's all. Know what else? Just like a wolf, if a member of the pack turns bad, the hyena will hunt it down and kill it. Or at least drum it out of the pack, keep the pack clean."

Harrington was frowning, puzzled. "What're you getting at, Yount?"

Yount put a hand gently on Harrington's shoulder. The other man didn't pull away. Detective Yount continued, "It's like you guys in Stakeout. The lions are all over you, the papers, the mayor. Sure, the chief may think you're the neatest thing since sliced bread, but that's 'cause you guys are his brainchild. All the way down under him—down a pretty fat slice of depth between him and you guys—there's a whole lot of deputy chiefs just waiting for Kearn to fall on his face so they can take over.

"Dan, between you and I, there's a whole lot of folks figure Stakeout's going to be his downfall. When that happens—not if, but when it happens—Stakeout will be the Judas goat."

Harrington glared at him from under furrowed eyebrows. "What makes you so damn sure?"

Bruce Yount smiled benevolently, raised his hands palms up and shrugged, the studied body language of a man trying to look selfless and helpful. "Dan," he said cheerfully, "come on. They must've given you the history of all the big-city special teams they studied before they made you guys. They took a little bit from LAPD's Special Investigations Section. A little bit from Philly Stakeout. Some from the New York City Stakeout Squad. Am I right?"

"Yeah, I guess," mumbled Harrington suspiciously.

"Well," Yount went on, "maybe they didn't tell you how SIS became a bastard child of LAPD after Chief Gates left. Maybe they didn't tell you how the day after a certain police commissioner went down in New York City, the whole damn Stakeout Squad there found out they'd all been reassigned. Wiped out. Not a one of them ever got a promotion for the rest of their careers, Dan! Not a one of them ever got the detective shield they'd been promised for all that high risk to their lives all those years. Not one! You hearing me, Dan?"

Harrington nodded dumbly, and Yount went on.

"It's going to happen here in Miami, Dan. It's only a matter of time. Whole lot of people will go down with that ship when it sinks! You read me, Dan?"

Harrington nodded again. Yount realized that gestures wouldn't pick up on his pocket tape recorder. "C'mon, Dan, talk to me," he said urgently. "Are you hearing what I'm saying here?"

"Yeah," Harrington blurted. "Yeah. I hear you."

He was seasoned enough a detective that he should have picked up on the fact that he was talking to someone who was wired. But the alcohol he'd consumed, and his anger about the insult of the hyenas, had thrown his natural intellectual defenses off kilter.

"I hear you good," Harrington said.

"Okay," replied Yount, rewarding the other detective with a smile and a pat on the shoulder. "Now, listen up. I know you, partner. You and I are two of a kind. Sure, we never worked together. But we're both detectives that don't get credit for it, right? Both get shit on by glory grabbers 'cause we do our job better than they do theirs, right?"

For the first time Dan Harrington gave an enthusiastic answer. "Damn right," he blurted.

"Okay, then. Now, listen, Dan. When that whole boat full of losers goes down, they're going to be looking for scapegoats. A lot of cops on this job figure that's *my* job, right? Pinpointing scapegoats? Well, let me tell you, partner, the scapegoat's already pinpointed for when Stakeout goes to the bottom. I don't think that's altogether fair, so that's why I'm here."

Harrington squinted at him, confused. God, he needed a drink. "I don't get it."

Yount forced himself to be patient. "You don't get it, Detective Harrington? You still don't get it? Dan, the scapegoat will be you."

Harrington staggered back a step, as if an invisible hand had struck him. "Me?" he cried incredulously. "Whaddaya mean, *me?*"

Yount continued smoothly, slowly. "Dan, Dan, stop and think! I'm the guy from Professional Standards, right? I'm the guy who's got your whole history including stuff you don't know about, right? Just listen to me for a moment, okay?"

Yount raised the index finger of his left hand. He didn't know how bad Harrington was going to spook on him, and he wanted to keep his gun hand free.

"One," he said. "Your own lieutenant thought you were a phony piece of work when you told him about all the shootings you'd been in."

He raised his middle finger to join the first. "Two. The killing of the guy in the Mart was something close to manslaughter. I get to read the reports, remember? All the reports, including the witnesses' statements. Poor bastard didn't even have a loaded gun when you slaughtered him."

"Stop it," wailed Harrington, raising his hands to block his ears. "Just stop it! That thing you do, counting with your fingers, it's like the fuckin' lieutenant!"

Yount lowered his hands. "Okay," he said softly, calmingly. "I understand. But believe me, Dan, you have to hear this.

"Three. The guy you shot in the arm during the ATM robbery. Everybody said you should have shot him in the head. SWAT said so. Firearms Training Unit said so. Everybody thinks you got the shakes, messed up, shot an armed man who was about to kill another cop and shot him in the wrong place, damn near got her killed. Christ, Dan, your own lieutenant thinks so!"

"To hell with both of yous!" stammered Harrington. "Damn nigger's been out to get me since before I even got on the squad!"

Yount paused to savor the sound of those words. He had Harrington on tape calling his own lieutenant a "nigger." Music to his ears. But he was close to the kill now, and instinct told him to press on.

"Just hear me out, Dan," he said, his voice loaded with sympathy but insistent. He had spent his career learning to play his voice like a musical instrument to get the effects he wanted. "Think about number four, Dan—your own partner said you weren't there for him on that kidnap thing."

"No," wailed Harrington miserably. "Nooo! They came from nowhere! Blindsided me before they ever got close to Frank! I came to after Frank was down, just in time to save him and the others! I killed two of the bad guys, for Christ's sake! I was a *hero!*"

Yount forced a gentle smile and shook his head sadly. "Dan, Dan... this is me you're talking to, remember? I saw the reports, Dan! Blood-spatter evidence from at least one you shot indicates he was on the ground and helpless when you killed him. Keys in perfectly with your partner remembering knocking two of them out before he was disarmed and shot. He was out of it. You set it up good, Dan. You fooled almost everybody, but you can't fool me."

Dan Harrington's jaw hung slack, his rheumy eyes unfocused. Finally, after a long moment, his words came in a ragged whisper.

"What... what do you want from me?"

Yount grinned. "Information, Dan." He spoke in the same whispered tone as the beaten detective, but he spoke clearly, with confidence.

"I... I can't..." Harrington was beginning to cry.

It was Yount's cue to put his hand on the other man's shoulder again reassuringly. "Dan," he said in the same whisper, not caring now if the tape could pick up their words. "I want the big fish!

"When those cultists got fried, Christ, if the Waco thing hadn't been bigger and happened just a couple of years before, it would've been on the cover of *Newsweek!* Only reason it didn't hit back at the whole Miami PD the way Waco screwed up the Department of Justice was that the Miami cultists were ten times worse than the Branch Davidians! What can you give me about that, take the heat off you?"

Harrington shook his head numbly. "Damned if I know! *I* didn't have nothing to do with that!"

Yount didn't allow his disappointment to show. He knew Harrington was telling the truth, but it had been worth a shot.

"Okay, then," Yount pressed on. "Your sergeant, Cohen. He's going through a divorce. His wife is telling his friends he's gone nuts from being on Stakeout. That true, Dan?"

Harrington's eyes were wide. "I know nothing about that. Cohen's okay, I guess. He don't screw around with me. It's Bartlett, that damn nigger lieutenant! He's the one!"

Yount grinned. He was getting closer. "Okay, Dan, good," he said urgently. "Tell me. Tell me about Ken Bartlett."

"I told you," Harrington bleated. "He hates me! He screws with me!"

Yount wanted to slap the drunken fool across the face and snap him back to reality. He resisted the urge. He forced himself to remain patient as he said, "No, Dan, that's not what I mean. I mean, what's he done wrong?"

"Huh?"

"Done wrong, Dan! What's he covered up? What's he dirty on? Dammit, ***what can I get him for?***"

Hell, Yount realized, I'm losing it. Stay cool.

Too late. Harrington was backing away from him, still slack jawed, shaking his head sideways as if to say, No! No!

But Detective Bruce Yount was always able to think on his feet. He raised both hands, palms toward the other detective in the gentle, calming gesture they'd taught him at body-language school.

"Never mind Bartlett for now," Yount intoned softly. "What about your partner? What about Frank Cross? Tell me about him."

Yount couldn't believe the change that came over Harrington when the words were spoken. It was as if Harrington's face had gone instantly from a mask of fear to one of hate. It's not too late after all, Yount realized exultantly. I've hit the nerve ending. He hates Cross even more than he hates his black lieutenant.

Harrington's eyes narrowed, and his face lost its slackness and became a tense red ball of muscle as he began to speak. "Yeah, Cross! He's the one you need to go after! Everybody says he never should have got that Combat Cross from that shooting he was in before Stakeout. Everybody says he turned chicken-shit, panicked, got his buddies shot!"

"Yeah," said Yount softly. He didn't realize his lips were coming back from his teeth as he spoke. "Yeah. Tell me about that, Dan!"

"He went crazy in the Mart," Harrington babbled. "Went up on that guy with the shotgun like he was bulletproof. Stupid motherfucker! Didn't do nothing I taught him. Got lucky, that was all. Got lucky, and they called him a hero!" Harrington's voice cracked off into a bitter sob.

Softly, almost inaudibly Yount urged, "Go on."

"Stupid bastard's got everything," Harrington whined. "He's got looks, and now he's a *hero!* He was putting it to that bitch we were supposed to protect, still putting it to her to this day! *He* ain't never been kicked in the—"

Harrington's voice broke off in a choking sound. His head came forward into his hands. He was sobbing, his shoulders convulsing in time with the tears.

Yount forced himself to put an arm around Harrington's shoulders. "It's okay, Dan," he whispered. "It's okay. I'll take care of you. You aren't the bad guy in this, Dan. You just keep talking to me, partner. I won't let you take the fall. It's the others, just like you said. I'll see to it that it all comes down where it belongs. . . ."

Harrington's knees buckled. He collapsed against Bruce Yount, his head on the other detective's shoulder, the sobs racking him uncontrollably. Yount put his arms around him protectively.

"It'll be okay, Dan," he said softly as if he was talking to a baby, the Sony in his pocket picking it all up. "It'll be okay. You'll see. You'll see. . . ."

9

The small man lounged against the wicker chair in his study, exhausted. He brought the marijuana cigarette to his lips, sucking in the smoke greedily and holding it in his lungs as long as he could. At last he exhaled slowly, watching the pungent smoke float up toward the ceiling fan.

He wore white cotton pants, a matching jacket and a black silk shirt with its wide collar open. Gold chains cascaded down his hairless chest, and a diamond-studded Movado wristwatch hung stylishly loose from beneath his slender left hand. Even now, indoors at night, he wore Serengeti aviator sunglasses.

A white plantation hat, the most broad-brimmed that Banana Republic made, covered his balding pate. He inhaled again and glanced covertly at one of the mirrors that adorned almost every wall of his study.

Yes, he thought, smugly satisfied. The reflection looked like Hunter Thompson, the journalist he most sought to emulate.

But admittedly scaled down.

The man in the wicker chair had read everything Dr. Thompson had ever written and everything that had ever been written about him. The only thing wrong was the scale. Thompson was supposed to be over six feet tall and was reputed to carry a .44 Magnum revolver.

There was a public him, and a real him, and he smugly reminded himself often that only he knew the difference.

In his public persona he abhorred firearms. Hundreds of thousands of people had read his words in which he'd made it clear that firearms were the root of America's violent evils. That if even the police abandoned guns, like Britain's bobbies had, there would be a chance for children to grow up without being killed in drive-by shootings and that even if it didn't work, well, at least we would have given peace a chance.

That was for the stupid to consume. In real life he was seldom far from his shiny .22 Magnum.

When you had, you kept what you had. If others had, they might have enough to take yours. That would not do.

If cops hadn't had guns one terrible and formative night in his life, he could have used his gun to kill a couple of them, and everything would have been fine.

You take the power. You keep the power. You do not share the power. That was the immutable law of the powerful as he knew it. Like the famous movie actress who had campaigned for banning private ownership of guns, yet when the cops came to her house when the alarm went off they found her holding a loaded automatic. When they reminded her of her public stance, she said righteously, "That's not for *us.*"

He reached down and touched his loaded .22 Magnum. He understood completely.

The man under the Banana Republic hat stood just barely five feet four inches. The revolver tucked in his waistband was only a .22, but it was a .22 Magnum, thank you very much, and its bright nickel plating made it look larger than it was.

He sucked again on the cannabis. It made him feel bigger.

At birth, some forty years before, he had seemed a normal baby, just very small. His mother told everyone he was a premature infant, even though he was not. By the time he was two, they told his mother the truth: he was a dwarf.

Mother had the money to deal with that. Father—the pig!—didn't have much to do with her after the birth. Stretch marks, and guilt things, and more than he wanted to think about. But the guilt kept Father's unstoppable flow of money coming.

At that time, in Florida in the fifties, the rich already had their Dr. Feelgoods and their clinics. The vogue then for children with his problem was hormone therapy, expensive extracts drawn from the glands of thousands of corpses, in a time before organ-donor cards were the politically correct thing to carry.

When doctors did things under the table for money, they didn't mind doing things that were no more medically correct than politically correct.

There was no refund when his growth had stopped at five feet four. Nor was there any refund when he reached and passed adolescence without a full puberty ever setting in.

A few tendrils of pubic hair still curled at his groin. That was all there had ever been. No beard to speak of, except the silky wisps over the upper lip that one would see on some women after the change of life. One day, in a fit of pique, the man in the wicker chair went to an electrologist and had them removed.

The doctors had given him growth drugs. Why had the fools not thought of testosterone? They'd pillaged practically everything else from the bodies they'd tapped into him, like Frankenstein's monster—why not that specifically male hormone?

He sighed. It was too late for that. A person had to go on. He didn't think of himself as a man. He thought of himself as a person.

No. Something more.

He thought of himself as an entity.

He had inherited his father's intellect and his mother's arch wit. And, of course, the guilt money from Father.

He glanced down into his lap. He hated the thing that the cotton slacks covered, the tiny worm that masqueraded as a penis. In time he had come to think of himself as beyond gender. He was a former of opinions. A doer of deeds. A power behind the throne. A kingmaker!

The mayor understood and accepted him as such. It gave him a warm surge of strength, the same roaring power he felt when he saw his thoughts transformed into words on the printed page. Words that would bend others to his awesome will.

The marijuana cigarette was almost gone. He picked up the gold roach clip and fixed the stub in place to take the last, most powerful hit. As the impact rose from his lungs to his brain, he thought of the people he hated the most, the people he would crush.

The pigs, the blue-suited pigs!

His mother had shielded him from the cruel hatreds of the world. It was she who convinced him that the scorn of others was the mark of their fear of him, convinced him that he was the most powerful, most dynamic human being on Earth. That even Father, wealthy enough that Mother showed him Father's picture in *Forbes* magazine, would cringe in fear of his power!

And yet poor Mother, still herself a child of society's tight-assed and plebeian mores, was to the end bound by hated conventions and standards. This was what killed her.

Or, rather, it was what allowed the pigs to kill her.

He still remembered that terrible night, remembered it with a rage so forcible that he crushed the stub of the marijuana cigarette into his crystal ashtray in the anger of the memory.

He had been seventeen. He and Mother had never discussed sex at all, let alone homosexuality. Mother didn't know that at night, after the sherry and the sleeping pills had closed her eyes, her son was out and about, burying his face in the laps of young men who had what he had been denied, who had what he needed to possess any way he could consume it.

Life was good. Life was his, to take and do with as he chose.

Until that night.

Until the night of the policemen.

He was in an alley downtown at the time, on his knees before a young black man, when the stealthy feet of the police officers approached from behind him. Suddenly everything was bathed in a shameful light, and there were loud, deep, harsh voices.

He could hear the deep, gruff voice of the first cop as if it had happened this morning. "Dammit, Anthony, didn't I tell you, stay off my beat? Didn't I fuckin' *tell* you, get your kicks from these white faggots someplace I don't have to see you?"

He was outraged. No one interfered with him and his pleasures. No one!

"Leave us alone," he shrieked. "You want money? Here, you troglodyte, take the money and go away!"

He reached for his wallet.

The other cop yelled, in a terrifying tone of voice, "Don't move! Keep your hand where I can see it!"

He realized with horror that the cop had drawn his gun.

"Oh," he had cried in disgust. "Oh!" But he moved slowly when he took his hand out. The cop lowered the gun.

That made him feel bold. He cried shrilly, "What's the matter, Piggy? That gun the only thing you've got that's big and hard?"

The man he'd been with, who was hastily zipping up his pants, saw what was happening. He started to say, "For Christ's sake—"

But the young man wasn't able to finish it.

The man who now sat in the wicker chair had screamed, in his still-high-pitched voice, "You dumb nigger! This isn't about you! It's about me!"

He turned toward the cop, flouncing defiantly, his hands on his hips. "Just who do you think you are? I can buy you and sell you! Just get out of here!"

The cops looked at each other and grinned. The cop who had drawn the gun holstered it sheepishly. Then he said, "Sir, or ma'am, or whoever or whatever you are, you are under arrest for lewd and lascivious—"

He didn't let the cop finish. A red haze seemed to descend on everything he saw, and he lunged at the cop's gun to kill him with it.

At that point, all bets were off.

The cop tried to knee him in the groin as he came at the holster, but misjudged his height. The officer's knee caught him at the solar plexus instead, expelling his breath in a gagging whoosh of air.

The first cop, the one with the gruff voice, also lost his humor instantly. His long black flashlight came down, striking the seventeen-year-old in the face and shattering his jaw.

Lying on the sidewalk, he burbled hysterically, "I wah muh mumma! I wah muh mumma!"

The cops obliged. They roughly handcuffed and searched him and took him to a hospital where his broken jaw was wired shut, then brought him to a downtown station house from which his mother was called.

When Mother arrived, they told her everything.

A day later he limped from his silken bedroom, his jaw still wired shut, into her room to talk to her and thank her for paying the bail. He brought a notepad on which he'd written his demands.

The pigs who beat me must be fired!
The pigs who beat me must be sent to prison!
The pigs who beat me must be sued for every penny until their children are on the public dole!

But he never had the chance to share that with Mother. He found her enshrouded in her own satin sheets, her face white and her mouth blue, the bottle of barbiturates empty beside her and the stench of bodily wastes rising from the satin bedclothing.

He knelt there for a very long time, smearing his face in remorse with the mucky stuff from the bed, unable to speak a coherent word because of the wires that held his jaw shut.

Keening in a terrible, high-pitched wail of grief and of pain.

It was the cops who had done it. The pigs!

He swore then that he would spend the rest of his life making them pay. Them and their kind. Filthy, crude things who didn't understand people's needs and feelings, who waited in the darkness to pounce on them and hurt them for doing things that they simply didn't understand.

And now, today, it seemed that he was winning.

The doorbell rang.

He sighed deeply and slowly brought himself to his feet. As he stumbled toward the door, he caught sight of himself in one of the ever-present mirrors.

Yes, he thought with self-satisfaction, I look just like Hunter Thompson. I use all the drugs and liquor I want, and they only make me better. The Magnum gun, the shades, the hat... it's all there!

The bell rang insistently. The man behind the Serengeti sunglasses frowned in exasperation as he flounced forward.

He checked his image in the mirror one last time and decided to cover the gun.

Some of the boys coming might become frightened by it.

BRUCE YOUNT didn't even like other cops. He had no use at all for security guards.

It was already dark when he walked into the foyer of the exclusive apartment building in Coconut Grove. The knot of his necktie had been pulled down level with the top of his shirt pocket, and the brown sport coat that he held over his right shoulder to hide his pistol smelled of armpit sweat.

He was in no mood at all for the dark-skinned man who approached him in a crisp white uniform shirt and said, "Security. Do you have some identification?"

Yount's nostrils flared like a hyena's as he flipped the coat off his shoulder, revealing the Glock automatic in his hip holster and the gold shield clipped in front of it. "Detective Yount, Miami Police. That enough ID for you?" he snarled.

The guard swallowed, his mouth suddenly dry. "Please, *señor,* I'm only—"

Yount cut him off. "You're only nothing," he barked. "You're only a useless rent-a-cop! You gonna get outa my way, or am I gonna run you in for obstruction of justice and interfering with a real cop in the performance of his duties? Huh?"

The guard stepped back obsequiously.

"Officer...Detective...I'm only trying to do my job."

Yount grunted and brushed past him, deliberately bumping him as he headed to the elevator. He knew where he had to go.

He pressed the button. After a long time of nothing happening, he turned and snapped, "Are you gonna turn this damn thing on, or do I have to..."

Nothing more had to be said. The flustered security guard stepped behind a podium and pressed a button. The elevator door opened.

Grinning in triumph, Yount entered the little cubicle and pressed the button for the appropriate floor. The door silently closed, and the elevator began to rise.

Yount was fuming. That drunk detective was his! It was only a matter of time.

He felt dirty, shaming himself, comparing himself to Harrington. But, hell, wasn't that what the best interrogators, the best detectives, always did?

They taught you how to get a confession out of a murderer. *"Yeah, buddy, I know how you feel. If I'd been having to put up with that garbage all the time, and she burned my breakfast on an important morning like that, well, hell, I might have stuck a knife in her, too! But, see, you gotta tell me how it happened...."*

Or you were doing the interrogation on some rat bastard who had put it to his own daughter. *"Hey, I understand, man! They get that age, they get real seductive, you know? Can't nobody blame you for doing what comes naturally, right? I understand.*

But, see, I need you to talk about it, tell me how it happened. . . ."

Yount shivered. He felt dirty. Sometimes this whole internal-affairs trip made him feel dirty.

But, what the hell, you did what you had to do. There were over a thousand men and women on the Miami Police Department and only a handful of chiefs, and only one real chief on top of them. You could die of old age waiting for somebody to retire or get a better job or move out of the way for some other reason and make room for you.

Yount would make his room. His own way.

Detective? Big deal! Not even a take-home car. No salary advantage to go with the gold shield. Professional Standards detectives could at least get the overtime, but Bruce Yount was beginning to really hate working the internal-affairs beat.

The elevator stopped, and the door opened smoothly, silently. Just a couple of steps across the deep-pile carpeting of this fancy building where the fat cats lived, and he'd be where he needed to be.

He'd be with the man who had the inside track to the real power in the city. The man he had to serve, to feed information, so he could go up, up the ladder to where the true power was in the police department.

Yount rang the doorbell.

He waited for a long time and was about to ring it again when the oaken door swung open suddenly.

In front of him stood a very small man. The little guy was wearing white cotton pants and suit coat, and a black silk shirt underneath. He wore a floppy white hat with a wide brim, and although designer sunglasses shadowed his eyes even at this late hour, Yount could see that he was squinting to see who his visitor was.

The small, beardless face smiled. "Detective Yount," the little man said in a high-pitched whine. "Do come in. I hope you were able to deliver for me today."

Christ, moaned Yount to himself, what a little fairy.

But what he said out loud was, "I think you'll be happy with what I have to share with you. It may give you something to work with in the future. I'd be the last person in Miami to disappoint Oliver Teasdale."

10

Bobby Donahue guided the big Regional Parcel Service truck out through the gates of Southland Distributors and turned right on the access road that would take them back to the interstate. He turned to his trainee, John Kellerman, and said, "Amazing, isn't it? You'd think they'd ship this many guns by armored truck with a bunch of guards with machine guns, wouldn't you? Instead, every day we truck enough weapons out of here to take a beachhead in Cuba."

"Weird," agreed Kellerman. "I always thought it was against the law to ship guns by mail or RPS or like that."

"That's just for regular people," Donahue explained. "They gotta get to the sporting-goods store somehow, right? The manufacturer ships them to a distributor like Southland. The distributor ships them wholesale to the sporting-goods stores and the gun shops, like the load we got here. Just freight, that's all."

Kellerman said, "Guns everywhere, huh? Hey, you hear about the tourist in Miami?"

"I don't think so."

"Well, there's this tourist, see, comes to Miami for the first time. He's sitting at a bar, looking over his shoulder like he's real paranoid, right? Guy sitting next to him says, 'Hey, buddy, something wrong?'

"Well, the tourist says, 'Gee, everybody told me Miami's all fulla crime, you know?' Guy sitting next to him says, 'Hey, buddy, that's bullshit. They just say that to scare the visitors. I've lived in Miami all my life. There ain't no crime problem here.'

"Well, the tourist says, 'Hey, man, it's a relief to hear that! By the way, what do you do for a living?'

"And the guy from Miami says, 'Oh, nothing special. I'm a tail gunner on a bread truck.' "

Donahue burst out laughing. Then the laughter stopped.

"What the fuck?"

Up ahead of them were two sedans parked across the lonely access road, blocking it. There were three men standing around outside the cars.

"Hell," said Kellerman. "Looks like a fender bender. Want to stop, help them push the cars outa the road? Can't get by them anyway."

Donahue sighed and applied the brakes. When were regular motorists going to learn to drive like he did, like a professional? He pulled the RPS step van in behind the two cars and set the brake. Couldn't be too bad. There wasn't any damage that he could see from here.

The RPS men walked up to the three guys in the road. One with a cowboy hat and an unkempt sandy beard looked at them with a big, welcoming smile.

Donahue said, "Can we help you, fellas?"

"You bet," said the bearded guy, casually reaching under his cotton vest and producing the biggest, ugliest automatic pistol the RPS driver had ever seen. Donahue went cold. He heard someone say, "These guys are lucky they're white men. They behave, we'll let them live."

Donahue wished he had a tail gunner.

IT WASN'T QUITE NOON.

Bob Carmody pushed himself up on one elbow on the clean, cool sheets and looked down at the woman beside him.

Melinda Hoffritz's eyes were closed. The fine blond hair cascaded down the sides of her unblemished, tan cheeks. The tan line ended on the firm, round breasts. They were milky white, the nipples so pale a pink that the color almost blended with the flesh around them.

Her chest rose and fell gently above her firm, flat abdomen. An almost invisible line of soft blond down began just below her deep, oval navel, trailing down through another tan line and blossoming into the pale blond puff of her silken pubic hair. It was still damp.

She opened her eyes, looked at him, smiled. Behind the gorgeous face, through the windows of the wide eyes, he saw something surprisingly vulnerable. He touched her face, tracing the tip of his finger down her soft cheek.

"Hi," she whispered.

"Hi."

"What are you thinking?"

He smiled tenderly. "I'm thinking how cute that little crooked tooth of yours is."

Hoffritz blinked. Everyone—from men to her sister, the model—had always told her how perfect she was. Her hair, her face, her figure. She couldn't remember anyone ever saying they liked her imperfections. She felt something start to well up in her eyes, so she closed them hard and buried her face against his smooth, hard chest.

"What's wrong?"

She caught the gentle concern in his voice.

She shook her head, as if to say, Nothing at all. What she said aloud, barely a whisper, was, "Hold me."

He did. She squeezed back. She was stronger than she looked.

Carmody felt warm moisture on his chest. He sensed that it was the wrong time to ask why she was crying.

Instead, he hugged her a little tighter, and she responded. He let his fingertips trail gently down the curve of her back, into the hollow where her spine met the smooth, round buttocks. She quivered. He touched her again.

She had been so responsive! When he'd come by to pick her up to go to the range, she invited him in. She looked soft and lovely.

Their eyes had met. There was no mistaking the meaning of her look. But she was projecting something else, too... a feeling of pain, of hurt, a silent plea that she wouldn't be hurt again.

He had reached his hands out to hers. Her fingertips slid against his, and then she was grasping his hands firmly, almost desperately. He saw her eyes close, her chin tilt up toward him.

He barely touched her lips. They were soft and moist and sweet. Tentatively he brought the tip of his tongue between them, and hers moved in response, and then she was in his arms. The softness had become firm, and the hesitancy changed to a strong animal resolve.

She looked up at him now. "You were so gentle," she murmured.

He was glad. He knew how strongly most men came on to her. He didn't want her to think he was like them. He had wanted her from the first moment he'd seen her, more than a year ago. Knowing her, coming to appreciate her keen mind and her clear judgment and her unhesitating courage—and sharing with her dangers that had brought them both to the edge of death—he had come to want her all the more.

I've needed you for so long, he thought. "So very long." He realized that he had actually said the last three words aloud.

She smiled at him, the tears fading rapidly. Her fingers reached down between his legs.

She said impishly, "It is, isn't it?"

Then she was pulling him toward her with the same urgency as before.

THE SIX MEN plus their weaponry were a full load for the Beechcraft KingAir, but the pilot didn't mind. He was being well paid, the plane was rented anyway and besides, he was a sympathizer.

Two of the men in the back, who wore black jumpsuits and nylon military webbing over jeans and T-shirts, sat together. Each had a GI .45 automatic in a holster tied halfway down their thigh and a black baseball cap. The nylon pouches on their belts contained spare magazines for the M-16 machine guns racked in the cargo area in back. None of their clothing bore any markings. The bigger of the two spoke.

"What they tell us, it oughta go smooth," he drawled. "Shame to do it, though. My way of thinking, them assholes been doing patriots' work, even if they are a bunch of dip-shit dorks."

In the seats on the opposite side of the fuselage were two more men, Caucasians like the others. This pair was also dressed alike. They wore khaki BDU pants and oversize shirts the same color that were tails-out and bulging underneath from their Matthews bulletproof vests. Their Smith & Wesson 9 mm automatics were hidden under their shirttails, along with the spare high-capacity magazines. Their flight caps were also khaki. One of them said, "If that's what CCC thinks, maybe CCC should be running with them instead of with us. Hope we get our minds made up before we get on the ground and have to deal with the crazy bastards."

In the rear seats were two more identically dressed white males. These each wore sport slacks, oversize golf shirts that concealed body armor, and shoulder holsters. They had taken off their light summer tweed sport coats. "Goddammit," said the leaner of the two, "this is supposed to be a unified operation. SOLID wants ARM *and* CCC to be working together with us on this. If good white men can't work together to solve this problem, our grandchildren won't ever know anything but a nation of mongrels."

"Shit-fire," said one of the men in khaki contemptuously. "Does this deal look like any of us got our shit together? CCC can't make up its own mind whether they wanna be strutting around running for office like them David Duke wimps in their Brooks Brothers suits, or combat-jumping like a SWAT team with their bad-ass blacksuits and M-16s. Ain't even got *this* deal organized right. Instead of mixing us all up like this, like a one-world Commie UN, we shoulda planned it like the great leader would of. He had his storm troopers do the lightning war, had the Italians come in all by themselves on the flank for backup, and had his Gestapo spies and stuff on the ground to get everything ready for both of 'em. Not all mixed together like we are!"

"Yes," said one of the men in sport clothes placatingly, "but it didn't work. Nobody here wants to be reduced to being the Italian army. We all want to be the storm troopers. Come the new beginning, there'll be room for all of us. Besides, we do have people on the ground, perfectly situated to guide us in and come in from behind to back us up."

"Yeah, right," said a man in blacksuit sarcastically. "Mishmash of us, mishmash of them. One thing that will make it work, them Blizzard guys ain't got no idea how to work nothing! We gonna smoke 'em so fast they ain't gonna know what hit 'em. Serves 'em right, I guess, making the rest of us patriots look bad, bringing this whole ZOG storm down on all of us. They got no sense of timing."

The man in khaki laughed. "Timing," he cried incredulously. "Y'all mean, put your blacksuits and M-16s in mothballs and get all yuppie-fied and pussified like that there David Duke done with the Ku Klux? Shit, is that CCC's idea of timing?"

"No," snapped Blacksuit. "Our idea of timing is to penetrate the heart of the beast. Ten years, twenty years tops, we'll have our people on Capitol Hill. Our people will do the coup properly. Instead of fighting the entire U.S. Armed Forces, we'll *com-*

mand them! *That's* when the Newest Testament will become a reality!"

There were a couple of cheers at the mention of the Newest Testament, which was Aryan supremacist code for the underground novel *The Turner Diaries*. It depicts a future revolution in which all nonwhites and all Jews are hung from lampposts in the streets, and a new reich in the spirit of Adolf Hitler takes over the United States and then the world. This work, like the mention of the Bible to the religious, brought a second of reverence to their faces.

"All right, but that's twenty years from now." Sport Clothes brought them back to the matter at hand. "Let's just think a few hours ahead for now. What do *you* guys have for fallback if things go wrong? The plane becomes disabled, for instance."

Blacksuit and Khaki looked at each other blankly.

"We got fallback," said Khaki. "Gonna bomb on outa here soon as them Blizzards are all down, scoot on up to Jacksonville, dump this bird at the hideout airstrip and take off on our own in the different Cessnas."

"Hah," barked Blacksuit. "Don't forget, they want us to bring back at least one prisoner for interrogation." He undid a Velcro pouch on his black nylon utility belt and pulled out a pair of handcuffs, waving them as if to tease. "ARM and SOLID can do what they want. We're bringing CCC back an intelligence source." He glowered at the man from

SOLID. "We don't like being kept in the dark about shit until it's already going bad," he added acidly.

Sport Clothes shook his head with irritation. "That's not what I mean, guys. We've always gotta have a worst-case-scenario fallback. What are you gonna do if the plane gets disabled, for example?"

Blacksuit shrugged. "Gonna dump these clothes and the M-16s, keep our .45s. We got jeans and T-shirts underneath. Steal a car, drive the hell out, get to a safehouse, I guess."

Khaki frowned. "Y'all only need a plan for defeat if you're gonna get defeated. That's why the white race is in such trouble these days. Everybody thinks defeat. Nobody thinks victory, like we do in ARM!"

Sport Clothes sighed. He thought about the keys to the rented van that were in his trouser pocket. An identical pair was in the pocket of the SOLID man next to him, and a third set in the pockets of SOLID's man on the ground. The van would be parked within a hundred yards of where the arms transfer—which would turn into the wipeout of the Blizzard—was scheduled to go down.

The van would take them and their prisoner to the Gulf Coast, where a chartered boat already waited to bring them across the Gulf to Louisiana. Other stalwarts of SOLID would meet them there, snatching victory from the jaws of any possible defeat.

Sport Clothes wondered if he should tell the CCC blacksuits and the khaki-clad ARM soldiers about the van and offer them a lift. He decided against it.

People that stupid would just slow them down anyway.

MELINDA HOFFRITZ and Bob Carmody checked out their powder blue Chevy unmarked before heading out on umbrella patrol. Everything worked. They inspected their twin shotguns, Benelli Super 90 entry guns. Each automatic shotgun had a full four rounds of double-O buckshot in the magazine, chambers empty. They each had more shells in the pockets of their Hidden Agenda vests.

The vests were the kind that photographers wore. You saw them all over Miami. No one looked at them twice. But sewn inside hidden pockets were pull-down tabs. The one over the right chest said Police. The one over the left chest carried the embroidered shield of the City of Miami Police Department. The one in the back pulled down and said Police in even bigger, reflective letters. Each had a fistful of spare shotgun shells in the lower right pocket of the vest. And each vest concealed a Colt .45 automatic in a Bruce Nelson holster.

They always took turns driving. Today was Carmody's day. He wheeled the car out of the parking lot and onto the street. As he drove, he looked at his partner sheepishly and said, "You're sure I'm not dreaming?"

She reached across the front seat and squeezed his hand firmly, down low where no one could see. It was the kiss of death in the department for male and female partners to become intimate with each other.

"It was real," she said quietly but firmly. "It was real and it was beautiful."

After a long moment he asked, "Why today?"

"I'll tell you sometime," she answered slowly. "Bob, I don't want to analyze it. I don't want to intellectualize it. I loved the way it happened. I needed it. It was great. *You* were great."

He just blushed.

"Sometime," she continued, "I'll even tell you how long I've been wanting to. How about you?"

"Probably since I first saw you," he blurted honestly.

She squeezed his hand again reassuringly.

The question hung in the silent air for a long time. Finally Hoffritz said, "Are you sorry?"

"God, no!"

"I mean, it might change things."

"How?"

"You know. Cops who are intimate aren't supposed to ride together. I've heard the horror stories, when things go wrong, either because the woman officer feels the need to prove herself, or because the guy feels obliged to protect her, or just acts on his protective instinct toward women. A lot of wrong conclusions can be drawn while people make split-second decisions. And then the dynamics change, potentially setting off a chain reaction."

"Don't worry," her partner retorted. "You and I have been in a lot of bad scenes together. You never misstepped once. I never doubted you once. You never had to prove anything to me."

"Sure I did," she sighed. "Every woman who's ever worn a badge has had to prove herself. Prove she wouldn't lock herself in the patrol car screaming if things turned ugly."

"Hell," her partner answered, "so does every male rookie cop. I remember the vibes I got from the other guys when we all came onto Stakeout together. 'So, here's the baby-faced kid, won all the shooting medals. Well, kid, think you can handle it when the target's shootin' back?' We all go through that, Melinda."

"I guess," she said. She didn't want to pursue the point. Instead, she asked, "Sure you're not sorry about today?"

"Not hardly!"

"Me, neither," she said warmly. She'd needed it so bad. Not just the sex, either. The warmth. The caring. Being cared about by somebody who knew who you were, not just what you looked like or seemed like.

Carmody couldn't contain the question any longer. He asked very softly, "Where do we go from here? Do you want to. . . you know. . ."

"Yes," she said firmly.

"I can be discreet."

"That won't be enough," she said flatly, knowing.

"Why not?"

"Things will change. You know how everybody's looking at Frank since he moved in with Monica Wollman. It started with him bodyguarding her on duty. Everybody's going, 'ooh, naughty, naughty.' It's as if we're the only job in the world where you can't have a meaningful relationship with someone you met at work."

Carmody took hope in those words. *Meaningful relationship.*

He said insistently, "We're different."

"How?"

"Dammit, Melinda, you're the best partner I ever had! That won't change! All I want is to be with you . . . more."

"Me, too," Melinda Hoffritz murmured. "But that's two things right there. We're together more, maybe we'll get sick of each other. I don't want that. Bob, I can't tell you how I feel right now, how good this morning made me feel. It's something I've needed for a long time. *Wanted* for a long time. I'm just afraid how it could affect us out here.

"And that's the other thing. Stakeout's the best thing that's happened to me since I've been on the job, you know? Like you said before—nothing left to prove. Going home at night knowing I made a difference. Knowing that when I came to work there were...things out there, the worst kind of things that could prey on decent, innocent people. And knowing that after I went home, I'd done something so those things weren't out there anymore. They were locked up, or they were where they wouldn't hurt good people anymore."

She paused and added in a very soft voice, "I'm not ready to give that up."

Bob Carmody said, "Look, I know what you mean. I don't have anything left to prove to anybody, either. Tell you the truth, I wondered myself in the beginning. Wondered if I could stand up when it counted, if I could do it for real like I did on the range. I guess I did okay. If I had to switch to one of the other Stakeout teams, I could do it. If I had to even give up Stakeout and go back to teaching on the range, well, I guess I could do that, too."

They were at a stoplight. It was safe to turn and look into her eyes. He did.

"If that's what it came down to," he said sincerely, "I would." He was still squeezing her hand. His mind flashed back to this morning, the two of them nude together in her bed.

He said simply, "I want to be with you."

She squeezed his hand back and said, "I want to be with you, too. That's why we have to think this out."

A horn blared behind them, snapping them out of their reverie. Carmody blushed, let go of her hand

and gunned the car forward. They'd been mooning with each other long after the light turned green.

Hoffritz looked down at her now-empty hand, still warm from his touch. "You see what I mean," she said.

11

"Come with me," Dewey Huxley told Wallace Crowther and Tony Mann. They followed him obediently into the darkened basement of the expensive Altman house. Outside, in the huge garage, the stolen guns had already been transferred.

Crowther was proud of his part in the operation. He was a professional car thief, and his skills had kept things rolling. First they'd left the RPS drivers handcuffed and gagged in the dry culvert alongside the access road where the hijacking had gone down. Then he had driven the step van back up the access road to the empty lot where the stolen tractor trailer waited, the ramp already down to drive the RPS truck inside. The stolen cars that had faked the traffic accident were left where the semi had been.

Then, the convoluted track back, each step guaranteed to be another piece in an insoluble puzzle for anyone who wanted to find out where the stolen guns had gone. The guns now filled a minivan with stolen plates and tinted windows. In the garage. Waiting with the other vehicles.

Waiting for tonight.

Dewey Huxley spun the dial of the combination lock on the huge subterranean vault. It took him a few times to get it right. He was doing things rapidly, overconfidently, because of the cocaine he'd snorted.

Then the vault door swung open, and Huxley walked his Blizzard friends inside.

They said in unison, "Holy shit!"

Before them lay an armory they wouldn't have expected to see outside a U.S. military base.

Ten LAW rockets in their olive drab disposable plastic launchers were stacked in a row. Three M-60 .30-caliber machine guns were set up on bipods, next to case after steel O.D. case of linked belts of ammunition.

Huxley flipped open a wooden crate. Inside, stacked in a row, were blue plastic boxes. He undid one and pulled out a gleaming black Beretta 9 mm automatic pistol.

"Remember Hurricane Andrew? Well, there's a silver lining in every cloud, I guess," Huxley said triumphantly. "The hurricane wiped out Homestead Air Force Base, right down the way here. They were able to get the nukes down in the bomb shelters, no problem. Shoulda just put the F-16s in the air, man, had 'em flying up over the storm where they'd be safe or land 'em someplace else for a while. But, no, the Zionists who are supposed to be running our government just left 'em there on the ground to get trashed, man, sixteen million bucks apiece.''

Dewey Huxley's eyes glinted bright with something even more dangerous than the cocaine as he scanned the treasure trove of deadly weaponry. Then he went on.

''Most of their small arms were in the bunkers when Andrew tore the base apart. The Air Force assholes at least had the sense to see the looting coming after the hurricane was over. They sent out a big-ass truck to go around the base, distribute small arms to the people on base, establish a perimeter in case all the Miami niggers started coming to steal their shit. I guess they must of distributed the M-16s in another truck. There weren't any in this one. Just the Berettas and a bunch of magazines and ammo, and the M-60s with the linked belts and all them sweet little LAW babies.

''Anyway, when the storm hit, Ian had Ted and me head on out there in the two big station wagons. That was before you two ever heard of the Blizzard. Sent us out to, you know, see what we could see, grab what we could grab. Well, this here big-ass four-by-four truck was sitting on its side, blown over by what used to be the Gate Four to the base, and here's these two poor dumb-ass nigger airmen trapped in the truck. They was lookin' at Ted and me like we come to save 'em, you know?''

Huxley burst into hysterical cocaine laughter that stopped a few seconds after it began. He picked right up where he'd left off. "So, Ted and me, we just snapped their necks for 'em. They was all messed up, pinned in the truck, couldn't do nothin' about it. I guess everybody figured they broke their necks when their truck blew over. That's why nobody said nothing special about it on the news.

"Ted and me musta taken a good half hour to dig that shit outa the four-by-four, put it in the wagons. Wind and rain to beat hell, man! It was cool! Shoulda been there!

"Anyway, this's what we wound up with. I never heard hide nor hair of it on TV or in the *Crier.* I guess whatever chicken-shit junior officer ordered that stuff out of the armory, while he didn't have the balls to go out into the hurricane and supervise the transfer his own self, just shut up about it. Anyhow, nobody seems to know we got it." He chuckled. "At least, nobody come here lookin' for it yet!"

Wallace Crowther exploded in anger, his face turning red all the way past the gray edge of a hairline on his shaved scalp. "We been out there doing the job with these chicken-shit World War II Mausers, with fuckin' actions you gotta work the bolt between shots?" he screamed. "I been out there with that little three-hundred-dollar Mini-14 and that junk Charter gun in my belt? And you got this shit in the basement?"

Crowther had to stop to breathe before he stormed, "Man, if we knew we had *this* shit, we could have blown them first two ZOG dogs up from like a hundred yards or something! We wouldn't of got shot at. We wouldn't have almost got bagged by that fuckin' state trooper! Ted wouldn't of got killed, man!"

Huxley raised his hands in a placating gesture, a knowing smile showing through the bad teeth behind his grizzled beard. "Hey, whoa, be cool, man! Ian had to get to know you, all right? Had to be sure you was with us, you know? Be cool! You're gonna use this stuff tonight!

"Hey, Wally, you don't like that belly gun you got stuffed in your belt? Here ya go!" He tossed Crowther the pistol he'd taken out of its box, and Crowther grabbed it in midair. "Boxes of ammo for it, man! Couple thousand rounds. Lots of magazines. Sixteen bullets at a time. Shit, man, think positive! This ain't like he held nothing away from you! This is a reward! You're with us, now! You're the Blizzard!"

The eyes shone like hard, cheap, glowing jewels in the pockets of Huxley's baggy eyes. Crowther had seen that look before. These were the eyes of madness. He knew when to give.

"Hey," he said soothingly, "it's okay, Dewey. I understand now. But what's the deal? Why break out the heavy shit now?"

Dewey Huxley grinned insanely. "Because tonight SOLID's coming in! They want a piece of the action. The high-and-mighty bastards blew Ian off before like he wasn't worth shit, but since we dusted all them ZOG dogs, they want to join up with us! Not us going to them with our hats in our hands no more! Them coming to us saying, 'Yo, brothers, you doin' what *we* shoulda been doin'!' Don't you see? They got their hats in their hands for us, wanting a piece of our action!"

Finally Tony Mann spoke. "Something I don't understand, Dewey. If they're coming up kissing our ass, how come tonight's the night we break out all the doomsday machines?"

Huxley's eyes narrowed. "They treated us like garbage before. You never trust people who done that to you. Ian thinks they might try something real funny with us. I think he's right. If they do, they're gonna come in force. It's down to the three of us. You know Ian—he's the brains. He ain't ready for nothing physical.

"One of us gotta be ready to do the plans. One of us gotta be rear guard, 'cause if they fuck with us they'll come in from the ground. And I'm the son of a bitch has to meet 'em face-to-face.

"Now, you two wanna learn how to use these things or you wanna shoot the breeze some more?"

FRANK CROSS LAY on the sofa in their condo, his head in Monica Wollman's sweet-smelling lap. Monica's daughters were in school, and there was no one to see. She ran her fingers soothingly through Frank's dark hair and said, "You did right. It was time. What you did to Dan was right."

They had met the previous summer. Monica Wollman, Ph.D, had written a bestselling book on satanist cults and was visiting Miami on a book-promoting tour with her daughters when she was targeted by the Devil-worshiping cult that had been running amok with kidnaps that finished in savage murders. Cross and Harrington were the Stakeout cops who were assigned to guard Monica and her daughters.

Monica seduced him, just for his sheer good looks. He responded. She was a few years older than he, but strong, gorgeous, bright... the kind of woman he'd never thought a weakling like him would ever be able to attract.

When the cultists came for Monica's daughters, Frank Cross fought for them, literally to the death. That was the night that Harrington abandoned him. Disaster was averted—Monica and her daughters were safe. Cross was beaten, clubbed, shot, but survived thanks to the bulletproof vest. He could still touch his chest, all these months later, and feel soreness in the spot where the 9 mm hardball bullet had stopped before it tore through him—but he had done his job.

With that act of courage, he put the legacy of cowardice behind him.

The nightmares stopped, at least those in which he relived that terrible moment in the doorway when the bad guy had started shooting, and he had ducked behind another officer who took the bullet that was meant for him. The night one cop died and another became a human vegetable, and only he was alive to tell the tale.

The night he had buried with Monica's help.

Monica was the only living person who knew the truth. When he told her, he expected to see shame and scorn in her eyes. Instead, he saw understanding and compassion.

For Monica the relationship had begun as pure animal attraction to Cross's good looks and broad shoulders. It was convenient for her when his partner found an excuse to leave the hotel suite; the partner was drinking his secret booze, Monica was partaking of her secret needs with Frank and the girls were asleep, so what did it matter?

After the invasion of the kidnappers, things changed.

She found herself looking down at Frank Cross, wounded and bandaged and vulnerable in his hospital bed, and realizing that this man had risked his life for her and her daughters. Their relationship went beyond physical at that moment.

She had fallen in love with him.

Monica Wollman was a strong woman, as bright as she was beautiful. Her first husband had been an older man, a professor who was first enamored of her beauty and her intellect, and later, threatened by both. After the divorce, after she became a single mother who carved her way to money and success, she never found a man who wasn't threatened by her.

Men couldn't handle a woman who wouldn't put up with any crap. Nor could most of them handle a woman who made more money than they did. The only kind left were the ones who wanted a mother.

Frank Cross was none of the above.

The seduction was spur-of-the-moment. She liked his body, loved his looks and felt safe with him. She knew he wouldn't live up to her standards afterward, but at the time, she didn't care.

Frank Cross surprised her.

After the trauma that she remembered as The Night of the Invaders, things changed. Her last memory before being knocked unconscious was Frank standing there, obviously about to be murdered, fighting against hopeless odds for her and her girls.

That wasn't something she could set on a shelf.

Afterward, on that quiet night alone when he told her about what had happened in the doorway so many years before, she held him. She reassured him that whoever that person was who doubted himself in the gunfire of the doorway, he no longer existed. Frank Cross, the Frank she knew, had replaced him.

She knew now that it was true. In the months since, she had seen an intelligence in him, a strength that he didn't know he possessed.

She had fallen in love with him.

As he lay on her lap on the sofa, she ran her fingers gently through his hair and said, "Frank, look at me."

He did.

Few men could look into those emerald eyes without flinching, but Frank Cross could and did. She said, "Darling, I love you. I know how strong you are. You don't really appreciate it yet, but you've got a better strength than the kind you're born with. You've got a strength that you've earned!

"You learned it on Stakeout. I understood that. That's why I never once asked you to leave. But you told me tonight, not in so many words, that it's turned bitter for you. It isn't just Dan."

Tears came into her eyes, and she continued, "Stakeout's done everything for you it needs to. Everything it can. You're a hero cop, Frank, a real hero cop! Do you understand what you've done? You conquered your fear. You learned how to teach other people who are afraid to do the same thing. I came to live in Miami just so I could be with you—you know that, darling. But maybe it's time for us both to leave.

"I go on TV talking about my books. You can go around the country doing something more. You can teach people how to overcome the kind of fear that cripples them. Think about it, Frank. Not just that you'll make ten times as much money as you do here. You'll leave the bullshit behind you. No more Dan Harringtons. No more getting shot. Think what you can be!"

There was a long moment before Frank Cross said, "I'll think about it."

MIAMI INTERNATIONAL Airport had left Tamiami Airport in the dust of commercial air traffic long ago. The aging airfield now hosted only cargo planes, private jets, low-budget flights and some of the region's emergency aircraft.

There was no U.S. Customs Service, no Dade County police officers assigned on routine patrol, and certainly no mini-SWAT team as you'd find at the big airport that was code-lettered MIA. People came to Tamiami Airport to be discreet, to quietly do business. The airfield lay at the northwestern edge of the city, on the border of the hinterlands that came so close to the narrow band of suburbs that separated the Miami metropolis from the primitive swampland it had risen from.

The Beechcraft King Air touched down on the far end of the farthest runway, smooth and steady.

Inside the shell of the King Air, two men in blacksuits flicked the safety levers of their M-16 automatic rifles down to full auto. Two more reached under their newly donned sport coats and touched the checkered walnut grips of the Smith & Wesson .357 Magnum revolvers in their shoulder holsters. And two more, clad in khaki not unlike the flight uniforms of a private pilot's service, pulled down the hems of their shirts to hide the butts of the 9 mm pistols holstered inside their waistbands.

The plane was slowing down, taxiing now.

The man in the sport clothes picked up a walkie-talkie. He keyed its microphone and said, "The hawk has reached the nest."

A voice came back that said, "The wolf is ready, hawk. Pull right up to the hangar they directed us to. There's a van right there, fits our man's description of the guy with the bushy beard that visited our friends with you know who. Seems to be alone. We're alongside the next hangar down from where you'll stop, around to the side. We'll light things up and come in when the Eye tells us to."

"The Eye" meant the infrared goggles the ground people were using. The CCC ground man was at the wheel of the darkened Pontiac that had been rented with fake ID. In his belt was a cocked Colt .45 automatic, and beside him was a CAR-15 automatic rifle with its stock folded.

In the right front seat, wearing khakis over a bulletproof vest and a Smith & Wesson 9 mm pistol, was an ARM member holding a lamp that sent out infrared light that bathed the incoming plane. The light was invisible to the naked eye.

Behind him, in the back seat of the rented car, was a man from SOLID with his heavy infrared goggles braced against the middle of the front seat, lined up through the windshield with the plane and the car and the hangar. One hand steadied the infrared-vision device, while the other held the walkie-talkie. He said, "Good, coming right along. He's waiting there in the van. Can't see what's in the back."

The CCC man in the front seat of the car said, "Get out the rifle with the night scope, dammit! This doesn't feel right!"

The one beside him said scornfully, "Don't piss your pants, all right? We scanned the area, man! There's just the one dumb guy! We need the rifle, it's right here! But we don't need it. Our brothers will just take him on the plane and scoot right on outa here."

The KingAir coasted to a stop perhaps ten steps away from the minivan. From inside the plane, powerful lights were turned on, bathing the van in a hard white glow.

Inside the van, Dewey Huxley forced himself to grin broadly despite the pain of the light in his eyes. He raised his hands to show that they were empty. The Colt Commander automatic stuffed into his jeans behind his right hip didn't feel nearly as comforting as usual.

The door of the plane opened, and a stepped exit ramp folded itself downward. Squinting against the bright light, Dewey Huxley saw the two men appear from the corners of the black ovoid that was the open jetway in the side of the plane. Their stainless-steel pistols were pointed directly at him. He heard someone say, "Don't fuckin' move!"

He was obeying that already.

Two more shapes came out of the doorway—black-clad men holding Army M-16 assault rifles. Behind them, cautiously, emerged two more, a couple of bulky guys wearing sport coats over golf shirts, their hands inside their coats as if touching the butts of guns in shoulder holsters.

"Be cool, man," Dewey Huxley said loudly, clearly and calmly. "The Blizzard delivers! You need help loading this stuff on board?"

"All we need on board is you," said one of the black-clad men, shoving the muzzle of his M-16 against Huxley's throat. "Where are your asshole friends?"

Huxley let out a sigh of disappointment. He'd hoped it would go better, but this was what he was expecting.

He shrugged his shoulders. That didn't mean anything to the men with the guns.

But it meant everything to his brothers of the Blizzard. It was the signal.

AS SOON AS TONY MANN SAW Dewey Huxley shrug his shoulders in the bright glare of the spotlights, he knew what he had to do. He didn't hesitate. After all, it wasn't as if he was in the line of fire.

The LAW rocket launcher was already set up, braced, armed and off safe. He looked once through the viewfinder to verify that the launcher was on target and then he pressed the lever.

Fire bloomed behind him in a hissing rush. The rocket was on its way. It streaked toward the car he had targeted, inside which he could make out a black-clad man behind the wheel, a man in khakis in the right front and somebody else in the back seat.

And then something happened to the car as he looked at it through the goggles, something so blinding that the goggles flared into a bright flash that plunged him into green darkness. Mann ripped off his night goggles in time to see the car with the three men in it disappear into a giant fireball of roiling black and orange, with things flying away from it.

He knew the three opponents in that car were dead.

He dropped the now-empty-and-useless LAW launcher, dropped the night goggles, too. His target was lit up. It provided enough light to see by.

It took less than a step for Mann to move himself inside the ditch at the edge of the airfield and grab the M-60 that had already been set up on its bipod and triangulated for exactly where the plane would be, its side presented cleanly to him.

Tony Mann's left hand grabbed the top of the M-60's wooden stock and held it hard against his right shoulder as his right hand went to the pistol grip of the already aimed weapon. He pulled the trigger back, exulting in the explosive din of machine-gun fire that roared from the M-60's barrel as he swept his cone of deadly, high-powered, fully automatic fire from left to right and back again.

DEWEY HUXLEY loved it when a plan came together.

No sooner had he shrugged his shoulders in resignation than there came the flash from the other side of the plane, about fifty yards to the side. Instinctively the others looked.

Looking away from Dewey! That was the key!

The shock wave and the blast of the explosion hit them all an instant after the car with the three backup men exploded into a fireball of Halloween black and orange.

At that same moment the man who was holding the muzzle of the M-16 at Huxley's throat turned with the others. It was instinct to look toward something that happened in the dark without warning. They couldn't help it.

It was then that the blacksuited man's head exploded.

Blood and thick, wet, spongy matter sprayed Dewey Huxley's face. He ignored it. Instead, he dived forward, toward the belly of the Beechcraft, sliding underneath the plane's fuselage. Out of sight of the two khaki-clad men in the doorway and out of their line of fire.

As he got to his feet, he glanced under the plane. He drew his lightweight .45 pistol instinctively. He was coming up with it when the other black-clad man jerked violently and then collapsed like a sack of wet laundry, his expensive rifle clattering to the tarmac of the airstrip.

The guys with the sport coats were ducking now, bobbing and weaving. Their hands came out from under their jackets holding revolvers. But they weren't looking toward Huxley anymore. One was looking toward the raging funeral pyre that was their friends' car fifty yards away, and the other had his back toward Huxley, scanning the darkness with his revolver raised, trying to find the source of the gunfire that had killed his black-garbed friends.

Huxley was safe.

He had a clear shot at the guys in the sport coats, but that didn't matter now. He turned and ran in the opposite direction, into the darkness. Ran for his life.

He knew what was going to happen now.

FOR THE FIRST TIME in a long time, Wallace Crowther was impressed with the planning of Ian Altman and his friend Dewey Huxley.

He had watched everything happen through the brilliant magnification in the German lenses of his telescopic-sighted Mauser rifle.

He saw the others come out of the airplane.

Saw them point the M-16s at Huxley.

Saw them, from his vantage point atop the hangar across the way, where the interlopers' backup people couldn't spot him with their infrared lenses, take their positions. It was then that he put the cross hairs of his rifle scope on the head of the most dangerous target, the one holding the gun muzzle to his colleague's throat.

Wallace Crowther let out part of a breath, took up the slack on the trigger and waited.

Then from the side came Tony Mann's LAW rocket, obliterating the backup car of the interlopers. Through the scope he could see the shock on his target's face as he turned.

Now!

He finished the squeeze on the trigger. The old German army rifle bumped against his shoulder with the recoil, but he kept the butt in the pocket between his pectoral muscle and the deltoid of his shoulder as he worked the bolt mechanism with his right hand, reaching back for the trigger even as the scope's image came back onto the face of the second black-clad man, who was ducking and dodging, wondering what had happened.

Wallace Crowther didn't give him the chance to find out. He rolled the trigger back. The cross hairs were centered on the base of the second blacksuited man's skull when he pressed the trigger.

Crowther worked the bolt again. Through the scope he scanned the scene.

Both the guys who'd had Huxley were down and out.

The guys in sport coats were jerking around, not knowing what to do next. Not realizing that Huxley was already safely out from under the plane, running the opposite way, something Crowther could see now in the powerful light-gathering lenses of the rifle scope. The plane was shuddering from the impacts of high-powered machine-gun fire. Crowther saw the holes appear, saw one of the sport coats spin and fall as the swath of the bullets tore through him.

Now!

Crowther dropped the rifle unceremoniously and scooped up his LAW rocket launcher. He swept its viewfinder across the plane from the tail toward the nose, in time to see the khaki-clad men ducking back inside. He knew they had to be screaming to the pilot to move out.

Crowther thought, Too late, lousy double-crossers!

The plane was rolling slowly forward now, gaining momentum. Crowther triggered the release on the LAW rocket.

He watched the missile, as if in slow motion, arc toward the Beechcraft KingAir, homing for the cabin up front.

As if in slow motion, a large hole appeared in the fuselage.

Then everything blew back out in a giant orange fireball, a thick jet of flame shooting out from the hole where the rocket had just pierced the skin of the dying plane.

The aircraft's momentum seemed to spin it around when the explosion occurred, the wings going up and down as the tires caught against the friction of the airstrip, and the plane came to a dead stop.

He knew Huxley must be safely in the ditch on the far side of the field by now.

Tony Mann must have known it, too.

From Mann's position on the other end of the field-side ditch came a flickering tongue of fire. The M-60 did its thing.

Mann's first burst had been regular bullets. Huxley had craftily linked the ammo belts up that way. But now the belt of ammo had been sucked through the machine gun until it reached the hard stuff.

Crowther saw the red lines of fire draw themselves from the machine-gun pit to the dying airplane. Tracer bullets. He knew what came next and he wanted to duck and brace himself, but he couldn't. He had to watch.

Now came the rest of the deadly belt of machinegun bullets. The API, or Armor-Piercing Incendiaries.

Crowther saw the little flickers of fire when the bullets hit the plane, different from the red lines of the glowing tracers that had been fired previously.

And then—

The blast was awesome, unbelievable.

The incendiary bullets tore through one of the fuel tanks of the KingAir, igniting the jet fuel and sending sympathetic flames racing through the entire fuel train of the aircraft.

The plane exploded.

The blast lit the field with a blinding light, and it sent a breathtaking shock wave of superheated air out a hundred yards in every direction. The blast wave blew Tony Mann back into his ditch, out from behind his M-60. Bowled Dewey Huxley ass over cowboy hat into the weeds at the edge of the airfield. Damn near blew Wallace Crowther off the roof of the airplane hangar, and even then nearly seared the eyes out of his sockets even though he had instinctively ducked his face away and shut his eyes tight.

It was over, the plane burning intensely on the airfield, and sirens sounding through Crowther's ringing ears from someplace that seemed very far away.

Wallace Crowther screamed joyously into the night. "Yeee-*hah!*"

For the first time he could remember, it felt good to be alive.

12

John Kearn sat behind his desk as if it was a fortress.

He wondered why. The answer came to him quickly. As soon as he ventured out from behind this desk, he had to speak at the funerals of cops. As soon as he left the secure barricade of the mahogany, the mayor was in his face, asking insistently when the cop-killings would end.

And if, God forbid, he went home to his wife, she and the kids would ask him the same thing.

It was better here.

He ncver wanted to see another policeman go to his grave again. He had been through the spectacle of the "inspector's funeral" too many times already.

Police cars snaking in a long, silent caravan, as far as the eye could see. Thousands of cops—not hundreds, *thousands*—coming to march in silent respect, as if their show of force could mean anything now. The cops for the last couple of funerals had come from more than thirty states, once CNN made it apparent nationwide that a conspiracy to murder police officers was afoot in Miami.

Overhead the police-department helicopters had roared. To the citizens and the police families, Kearn thought, it must have seemed like a powerful show of force, the turbojet engines screaming a warning that said, "Don't tread on us."

But to Kearn it had been a symbol of frustration, the impotent rage of the police force's power, as hollow as the contrails of their exhaust that wafted on the warm spring Miami wind and then dissipated and drifted away.

Six cops dead. Six! Five of them his own! It was like swallowing the grief of five dead children.

Kearn had begun as a young black street cop working the Twenty-fifth Precinct, in the depths of Harlem. Everything he'd seen there taught him that education and knowledge were the way to the power that would get you out of the ghetto. It had worked for him.

Even when he'd been an ordinary street cop, the others had seen, had felt John Kearn's sense of leadership. They had voted him onto the board of the Guardians, the African-American patrolmen's group within NYPD, and cops of all colors had later made him their representative with the PBA, the Patrolman's Benevolent Association, the most powerful of all police unions. Before John Kearn ever supervised field-patrol officers, he had been their advocate and their champion, speaking on their behalf against management.

Against the thing he had become.

He wondered why he had ever forsworn those roots, why he had climbed a chain of command that led him out of NYPD and into a series of municipal police departments, the promotions going higher each time until he was selected as the chief of the Miami Police Department. Couldn't he have been just as happy as a patrolman, working out his need to change and improve things as a senior member of the union?

No, he realized, he couldn't. The infantry private could never change the overall attitude of high command. Only by climbing the ranks could Kearn make the changes he knew had to be made for cops to not only take care of their own, but to truly fulfill the public trust.

And he had tried. Affirmative action was already in full swing when he took command of Miami PD. A respected black chief had retired, creating the opening. A respected Hispanic man, Miami's mayor, had recently been voted up from city hall to the governor's chair.

Kearn knew he had tried to be as good a leader as the strong chief he replaced. He knew with equal certainty that the new mayor was not nearly as good as his predecessor.

It was clear from the beginning that Mayor Orlando Hernandez had won control of city hall the old-fashioned way: he'd bought his way in with a mix of false promises, a great smile and cold, ruthless political calculation. He'd hired Kearn because he knew that he needed another black man to head his racially torn city's police department. Also no honest man of any color in Miami PD's high command would go along with a cutthroat blowhard like the new mayor. A further advantage was that someone he promoted from within the department could always fall back to the civil-service rank and pension benefits of a full captain, but an outsider would be left with nothing if he incurred the new mayor's wrath. Hernandez felt it gave him more leverage.

It was not surprising, then, that one of Kearn's first acts as the new chief was to implement the controversial Stakeout Unit. He remembered from his early days on NYPD that stakeout cops had been put in place inside the most robbery-prone establishments, places where black entrepreneurs and Hispanic bodega owners were fighting to carve out a piece of the American dream, only to be ripped off by gunmen who didn't care that the insurance companies had redlined districts like Harlem and Bedford-Stuyvesant and the South Bronx. The predators didn't care that their stolen money meant food out of the mouths of little kids whose parents worked hard for it. They didn't care, either, when they killed those parents for the sheer fun of watching them die.

Enter the NYPD Stakeout Squad.

During the tumultuous years of the NYPD unit's existence, they blew more than thirty criminals into cells where the walls were six feet of soil in potter's field instead of just iron bars. Countless more were wounded but taken alive, and more yet captured without resistance as soon as they realized just who was pointing those guns at them and commanding, "Police! Drop your weapons!"

In the end, the NYPD Stakeout Squad was simply too politically incorrect for its time. It was disbanded. It had killed too many people, some said; Kearn, a former New York cop himself, knew that the real reason was that virtually everyone they'd killed was black.

This was in the forefront of his mind when he sent his people out to research, not just the NYPD experience, but that of Philadelphia and Los Angeles, both of which still had stakeout squads in operation despite heavy media demand that the units be disbanded. Kearn's impartial researchers returned to tell him that the reason stakeout units still worked in Philly and the City of Angels was that ultimately they protected the innocent and either arrested or killed the monsters who preyed on those honest people.

Kearn, who had inherited command of the Miami Police Department at a time when a gang of particularly vicious, homicidal robbers was running rampant, knew what he had to do.

He created the Stakeout Unit.

He deliberately chose men like Mike Cohen and Ken Bartlett for command positions. Bartlett was clearly an African-American like Kearn himself, not only relatively immune from racial bias if there were politically incorrect shootings, but a man who had no Rambo in him at all, indeed, a man who was a careerist who had no use for the kind of Rambo cop who packed a gun off duty when he didn't have to. Cohen, one of his field sergeants, seemed to be cut from the same cloth.

In the past year or so, however, Kearn's perspective on that had changed.

Miami was, per capita, more violent than even New York City—no question about it. Stakeout from the beginning had its hands full. But it had dealt with its mission well.

The gang that had brought them into existence was soon extinct. They had, in their way, forced Kearn to create the Stakeout Unit; it was the Stakeout Unit who annihilated that gang, in turn. Kearn remembered thinking, "As ye sow, so shall ye reap."

When that crime wave was over, he thought of disbanding the unit. Everyone expected him to. But instead, he kept it going, which turned out to be one of the best things he had ever done. Today Kearn's enemies accused him of favoring the unit because it had been his pet project.

All Kearn knew was that they'd been in some trouble but they hadn't yet shot anyone they didn't have to shoot, and they had kept a whole lot of good people alive. Truth to tell, the public had come to appreciate, if not exactly love, the Stakeout Unit, Oliver Teasdale and his editors at the *Miami Crier* notwithstanding.

The mayor, however, was not a Stakeout fan. Indeed, he had vehemently opposed the unit's creation—political incorrectness, and all that—and Chief Kearn had in essence told the mayor to screw himself and established the Stakeout teams anyway.

The relationship between the chief and the mayor had been in the pits ever since.

Chief John Kearn had a feeling that Mayor Orlando Hernandez just couldn't get past the race thing. Any mayor wanted a stable community, and in Miami the mayor was particularly demanding of his police chief in that respect, for reasons the city had burned into history with fire and with blood. Kearn had studied what had gone before in the city and the police department he had come to.

In 1980 Metro Dade police had chased a black motorcyclist in a high-speed pursuit. When they finally caught up with him, witnesses said, they beat him unmercifully. Arthur MacDuffee's head was on the pavement, according to the medical examiner's office, when a heavy flashlight smashed down into his skull and crushed his cranium like an eggshell. The city exploded into a riot of the kind that hadn't been seen in the United States in more than a decade. When the fires were put out, numerous people were dead.

1982 was no better. A City of Miami cop named Luis Alvarez shot in the head and killed a young black man named Nevell Johnson when a routine pat-and-frisk in a video arcade in Overtown turned ugly and Johnson went for a gun. The dying Johnson fell on top of his gun after the shot, and witnesses only saw that an ostensibly unarmed man had been killed by Hispanic cops. The riot was already beginning when Alvarez and his young rookie partner, Luis Cruz, were escorted out of the arcade by SWAT cops amid a hail of flying rocks and bottles. The riot spread, taking more life and causing millions of dollars in property damage.

Then, in 1984 the same cop, Alvarez, stood trial in what was then the longest criminal proceeding in Florida history, some eight weeks in court. After only two hours of deliberation, the jury found him not guilty of manslaughter. Another riot flared. It would have consumed the city except for the lessons learned in the past two conflagrations. By the time the verdict was announced, a thousand helmeted, riot-equipped Miami police and Metro Dade officers were on the street. Even with the Field Forces in place, there was disturbance and violence.

Miami had become the source of a new phenomenon: the miniriot, a riot held somewhat in check only by massive, carefully placed police presence.

Five years later, in 1989, a drug dealer on a motorcycle turned what would have been a routine speeding ticket into a high-speed pursuit through

Overtown, one of the black population centers of Miami. An officer named William Lozano, taking a black citizen's crime report at the time, stepped off the sidewalk to see what the hubbub was about as the pursuit roared toward him. He came out from behind his cruiser to see a black man, Clement Lloyd, swerving from his path and now bearing down on him at high speed. As he ducked out of the way, Lozano drew his Glock and fired. The bullet destroyed Clement Anthony Lloyd's brain immediately, and moments later the bike crashed and killed Lloyd's friend, also black, who was riding pillion on the high-powered motorcycle.

High on cocaine, marijuana and alcohol, Lloyd nearly ran down several little black kids in his reckless attempt to escape capture. There was no need for a riot. But things got out of hand, and the next thing anyone knew, the bottles were flying. It had become a verb unique to Miami by then: *Bottling*.

And then the riot was under way. More burned neighborhoods, more tragedy, more unnecessary human suffering.

Miami Police Chief John Kearn rubbed his forehead, as if to wipe the images away. But they wouldn't go. They were part of the reality of this city, part of the reality he faced, part of the history he knew would be doomed to repeat itself if things weren't handled differently the next time.

The racial hatred in Miami was clear and present. You could smell it in the air, the way you could smell the polluted river in Cleveland.

Were there whites who hated nonwhites? Yes. Kearn had five dead cops, five grieving police families of different colors, to prove it.

Did the city's heavy Hispanic population harbor in any corner a resentment against blacks or a sense of having been held down by Anglos? Of course. The evidence was visible before John Kearn had arrived in Miami, and remained.

Were there African-Americans who felt so oppressed by those of lighter colors that certain incidents could trigger them to deadly violence? John Kearn looked down at his own chocolate brown hands and knew the answer. He had seen the videotaped horrors of what were known in the city as the MacDuffee riot, the Alvarez riots and the Lozano riot.

He knew that he and the city he had come to love were sitting on the edge of something just as explosive. The white-on-black racial violence of the past few days, had the victims been civilians instead of police officers, would have set the spark to another wildfire. That, Kearn knew with certainty. He feared that soon the nonwhite community would wake up to the fact that Aryan supremacists were murdering their own people, this time beyond doubt for no other reason but the color of their skin, and the chief wondered if the next fire would burn with an even greater intensity than the last.

Amazingly what came closest to lighting the tinder was the death of the albino black man a few days ago after he had shot at white cops and been chased by them. What prevented the fire from blazing up was that it was obvious that the cops had thought it was a white guy they were chasing, and the guy had killed himself through his own stupidity anyway. But things like that happened all the time.

Kearn understood that the powder keg would explode and it was only a matter of when. He had already told his subcommanders to have Field Forces ready to roll, and had agreed on that with his counterpart, the head of the Dade County Police.

His people were already on twelve-hour emergency shifts because of the Blizzard cop-killings. It was gobbling up his salary budget with overtime. Soon he'd have to go before city council to request additional funds. His people would soon burn out on that twelve-on-twelve-off schedule. If the killings didn't abate, if they couldn't find a solution...

Kearn didn't want to think about it but he had to. He could picture a worn-out cop making a split-second mistake in judgment that would plunge the city into another firestorm.

In the meantime the violent city kept up its pace. There were still robberies. There were still homicides. Just hours ago Tamiami Airport had been the site of a military-weapons shoot-out between some gunrunners. A plane and an automobile had been blasted to shreds, with at least five known dead. His evidence people told him that the combatants had been using heavy-duty M-60 machine guns and LAW rockets, the kind of technology you expected to see in a Middle Eastern war, not in the streets of one of America's largest cities.

Kearn's cops were too thinly spread to deal with all of that.

The chief dropped his head into his hands. He felt a terrible foreboding that things were about to get worse, that the roller coaster had just hit the top edge and was about to plummet down.

He just didn't realize how soon.

DAN HARRINGTON SLAMMED the door of his tiny apartment shut behind him. The ache in the side of his face from Frank Cross's punch didn't hurt him nearly as much as the aching emptiness inside him.

God, he needed a drink!

Harrington kicked his way through the accumulated trash that littered his apartment floor and made his way past the liquor cabinet and to the kitchen counter. It had been a long time since he'd bothered to stock the liquor cabinet. Lately he just drank from the bottle.

The case was there, half-empty but several fifths left. He had gone to eighty-proof blended whiskey a few weeks ago deliberately. Part of it was that it was lighter in alcohol than the ninety-proof premium stuff he'd been drinking before—and he needed to ease up—and part of it was that it was cheaper. He didn't care about taste anymore. He cared about effect.

Harrington ripped loose the label around the cap, tore the bottle open and brought it to his lips. The amber liquid went down his throat like cleansing fire.

Aaahhh... at last. Here safe. Home safe, he thought.

Still clutching the fifth of whiskey, he strode into the living room. He didn't bother to turn on the TV as he usually did. He had too much to think about. He took another swig, set the bottle down and began divesting himself of the Stakeout gear that seemed to stick to his sweaty body.

That sniveling little punk! The Hidden Agenda vest went flying. He took another hit of the whiskey. *Yella little bastard!* Harrington tore off the shirt that covered his Second Chance vest.

Punch me in the face like that, no fucking warning, damn coward sucker punch just like I'd expect from him! He ripped loose the Velcro straps and flung the bulletproof vest away from himself. The sleeveless T-shirt clung to his body, but he ignored it.

Dan Harrington's mind was raging. *I shoulda killed him! If he hadn't sucker-punched me, I would have! He's under a cloud from when he chickened out before! But I'm clean! They'll believe me!* He thought about taking off his Glock .45 service pistol, and then he decided to leave it on. It made him feel strong. He needed that right now.

He poured more liquor into his mouth. God, it was good to be home and safe and away from the prying eyes of all those little pricks who wanted to ruin you because you were smarter than they were.

Gotta think. Gotta think. I need a good one tonight, need to clean out the cobwebs, get serious about shit. Can't do another day at work. Not with this bruise on my face. Not with that stupid little whelp Frank Cross. Gotta call in sick, before they can say there's any booze on my voice. He took another gulp of the whiskey. The bottle was a third empty now.

Another thought hit him, and he grinned. The whiskey was making him crafty now. It was good for him, not bad for him; he'd always known that. Just don't call in at all. Pull the batteries out of the pager. Let 'em come to me. Whole idea is get a stress pension, right? Gotta show them I'm all screwed up from stress. They made me shoot people, my brain's all scrambled up. Any shrink in the country's gonna back me up. Why wait a few more months, hang out with assholes like Cross, yella little bastard? Why get out there in front of people's guns again? Take my pension, I done my whole year on Stakeout now, whole year on a high-risk unit, good as I'm gonna get for pension. Yeah. Forget calling 'em, damn right. I'll just wipe it all out, deal with it tomorrow. Yeah!

Dan Harrington swilled down another swallow of whiskey. It was good stuff. A few moments before, he'd felt like death. Now he felt great.

MICHAEL CARPENTER felt the ancient Plymouth's engine stuttering. Get me home to my boy, you goddamn rust bucket, he thought.

Carpenter was thirty-five, a black man who had grown up in the projects in Liberty City, one of the two ghettos that bracketed Miami. He had worked hard all his life. His mother had taught him that.

And what did he have to show for it? Twenty bucks in his cracked and worn billfold, the billfold he still carried because Mike Jr., twelve years old, had made it for him at Camp Garrity six years before. Camp Garrity? Screw the white rich bastard who'd named the camp after himself. Carpenter always thought of it as Camp Charity. Michael Carpenter was proud, proud of feeding himself and his boy even after his wife died of cancer. Even if he did make minimum wage mucking out floors at the white bastards' office buildings.

But Lord, Lord, it was harder than ever to make ends meet. Get that little chicken-shit paycheck at the end of the second week, you had just enough to keep the car running, keep the boy in clothes so the other kids at school wouldn't laugh at him and didn't have nothing for your only child's birthday, which was tonight.

Earlier that night, when he had driven by a sign that said Garage Sale, he'd stopped on impulse, wondering if the people there had something they didn't want anymore that still looked new, something he could buy for his son with the lousy twenty bucks in his pocket. He was browsing through the cast-off junk when a lady said, "Looking for anything special?"

"Yeah," Michael Carpenter grumbled. "Somethin' for my boy. Birthday present. He's twelve today."

"Ah," said the fat, frowsy woman who had spoken. "All my kids were girls, and all my jerk of a husband ever left me, I sold already. But I've got something my father gave me when I was about your kid's age. I never needed it, but it'd be just right for a boy. Come inside."

Michael Carpenter followed her. She went into a closet and said, "You can understand why I don't just leave it outside."

She pulled out a single-shot J. C. Higgins .22 rifle and held it aloft in triumph.

"Yours for fifty bucks," she said.

Carpenter was crestfallen. "Can't afford it, lady. Tell you right up front, I got twenty bucks in my pocket, and that's gotta buy me gas to go to work tomorrow."

The woman was unfazed. She remembered all those years ago, when her father had given her the rifle for Christmas, as he would have given it to the son he never had. She had looked it up in the Sears catalog—nineteen dollars and ninety-five cents, all those years ago.

"Close enough," she said. After all, the gun did have some rust on it, and what the hell, she could let it go for that. "Twenty bucks. You take the rifle, you deal with getting to work tomorrow."

Carpenter paid the money, took the rifle and left. He was surprised at how small and light the gun was. He had never fired a gun in his life.

But it didn't matter. He was on his way home now, driving through downtown, and he had a good present for his son. A manly present. Never mind that he didn't know how to teach the boy to use it. There had to be books, books in the library. He would have called his brother—his brother knew guns—but the idiot mixed guns with drugs, and *that* wasn't the example Michael Carpenter wanted to set for his kid. Hey, he'd work it out. He felt happy, eager. He'd be on Interstate 95 soon, homebound.

The red-and-blue lights came on behind him.

Carpenter glanced down at the speedometer in surprise. He didn't think he'd been *that* eager! He didn't even think the old Plymouth would go that fast.

The police lights flashed behind him insistently. Carpenter knew he was in deep trouble now. He had no insurance on the old Plymouth, no money to pay for a speeding ticket.

Michael Carpenter panicked.

He pressed the accelerator to the floorboard.

STAN BARANCK WAS TAKING his turn at the wheel of the pale yellow Chevy while Tom West rode shotgun beside him. Even on quiet nights, they enjoyed working together.

It puzzled some people in this racially striated city that they could get along as well as they did; Baranck was as white as a bowl of cream of wheat, West as black as the ace of spades, but they had more in common than not. They talked about their families and their houses and things only two people who were alike would discuss over a cup of coffee. Their families, like the men themselves, had become inextricably bonded in the year they had been working Stakeout Team Two together.

They were talking about the Miami Heat not being able to play worth spit in the wind but loving them anyway, when the radio came alive.

"... in pursuit, southbound on Southeast Second Avenue, crossing Flagler," the dispatcher said. "Vehicle is older-model Plymouth, blue, rusted." The dispatcher announced the Florida license tag number and the next cross street the vehicle had passed. The chase was obviously at a high rate of speed.

They weren't far from the scene. They'd been partners too long to have to say the obvious to each other. Stan Baranck was already spinning the Chevy into a racing drift as Tom West reached down to hit the switches that triggered the emergency lights and the siren.

Baranck countersteered out of the racing drift that headed them in the right direction as West, without any hint of urgency in his voice, keyed the radio microphone and said, "Sam Ocean Two Bravo, we are responding to back up on that pursuit."

The code meant SO-2-B, the middle squad of Stakeout Unit's Team Two. The dispatcher confirmed, and West slid the microphone carefully back into its steel-tongued track. Both of them had been in enough high-speed chases to know that anything not nailed down or held tight would go flying out of reach the first time the racing patrol car hit a bump or had to take a hard turn.

Stan Baranck talked slow but he thought fast, and he drove fast, too. Within a minute they were in sight of the flashing lights of the other pursuit cars, and in another minute they were in the thick of the chase.

The old Plymouth cut a corner sharply, and the cars ahead of them slewed in behind, one of them spinning out. West instinctively looked down at his partner's foot on the brake. When they'd gone through the academy years ago, they had been taught to stab their brakes repeatedly when coming into a corner like that, but that was before the ABS braking of today's police cars. West was relieved to see that his partner held a steady pressure and let the computer-controlled braking system do the work just before he spun the wheel and swept them through the corner with sickening G-force.

West heard his partner swear, then yell, "The drawbridge is up!" Baranck was already standing on the brake.

West lifted his head in time to see the tableau. In the old days Miami had been a city of canals. There were still bridges that were drawn up a few times a day to let high-topped boats through. One of those lay in front of them now, drawn all the way up. It wasn't a ramp the guy could drive over; it was now perpendicular to the water, a steel-and-concrete wall that had trapped the fleeing driver where he was.

The Plymouth stopped a few seconds before the Stakeout car did. So did the three or four police cars between the Stakeout unmarked car and the Plymouth. West didn't even think about reaching down for one of the buckshot-loaded shotguns. The spread of their fire would be too much for the distance; if West had to fire, the swath of the deadly pellets could spread out enough to strike cops between him and the vehicle.

Instead, he dropped his left hand to the seat-belt release and his right hand to his pistol. The double-action-only Smith & Wesson Model 4546 was already in his hand before his left came up to pull the door handle, and he kicked his way out of the car.

Other cops were bailing out of their vehicles, too, well ahead of West, their guns drawn.

So was the driver of the Plymouth.

Tom West saw the rifle in the man's right hand, swinging up. He had to be big; the rifle looked so small. West didn't dare aim his own gun; street cops were between him and the other guy.

Then Officer Tom West saw the flashes of fire at the muzzles of the street cops' guns and saw the man with the rifle fall.

13

Michael Carpenter suddenly saw the upraised drawbridge looming like a steel-and-concrete wall ahead of him. He slammed the brakes of the old Plymouth to the floor as hard as he could. The only thing that saved him was that the brake linings were worn-out on one side. When he hit the binders, the car spun sideways, coming to a dead stop from the rubber-burning tire friction just a few feet from the raised bridge.

Then all those lights were in his eyes. All those lights!

It wasn't fair, goddamn it! He was just trying to get home in time for his kid's birthday!

He had to declare himself. Show he was a man. Stand up and explain his indignation.

He grabbed the little rifle to show them he was just coming home with a present for his kid, then threw open the door.

In that last moment in the lights, he realized what it was he was holding, realized that they might mistake it for a real gun, a loaded gun, and Michael

Carpenter thrust his arms forward as if to say, "Listen!"

He never heard the shots. He only saw the twinkles of fire at the muzzles of the guns behind the headlights and felt a deep, burning pain in his chest and another in his abdomen. The same red-hot fire crippled both his arms, and then he was falling down on the hard macadam. He couldn't breathe, it hurt so bad, and people were yelling and he was afraid he was going to die and never see Michael Jr. again.

He heard a clattering sound. It was someone kicking the rifle away, across the street from where it had fallen. Deep, macho voices were yelling, "Police! Don't move!"

He couldn't move if he wanted to. He tasted blood in his mouth and choked on it in his nostrils, and he hurt all over.

A face loomed over him, a black man, a brother. The brother was holding a big silver-colored pistol in both hands. He wasn't dressed like a cop. He wore a golf shirt under a black vest like cameramen wore, only there was a tab hanging off one side that said Police, and off the other hung what looked like a badge.

Michael Carpenter tried to say "Help me," but he realized that he couldn't breathe and couldn't speak. There were only red bubbles coming out of his mouth.

He saw the brother shove the gun behind him somewhere, and then it was gone, and the brother's hands were reaching out. The brother was yelling, "Stan! Roll EMS! Now!"

Things were cold and dark, getting more so by the moment. Michael Carpenter could smell the river and the scent of his own blood, and he fixed on a mental picture of his son.

It was the last thing he saw before the darkness folded completely over him.

MAYOR ORLANDO HERNANDEZ was at a cocktail party in Coral Gables, being his usual suave self and charming the pants off everyone of both sexes, when his aide came rushing up to pull him aside and whisper in his ear about the shooting of the black man that had just gone down at the drawbridge. The mayor didn't bother to make excuses. He just put on a studied facial expression that showed he suddenly had very important things to do and strode swiftly out of the room with the aide.

In his limousine on the way to the scene, however, he allowed himself the luxury of gloating.

His advisers had told him this would happen, that it was only a matter of biding his time. They had been right.

It only stood to reason. Miami was more black and brown than it was white. The African-Americans and the Hispanics, whether by choice or by the whim of geo-economic politics, found themselves mostly in their own enclaves. Many of those enclaves were better described as ghettos.

Each such neighborhood became its own unique satellite of the city, a place of poverty as a general rule. When there was poverty, there was despair; where there was despair, there was crime; and where there was crime, there would inevitably be criminals who would be so violent that they would force police to shoot them.

The people who lived in those communities, Orlando Hernandez knew, had not historically handled that well.

In the old days, certainly, there had been brutality inflicted by an overwhelmingly white police force on an overwhelmingly black and brown minority. The new ways of policing had virtually stamped that out, but today's people had grown up with the stories of their mothers and their fathers from the bad old days, and no one ever let go of the values and the judgments of the forebears who formed them. Because Miami cops had been free with their fists and their clubs and their guns in the old days, the people of the ghetto today expected it to be true, and it was a rule of the human experience that what you expected to see, you would see.

Hernandez knew he had to look at this pragmatically. The job of a politician was first and foremost to win the next election. The handwriting for that was already on the wall: a certain Anglo woman, prominent in liberal prominority causes, would almost certainly be his next opponent. He had to realistically look at what he needed to defeat her.

The assessment was easy. If Spanish was your first tongue, you voted for those who talked in the same language. Whether the heavy Hispanic population of Miami liked him or not, Orlando Hernandez would be the only game in town for them in the next election, and they would vote for him automatically. His advisers told him that was a given.

The blacks, the same advisers assured Orlando, would vote for blacks. If no black was running, they would vote for whoever promised them the most and showed them intent to deliver. That was the key. Showing support!

The Anglos? Ignore them, the advisers said. They're the most malleable, the most manipulable of all. You want the right? Stop a riot from happening, and they'll drop their law-and-order asses right into your side of the ballot. You want the left? Say all the politically correct things, and it's open pocket, insert the liberal vote, end of story.

He and his advisers had gone over all the scenarios. What if we have another white or Hispanic cop who blows away a black man? His advisers told him the answer would be easy. Never mind if the shooting was justifiable. Just placate the blacks and keep them from having another riot, throw the cop to the wolves, ignore the Hispanics, who have nowhere else to go anyway, and you've just won the election!

Orlando Hernandez didn't pay for all that high-priced advice just to piss it away when the moment came that he could use it to his advantage. And it seemed to be happening now.

"Hurry up," he told the driver. "Get us to that drawbridge now!"

THEY CALLED the chief of police at his home. John Kearn listened to what his aide had to say and then told him, "Listen to me very carefully. You're telling me the people are already in the street, angry, ready to start bottling. Mobilize the Field Force immediately. Call the chief of Metro Dade, tell him I'll be talking to him in a few minutes, probably mobile to mobile. No, don't bother sending a car to my house. No time. I'll roll from here and meet you at the scene."

Kearn hung up the phone and thought, Goddammit!

At least the incident hadn't happened in the heart of Liberty City or Overtown. There was a chance of containment. But from what he'd been told, a crowd of more than a hundred people had already gathered at the scene, buzzing with rage.

Best-case scenario—with an early roll-out of the Field Forces, they'd contain it before the city caught fire at all. Worst-case scenario—the city would still go up but not as fast or as hard, because they had time to put a thousand riot police into the scene before the already burning tinder blossomed into raging flame.

His wife looked at him wordlessly. "You heard, darlin'. Gotta go."

Kearn had a bulletproof vest in the closet and a couple of uniforms he almost never wore. In the closet in his office was the utility jumpsuit for emergencies that he hadn't worn once, hadn't even tried on, and a flak jacket and a helmet. There was no time for any of that now.

There was only time to clip the still-black-banded badge onto his belt in front of the plastic holster he hadn't had a chance to take off. He shoved his little Glock 19 9 mm pistol into the holster, then he was out the door and running toward his compact Ford, his portable police radio in his hand. The department had given him a car, replete with all manner of communications like a mobile office, but he had let his driver take it home with him. Too late now, Kearn thought. Too late for a lot of things.

He slammed the car door closed behind him and rolled down the window. At least he'd had the foresight to equip his own car with a police scanner and a magnetic emergency roof light that plugged into the cigarette-lighter socket for power. He turned that on and gunned the car out of the driveway. Driving with his left hand, he keyed the mike of his portable and said, "This is Unit One. I'm responding to that scene, ETA fifteen minutes."

He continued driving with a fierce concentration, the urgency building in him. His Estimated Time of

Arrival was fifteen minutes from now, and a lot of things could happen in a mere quarter of an hour.

HARRINGTON SAT NUMBLY in front of his blank, turned-off television. Normally he watched TV to help get to sleep, but tonight it would have been a distraction so he had never turned it on.

Besides, the images in his mind were more exciting than anything a scriptwriter could ever have convinced actors to fake on TV.

He pictured Frank Cross sitting on the wrong side of an interrogation table, with Harrington and Bruce Yount from Professional Standards leaning over him, yelling. He pictured Cross bending over and wringing his hands, crying, bleating, "I'm sorry! I'm sorry!"

Harrington chuckled at the thought.

He became aware of an insistent pressure in his bladder. He hadn't pissed in a while. He looked down and saw that the bottle in his hand, his second fifth of the night, was almost empty. It seemed like just a few minutes ago that he'd started drinking. Time flew when you were having fun.

He tried to get to his feet but fell back on the sofa. He giggled. So long as nobody was there to see, it didn't matter. He wasn't going to go to work tomorrow anyway. He was going to wrap up this stupid show once and for all with a nice fat stress pension anyway, right?

He set down the bottle and forced himself to his feet, then turned toward the bathroom and started to move.

His feet betrayed him.

The next thing he knew, he was pitching toward the floor. There was a sensation of impact, no pain or anything, just a dim awareness of a blow as his head hit the hard, sharp edge of the coffee table.

He lay facedown on the floor, dazed. He was going to get up, but then he said out loud, "Fuck it. Why bother?"

The floor felt soft and comfortable. Everything was spinning. He'd had a lot to drink, he realized dimly, but he knew how to handle that. Just stay where you were. You weren't smashed if you could still hang on to the floor; that's what he always said.

He chuckled as his face rested against the soft, matted carpet. He was aware that the carpet was wet. He'd deal with that later. He had more-important things to worry about tonight, and it felt good, damn good, to be on top of all those things.

Dan Harrington passed out.

The puddle of blood from his lacerated forehead grew slowly, steadily wider on the carpet beneath his unconscious head.

EACH MEMBER of the Blizzard slept in a small bedroom in the lavish Altman house. The rooms featured small but comfortable beds, and bureaus and study desks were built into the walls. The beds were slept in these days, but no one used the study desks anymore.

A pounding on the door of his room jarred Tony Mann awake. Terror filled him when he first heard the sound, like when he was little and the old man was coming to beat the crap out of him again. That had been the stuff of his nightmares for all these years.

Not lately, though. Not since the first time he'd blown a cop away. Now he could sleep in peace.

Sleep was one thing, and pounding on the door was another. Tony Mann groped about frantically in the darkness, a silent scream on his lips, until his hand closed over the comforting hardness of the Browning 9 mm automatic.

Then he was in control again.

There was a false machismo in his voice, even so, as he screamed, "Whaddaya want?"

"Hey, man," came a familiar voice. "It's Dewey."

The voice sounded mellow. Mann knew instantly that Dewey Huxley had been at his drugs again.

"Whaddaya want?" he yelled again, more angrily.

"TV, man." Huxley giggled. "You gotta come down, see the TV!"

"Awright, awright," Mann mumbled, and he heard Huxley's feet go padding down the carpeted hall.

Mann forced himself upright and swung his feet off the bed. One hand held the Browning as he rubbed his scalp with the other. He stood up, still grousing about the manner of his awakening.

If those guys had ever been stuck in the bughouse, he thought angrily, they'd know enough to never do that to another guy.

He didn't have to dress. He always slept with his jeans on. When you slept with your jeans on, nobody could catch you asleep and shove their penis up your rectum, especially if you had a good, tight leather belt holding your pants up.

Tony Mann stretched, burped, stuffed his Browning automatic into his waistband—cold, hard, safe feeling against his belly—and went padding downstairs barefoot to see what the hell was going on.

He came into the living room, blinking his eyes. It felt good to be there. Not long ago it had been the scene of exultant celebration among the three fighters of the Blizzard.

Then, damn him, Ian Altman had waddled in and dropped his huge frame into the oversize recliner chair, like some hideously distorted and bulbous Captain Kirk taking command on the bridge of the starship *Enterprise.*

"What do you mean," Altman had said, "you killed them all?

"What do you mean, you won the battle?" Altman had shrieked. "I didn't tell you to have a battle! I told you to give them the guns so we'd all be together!

"What do you mean, you lost the guns? You took them for nothing? You should have at least got the guns back!"

The lardass sure knows how to spoil a party, Tony had thought to himself bitterly.

But as he walked into the room, the wall-size TV screen playing brightly, it was like a new Ian was there. A new, happy, forgiving Ian.

"Look," cried the huge, ugly cherub in the recliner. "Look what's on the news."

The screen showed a dark Miami street by a bridge where one side of the passageway was pulled straight up in the air, exposing the dark water beneath it to the swords of light that reflected off its surface from the high-powered light the TV cameramen were using.

A gorgeous brunette was saying, ". . . the scene of a shooting minutes ago where a black Miami man, Michael Carpenter, was shot and severely wounded by Miami police officers when he allegedly came out of his car after a high-speed pursuit that ended at this drawbridge."

There were blue-and-red strobe lights flickering all over the scene.

"Look," squealed Altman. "It's happening. It's happening!"

Mann's eyes met Wallace Crowther's from across the room. They seemed to be asking each other, "What the hell is happening?"

MAYOR HERNANDEZ SQUIRMED out of the back seat of his limousine and into the lights of the TV cameras. Behind them he could see the flickering red-and-blue lights of the police cars and the other emergency vehicles.

The streets were lined with people, but thinly. There weren't more than a hundred, a hundred and fifty at the most. It looked as if there were at least thirty cops there, the dark blue uniforms of the Miami Police officers intermingled with the tan uniforms of Metro Dade officers.

Perfect, the mayor thought as his plainclothes police bodyguards drew in toward him, close and protective. Enough to keep him safe, but not enough cops to keep the crowd in check if things got out of control half an hour or so from now, when he would be safely away.

Perfect. Once he was gone, anything that happened later could be blamed on that damn John Kearn.

The TV camera lights were blinding. Someone thrust a foam-covered microphone toward his face. "Mr. Mayor," a man's voice asked from the darkness in the officious tone of a reporter talking for the record, "what is your response to the events of tonight?"

Mayor Hernandez cleared his throat and then said, "I understand that a black citizen has been shot for fleeing the police. I don't know why he fled or what was going on yet, but you may be sure I'll get to the bottom of it. When the police go out of control, we lose the very fabric of law and order. If this is a matter of police brutality, you can be sure I'll make them answer for it!"

Realizing that his sound bite was complete—and that he didn't know what he was talking about yet—Mayor Hernandez decided that the best thing to do was to stride forward past the minicams and out of that terrifying circle of light, toward the scene of the shooting. As soon as he got past the halo of the powerful lights, he realized he was blind. He bumped into someone.

"Don't touch me," he cried reflexively, and whoever he had contacted seemed to melt back into the darkness as his bodyguards took a firm, reassuring hold of his elbows.

From behind him a pompous male voice said into the camera, "You've just heard Mayor Orlando Hernandez promising to punish the police brutality that he apparently feels has been displayed here tonight. We cut now to Jane Fournier at Jackson Memorial Hospital for an update on the victim's condition. 'Eyewitness News' will remain here at the shooting scene to bring you the latest news on what may turn into the next severe civil disturbance here in Miami. Jane . . . ?"

IAN ALTMAN'S rotund cheeks glowed bright red as he shrilled, "Don't you see? Charlie Manson said it would happen. He just had the words wrong. He said it would be helter-skelter. Helter-skelter! The final race war that puts the whites against the niggers in the street. Listen to the mayor! I couldn't make him say anything to piss everybody off more than what he's saying now. Oh, God, it's like I'd scripted him!"

There was silence from the other Blizzard people. Finally Dewey Huxley said, "Uh, Ian, I don't get it. I mean, we were on TV just a little while ago, with the burning plane and all, and you weren't half as excited about that as you are about this. I mean, we done that for you. And you were like—what's that word?—you were like *ambivalent* about it. Now somebody shot some nigger nobody ever gave a shit about, didn't even shoot him dead, far as we know, and you're all like fallin' all over yourself. Ian, I just don't get it!"

The huge man in the oversize recliner went into a tantrum.

"Oooh," he shrieked. "Oooh! You don't get anything at all!" The fat legs began to drum on the floor, and the pudgy fists pounded up and down on the arms of the recliner. "What you did tonight wasn't what I wanted! But this is! This is what I wanted!"

Across the room Wallace Crowther realized that he was seeing his future. I thought for a moment tonight that the son of a bitch was a genius, and I just hadn't appreciated him. But just look at this. Look at this! The blithering idiot is truly out of his squirming, wriggly mind!

14

John Kearn came to a stop at the police roadblock. The rotating police light that was attached magnetically to the roof of his car, powered by the spiral cord that went under his steering wheel and into the socket of the car's cigarette lighter, had impressed no one.

The Miami cop who loomed over his window said, "Sorry, bud. Unless you've got some ID says you need to be here—"

Kearn shut him up quick. "Look at my face, dammit," he barked. "You don't recognize your own chief of police?"

Kearn saw the man turn pale from fear, even in the artificial light. "Holy shit," the cop blurted. "Chief! Excuse me, sir! I didn't—"

Kearn didn't wait to hear the rest of it. He drove his car through the opening in the roadblock, threading his way through the myriad of marked and unmarked police cars from different agencies that surrounded the scene and stopped when he could go no farther. He killed his headlights but left the motor running and the keys in the ignition. He knew that one of his officers might have reason to move the vehicle and he didn't want to make that cop's job any harder.

Then Kearn was out of the car, striding toward the shooting scene. The cops recognized him and stepped respectfully back out of his path.

As he reached the back of the Plymouth, he saw big Bruce Yount leaning over Tom West, yelling in his face. Yount was raving, "Stakeout again...heavy shit this time...don't gimme none of your *Garrity* bullshit!"

There were a lot of cops he didn't know but still commanded. These two he did know. Tom West had stuck in his mind as a caring black cop who had taken the heat of a controversial assignment—Stakeout—because he'd known that it would be a way to protect the people he had come on the job to take care of.

And he knew Bruce Yount. Even as a young cop with an instinctive distrust of headhunters, Kearn had always known that the internal-affairs people had a necessary place in the scheme of things. He knew that some cops had to police the other cops. But that didn't mean they had to take pleasure in bringing another man down, and he had never liked the gleam in Yount's eyes when he testified against another cop, recommending that his career—his chosen life—be torn away from him.

Kearn stepped between the two of them.

Yount's face changed. "Oh, uh, hello, Chief," Yount stammered.

The chief indulged himself in a broad grin. It had been a long week, but things were coming back to him.

Ken Bartlett, the Stakeout commander who reported directly to the chief, told him that Sergeant Cohen thought Yount might be the mole in the department who was giving information to the truth-twisting columnist, Oliver Teasdale. Teasdale was the pet columnist of the *Miami Crier.* The *Crier,* in turn, was the politically powerful voice behind Orlando Hernandez's successful run for the mayor's office.

It was starting to come together only now, when the chief didn't have time for it.

Kearn leered down into Yount's pasty face and said, in a tone of voice that was deadly soft, "Go ahead, Bruce. Tell me what you've got here."

"Um, I, uh..."

Kearn wanted to laugh. He had a mental image of Jackie Gleason playing Ralph Kramden and babbling, "Homina-homina-homina..." Hell, Bruce Yount even looked a little like Ralph Kramden.

Chief Kearn changed to a stern command voice. "You're a Professional Standards detective, Yount. It's your job to be able to tell me how my officers performed here. Well? Tell me!"

"Um, ah, they shot a black guy, Chief!"

"I know that, Yount. Who shot the black guy?"

"Um, a cop, I guess."

"Are you telling me, Yount, that you don't even know who shot the guy?"

Yount kept stammering. "Uh, well, no sir, not yet. I've only been here for twenty minutes, you know, I'm trying to—"

He stopped talking when Kearn raised his hand, palm toward him. "Hold it right there. You've been here twenty minutes. The shooting went down a half an hour ago. You're my eyes and ears for Professional Standards, and you not only don't know who the hell shot the guy, you're just putting the blocks to the nearest Stakeout guy you can find? Yount, did this incident have anything to do with Stakeout?"

The investigator's pallid face had turned beet red by now. "How would I know?" he bleated.

The chief's eyes narrowed. "Then why were you getting down on this officer with that crap about 'Stakeout again'?"

"I, uh, I mean..."

"Enough," grated Kearn in a voice low enough that only Yount could hear it. "You're off this case. Report to my office. I'll be there when I get there. Wait for me. Go. Now."

Yount turned, his shoulders slumping. He looked as if he was going to cry. He disappeared behind the bank of flashing lights.

Kearn turned to Tom West. He asked, "What the hell happened?"

"We pulled in just as the shooting went down, Chief," West began, and proceeded to tell the rest of the story.

Several yards away on the sidewalk, the crowd was pressing in on the people nearest the action. There were mutterings. "What'd they say? What's goin' down?"

The black bystander nearest the conversation said, "There was this white pig, was fuckin' with a cop just 'cause the cop was a brother. This other brother, the big guy there with the pistol on, got there and gave it to the white cop, told him to get the hell out."

The word passed through the crowd like wildfire. Soon the story was rife that a black cop had put down a white cop who was screwing with a black cop.

It seemed like a small victory. People who had come in anger, ready to throw things if a man had been shot by whites just because he was black, had been given the taste of a small victory. It wasn't enough to make them go home, but it was enough to make them wait a while to see what was happening before they decided what to do.

Then the camera lights all seemed to focus in one place, on a car some ten paces away from where John Kearn stood. Kearn barked, "What's going on?"

One of the officers said, "Chief, it looks like the mayor is going to make a statement to the press."

Kearn felt his blood run cold.

WHEN HE'D BEEN SWORN in to office more than a year ago, Kearn was acutely aware that he was taking command of the police in the single most race-riot-prone city in the United States. He had studied the background of that situation before and since, in Miami and elsewhere.

He had come to believe that there were three things that led to riots after police use of force. He thought of them as the Three *M*s.

Media, Mayors and Mopes.

Mopes were the low-life scum who spent their lives looking for an excuse to run rampant and prey on decent people, stealing their property and burning what couldn't be carried away.

The media seemed bent on creating news and not just reporting it. If cops had to use force to arrest a bad guy, the media would take the bad guy's side and portray the cops as fascist oppressors who deserved to be "bottled" and rebelled against.

And then there was the role a mayor could play, frequently driven by a desire to secure future votes.

It had happened close to home.

When Kearn had become chief in Miami, his senior operations personnel told him of the incipient riot years before that was almost under control until a well-meaning mayor, trying to quell the unrest of black people he couldn't possibly relate to, had jumped up on the hood of an automobile and begun to talk to the crowd. He told the mob in essence, "Don't worry, it's obvious that racist hate police murdered this poor guy just for being the same color as you, but don't worry, I'll take care of it for you."

Those weren't the actual words the mayor spoke, but those apparently were the vibes the crowd got from the mayor's words, because the next thing anyone knew, a full-blown race riot was under way.

And now, only a few steps away, it was about to happen again. The mayor was already standing on the hood of a car; the crowd, grown to a mob of three hundred people by now, was listening; and the TV minicams were focused on the mayor, ready to beam his words into every home in the city.

Kearn felt a sense of dread. Déjà vu. He had seen this before. He just hadn't been there those times.

But he was here now, *this* time.

And, by God, if the mayor went out of control, Kearn would stop it before it started.

The chief moved closer as the mayor began to speak.

THE MAYOR BASKED in the beams of the lights that shone upon him. Behind those lights was the crowd, and near them were the reporters.

Orlando Hernandez felt at home.

The rumble of the crowd had been rising until the lights came on, and then they fell silent. It was as if all the people present were saying, "Shush! This is a media event. Let him talk, and then we'll do whatever we were going to do anyway."

Hernandez cleared his throat.

"My friends," he began, "I share your pain. You elected me to lead this sometimes tortured city because you knew I had no bias, no prejudice. I have the memories of this city burning because of injustice done to black citizens by white police officers who abused their powers.

"I promised you when you elected me that I would not stand for that sort of thing, that I would punish any cop who felt his color gave him a license to point a police gun at a man and pull the trigger just because he was black."

The mayor had a well-tuned sense of timing. He paused just then to allow murmurs of assent and scattered applause in the audience.

A few steps away, in the darkness beneath the lights, Chief Kearn turned toward his officers and snapped, "Who's in charge of this situation?"

"I am, sir." The voice from the darkness seemed small and light.

Kearn peered into the shadows.

"Lieutenant Marisa Arcaya, sir," said a tiny, dark-haired woman who stepped forward.

"Lieutenant," Kearn grated, "I'm going to ask you a question, and you'd damn well better tell me the truth. If you don't, a lot of people could get killed, including a lot of cops. What the hell happened here, and who shot the guy? Quick!"

"Started as a routine speeding stop, sir, and escalated into a chase when the suspect wouldn't stop," the lieutenant answered rapidly. "Full-scale pursuit. The guy in the Plymouth, a Mr. Michael Carpenter, black male, came to a dead end where the drawbridge was up, and stopped. He got out of the car with a single-shot .22 rifle, turned it in the direction of the officers and our people opened fire.

"I saw the thing with the Professional Standards guy getting down on the Stakeout cops. That was bullshit, sir. The black Stakeout officer was the first to reach the suspect while he was down and try to help him, but he and his partner never fired."

Kearn hissed urgently, "Who did fire, Arcaya? I know the suspect was black, but what I've got to know is, what color were the cops who shot him?"

"As of now, sir, it looks as if three of our patrolmen fired. Officer Sanderson, Anglo, male. Officer Ruiz, Hispanic female. And Officer Rockland, black male, sir."

"Okay." Kearn sighed. "Thanks. That's what I needed to know for now."

Up in the glare of the lights, Mayor Hernandez was reaching a fever pitch in the oratory.

"I promise you justice," the mayor cried. "I promise you that any white cop who shoots a black man just because of his skin color will pay the price!"

The crowd was responding, vibrating with cries.

"Right on, brother!"

"Tell it!"

"No more Rodney Kings!"

Chief Kearn knew where it was going. Like kerosene thrown on a fire. He hadn't even had a chance, in the darkness, to see if his subordinate commanders had activated the Field Forces, to see if the initial containment rings were in place if this scene went up for grabs right now.

And it was too late. He had to trust them.

"I share your pain," the mayor cried from the hood of the car. "I understand your rage at the injustice that has permeated Miami in the past!"

The echoes in the crowd grew louder.

"Amen!"

"Make 'em pay!"

"Kill the racist bastards!"

The crowd had to number four hundred now, maybe five hundred. The mayor was inciting them!

Kearn knew he couldn't wait any longer.

He sprinted forward and, with a long jump, landed next to the mayor on the hood of the car in the glare of the blinding TV lights.

The crowd collectively gasped.

So, involuntarily, did Mayor Hernandez.

Kearn shouted out one word in a booming voice, one word that stilled the humming sound of the angry throng.

"Enough!"

Suddenly there was silence.

"Enough," Kearn boomed again. "Brothers, sisters, look at me. My name is John Kearn. I'm chief of police in this city. I've been up as late as you are and I'm as tired as you are. I'm not wearing a bulletproof vest. I *am* wearing a badge. But look at it. *Look* at it!"

The suddenly silent crowd stared and squinted at the gold shield clipped to Kearn's brown belt.

The chief continued, "You see that black band around my badge? It's a thing cops do, a sign of mourning. Six police officers have been murdered in this past week! It's a record, a terrible and ugly record, for this city.

"You want to talk about losing one of your own? Hell, you want to talk about losing your own black brothers and sisters to the hands of white racists? Well, you all watch TV and read the newspapers, don't you? So, I guess you know why I've got this black band around my badge.

"Every one of those people—three black, one Hispanic, one Vietnamese and one white highway-patrol officer—were killed by white racists. They were killed by people who couldn't tolerate people who weren't like them, so they shot them to death! Shot one of them to death in front of his wife and his baby daughter."

Kearn paused to take a breath. The crowd was going, "Ooohh." The mayor was just standing out of the way.

"Dammit," Kearn roared, "do we remember Rodney King? During the Los Angeles riots? Do we remember King saying, 'Can't we all just get along?' "

By now a hush had fallen over the crowd. The group had swelled to perhaps six hundred.

"It isn't enough to try to 'just get along,'" Kearn told the crowd in his powerful voice. "Not when there are people out there who will kill you for just being the wrong color. But we're trying to deal with that. I've got more than a thousand cops out there trying to find out who's killing black people for not being white.

"Tonight, right where we're all standing, a shooting went down. That's why we're all here. A man refused to stop for police who just wanted to give him a speeding ticket. That man chose to race through the streets, endangering your children, instead of just pulling over and taking the ticket. When the cops chased him and he ran out of places to run, he came out of his car with a gun in his hand.

"I don't know why he did that yet. Neither do any of you. But when the cops who faced him saw that gun, you *know* there was only one thing they could think!

"They fired. The man went down and dropped his gun. They stopped shooting.

"One of those officers was as black as any of you. As black as the man who was shot. As black as I am! But does that matter? One of the other officers who fired was Anglo, and the other was a Latino. Does it make any damn difference?

"For God's sake, most of us standing here weren't even born when the last lynching of a black man took place here. Right now, right here, this past week, you've seen half a dozen cops lynched just for being what they were—cops and people of color. If I pulled a gun on you for no reason, I'd expect you to shoot me in self-defense—well, that's what these officers did. Are we going to lose our souls, revert to mob violence, because someone pulled a gun on a cop and the cop shot back? No! Dammit, I have to tell you—as a cop, as a black man, just as a man—*no!*"

Someone in the crowd shouted, "Right on, bro!" Someone else took up the chant.

It was too much for Orlando Hernandez. He lunged back into the spotlight and cried, "Don't listen to him! He's an apologist for the cops! He's the one who turned loose the damn Stakeout Unit! I'm telling you, I am the one who can give you justice! Listen to me!"

Later John Kearn would ask himself a hundred times why he did it, and a hundred times more if he should have done it. But at that moment it happened spontaneously.

Chief Kearn turned, cocked his strong arm and punched the mayor of the City of Miami on the jaw with as fine a right cross as had ever been seen on Friday-night boxing.

Every one of the hundreds of people present could hear the hard, bone-to-bone impact of the punch landing, could see the major spin violently away and fall off the hood of the car and into the crowd that broke his fall. Only a few could see that his eyes had rolled all the way up into his head before he started to topple off the vehicle and out of the lights.

There was a long moment of collective, stunned silence.

Kearn turned to the crowd and cried, "No more bullshit, all right? No more bullshit!"

The crowd murmured softly in awe.

"The hurting has to stop. The hate has to stop. Whether it's killing people because they're black, or whether it's trying to get your blood up 'cause it seems like the thing to do to get on TV, dammit, the hurting has to stop!"

Someone in the crowd cried, "Stop the hurting!" Someone called it out again. In moments it had become a rhythmic chant.

"Stop the hurting! Stop the hurting!"

Kearn ran out of words. He had nothing left to say. He stood alone in the lights, surrounded by what was now six or seven hundred people. The gun so clearly visible on his belt wasn't a weapon anymore; it was a badge of office, a mark of the protector, as surely as the black-banded gold shield clipped in front of it on his belt.

In the audience, someone clapped. The others picked it up. It became a thunderous, rolling wave of applause. And through it all, the chant continued.

"Stop the hurting! Stop the hurting!"

Chief John Kearn just stood there numbly on the hood of the car, bathed in the bright lights. Against all odds, somehow, he seemed to have won.

15

No one man's words were enough to stop a riot, but Kearn's had at least blunted the force of the storm.

TV news in the homes and bars had shown people yelling in the streets at the drawbridge. It was a riot mood that hovered over the city. Isolated incidents of bottling began at first outside the bars in Liberty City and Overtown. The Field Forces had not yet set up.

Fred Johnson armed himself inside his Overtown pawnshop as soon as the bottles had stared flying. When two men with a ball bat and a tire iron had started smashing through his locked door, he fired three shots. A fifty-six-year-old black man who couldn't get insurance since the last riot, he was determined not to lose everything he had worked for.

Two of his bullets missed. One, however, struck twenty-two-year-old Lawrence Prentiss through the heart, killing him where he stood on the sidewalk.

Responding Miami patrolmen saw the mood of the crowd. It wasn't something to stay for. They made a show of arresting Johnson in hopes of placating the mob—actually they were putting him in protective custody more than anything else—and as soon as the ambulance took the body away, they zoomed out of the neighborhood. If Homicide wanted to stand among a gang of angry rioters to guard the chalked outline of a looter's body, they could be their guests.

In the back of the white MPD Caprice, Fred Johnson was crying inconsolably. He knew what his neighbors would do to his shop now that he was no longer there to protect it. In the past three riots, the pawnshop had survived only because Johnson stood at the front door with a loaded shotgun in his hands.

Minutes after the police had left, the looters breached the door and the windows of the pawnshop. Twenty people pushed at each other to get at the guns first.

One of them was Radleigh Bingham. He had walked away from the hospital where they'd committed him, the bandage for his gunshot wound still on his leg. The haloperidol they had given him had never been swallowed; he had tucked it into his cheek and pretended to gulp it down, then spit it out. He had saved them, collecting them as evidence to prove the conspiracy against him. His pockets were filled with little green-scored five-milligram tablets, the aqua, octagonal ten-milligram tabs and several of the bombers, the salmon-colored twenty-milligram tablets prescribed when he had not responded to treatment and the dosage was increased to a massive one hundred milligrams per day.

Bingham was one of the first to smash through the locked showcase. He looked disdainfully at two semiautomatic pistols, passing them over his shoulders to others. You couldn't trust them. They'd go off in your pocket by themselves and shoot you through the leg. Get a revolver, one of the other patients had explained to him, with a round cylinder in the middle; it won't go off by itself.

He found one like that, gray and huge. He squinted at the letters on the barrel—Highway Patrolman .357 Magnum. He began looking for Highway .357 Magnum ammunition. They didn't have any so he settled for a box labeled PMC .357 Magnum. When he finally figured out how to open the cylinder, the bullets seemed to fit.

Now he was ready. The voices told him so.

"I CAN'T," cried Wallace Crowther. "They'll be watching for us. It's suicide!"

"You can! You will! Now!" shrieked Ian Altman hysterically. He put his hand on the Colt Python .357 beside him for emphasis.

Crowther hung his head. No sense arguing with a crazy man. And just when he was beginning to think there might be some sense behind that fat, jowled face.

Crowther turned on the microphone and began to speak into the tape recorder, in his most macho voice, reading from the sheet of paper in front of him.

"White patriot brothers. The time of battle is upon us. The blacks are in the streets. This time to burn your neighborhoods, not their own!"

Crowther knew that was bullshit, of course; the on-scene TV reports indicated that, as usual, the violence was limited to black neighborhoods. Man, it seemed, was the only creature that fouled its own nest when it became enraged. But Altman's hand was perilously close to that heavy revolver, and it didn't seem a good time to argue with his choice of words.

Crowther's booming voice continued, "Join us, O my brothers! We are already winning the battle. You've heard and seen the battle at the airport. That was us, the Blizzard. The blacks sent a cadre of well-armed Jews of the Zionist Occupation Government to murder us, but instead, we annihilated them, with no casualties of good white men.

"Come to the streets with us, my brothers. Join the Blizzard. We will fight the black beast on its own ground, in the streets of Overtown and Liberty City. Rise up, my brothers, and join the Blizzard in the name of the holy white race!"

He ended the tape.

Ian Altman clapped his hands like a grotesquely huge baby. "Well done! Well done!"

Tony Mann muttered, "He's got a point, though, Ian. After that's broadcast, they'll be looking for us. How we gonna get in and out of Overtown or Liberty City with our white faces, without getting shot to pieces?"

Ian Altman turned his neck inside the rolls of fat, grinning conspiratorially at Dewey Huxley. "Show them. Bring forth the monster!"

IN THE TRAINING CAMP at the edge of the Everglades, the heavyset colonel from ARM was ranting at a motley group of perhaps thirty men. Some wore khakis like his, some SWAT-style BDUs, the rest nondescript jumpsuits and cammies with a mish-mash of black nylon weapon and ammo pouches.

"I can't believe this shit," he yelled. "Mother-fuckin' Blizzard gets on the radio, calling our patriots, our real white patriots, a buncha fuckin' kikes! Are we gonna take this?"

"No," they chorused.

"I can't hear yew!"

They roared, "No!"

"Then, by God, lock an' load," the ARM leader shouted. "Come tonight, we gonna kick us some ass! We gonna teach 'em what it means to be back-shootin' *real* patriots!"

"IT'S NOT a full-blown riot yet, Chief, based on the ones I've been through," the chief of special operations was telling John Kearn. "We've got some outbreaks of looting, some arson but not all that much, and the fire department is still responding. Compared to, say, the MacDuffee riot, this is a cake-walk, so far. It's more like the looting and sporadic shooting that came from Hurricane Andrew. Our problem is manpower and blue flu."

Kearn frowned. Calling in sick, or blue flu, as it came to be known, was usually a response to a disliked policy affecting police life, but it wasn't aimed at avoiding responsibility or duty. "I'm not sure it's really blue flu. That usually means they got together in an orchestrated, union-approved kind of thing. This seems to be spontaneous."

"Can't blame them, really," the special-ops chief said. "Sons of bitches start killing cops in their homes, shooting at their little kids, can't wonder that some of them will stay home and protect what's most important. I packed my wife and kids off to her family's people in South Carolina yesterday."

"I think I've got a handle on it," said Kearn. "I spoke this morning with the union heads. I suggested that the union hall be turned into a guarded day-care center on an emergency basis. Cops can take turns providing security off duty—what time they can, on twelve-hour shifts—and I suggested most of the guard work be done by retired cops. They're all trained and they're all authorized to carry guns."

"Good move. What's the word on this latest bullshit from the Blizzard?"

"Have to take it serious," sighed Kearn, rubbing above his eyes at the growing headache. He'd been too long without sleep. "I want your SWAT teams out there at full strength. Metro Dade is going to field the same. The governor has agreed to roll in his best National Guard infantry unit for standby. As soon as the Blizzard took credit for the thing at the airport, I knew we needed the heavy stuff."

"No problem," said the special-ops chief proudly. "You haven't seen my guys shoot. A LAW rocket doesn't mean much when the operator's just been shot in the head with one of our countersniper rifles."

Kearn hated it. His city, the city he was sworn to keep the peace in, was turning into a war zone. What next? Tanks? Fighter bombers?

Kearn said dryly, "And you tell me this is a mini-riot?"

"Chief, take it from me—if the MacDuffee riot was Hurricane Andrew, this little civil disturbance we've got going here is a tempest in a teapot."

SARAH COHEN was meeting Rabbi Schiller for coffee. As devout as she was, she could no longer visit him in his office at the back of the synagogue where he had always counseled her and the other faithful before. It was in that office that what she thought of as the *thing* had happened to Michael.

"I'm not sure why I'm here," she began defensively. "Mike told me about his talks with you after the shootings. I know you're on his side."

A kindly smile appeared through Schiller's beard. He patted her hand. "Ach, Sarah. I am on both your sides. Now more than ever, I have been personally where both of you are right now."

"Yes," she sighed, "but now you're more where he is."

"Only in a sense," the rabbi answered softly. "You remember when we worked together on the committee? The committee to ban handguns?"

"Yes," she said. "I still belong. I'm not as active as I used to be. But you were the chairman."

He nodded. "Yes. The operative word being, of course, I *was* the chairman. I finally resigned, you know. After the...the incident, I felt like something of a hypocrite being there."

"I suppose you've joined the NRA," she said sarcastically.

He chuckled again. "No, but did you know they invited me to? I wasn't happy when they wrote about me without asking permission. 'Antigun Rabbi Shoots, Kills Satanist Gunman To Rescue Wounded Policeman And Kidnap Victim.' It was something I wanted to put behind me. I didn't appreciate having my nose rubbed in the blood I had spilled."

"But you had to," she conceded. "I know how hard it must have been. I never did thank you as I should have. Mike said without you, that man would have killed both him and the girl."

"Yes," the rabbi sighed. "I had to. I have probed my heart ever since, and it is so difficult to find remorse for that man after I learned the evil that he did, the evil that had motivated him. I console myself with the thought that in some small way I relieved the world of an evil thing that would have hurt the righteous if I had not. Whatever demons drove that man to become what he was, perhaps now he has peace. I think of it this way—how many of my Catholic-priest friends ever get to perform a real exorcism and remove a real demon?"

Sarah Cohen laughed in spite of herself. The ice seemed broken.

"Rabbi," she said, becoming serious again, "Mike was at the house the other night. He went to put something in the safe, something he bought for me. He saw the petition for divorce that I'd had drawn up. I hadn't decided to file it yet." She paused and added, "Jacob said Mike cried."

Schiller shook his head. "You still love him, don't you?"

"I love Michael," she blurted. "*My* Michael! The Michael I married, who fathered my son, who adopted our youngest with as much love as I did when I couldn't have any more. But, Rabbi, this is a new Michael. A Mike who calls me with crazy, paranoid delusions, telling me to get the kids out of the house. Who carries guns when he didn't before. Who wants *me* to carry a gun. That's what he left in the safe."

The rabbi's hand closed over hers, and he began to speak softly. "It's the same Michael, believe me. But it is a Michael who has seen, and had to do, things he never dreamed would be necessary when he became a policeman.

"I have known your husband, Sarah, since he was a boy. Since before you were married. All he ever wanted to be was a mensch, a good, honest man, a good, honest husband and father who did a good, honest job for forty hours and went home to his family.

"He took the job on the Stakeout Unit because he thought commanding an element of a high-risk unit would be a good career move, would allow him to move up the promotion ladder, make a better home for you and Jacob and the new baby. He's a family man, you see. Well, you know.

"But something happened on the Stakeout Unit. He bonded in a way he never had before as a police supervisor. He realized, perhaps for the first time, that the supervisor is the parent and the subordinate is the child, and now his children were going in to face the deadliest danger of their job.

"He had to be with them, Sarah. Would he let Jacob, oh, ride a jet-ski or a motorbike or something else even remotely dangerous without being with him? Of course not. It was like that with his officers. He had to be there to protect them. One of the men he shot, he shot to protect those occupational children of his. And the other, he shot to save his own life, to keep you from being a widow and the children from being orphans.

"That changed him, Sarah. Some of the psychologists call it cognitive dissonance. New values are thrust upon you that you have to accept, whether you like them or not. It has been like that for Michael.

"He has come to see the reality of a violent world in a way he has never known before. He cannot leave that at work, like a service revolver in a locker, when he comes home. Part of his new values involve protection and self-preservation, and he wants to share them with you."

He paused to assess her response.

"That *is* an alien sense of values to me, Rabbi. It goes against everything I've been brought up to believe. 'Turn the other cheek,' all of that. The lesson of Masada. The victim wins the moral victory in the end. The one who kills does not."

The rabbi looked at her with sad wisdom. "It's funny you should mention Masada," he answered. "I brought a book for you to read. A friend of mine gave it to me after the shooting. It's about self-defense. The writer, who is of Arab-American heritage, mentions Masada in a way I had never thought of until lately. Here, let me share it with you."

From his attaché case, Rabbi Schiller withdrew a paperback book, well thumbed and tattered at the edges, and turned to a page that had been marked beforehand.

"The writer asks rhetorically, 'If a criminal attacks me homicidally, isn't that God's will?' And he answers, 'Maybe. But if God allows you to fight back, then is that not also God's will?'

"And now, Sarah, the part I want you to hear. The author has asked rhetorically, 'Is it not a moral victory to surrender to a homicidal criminal assault, rather than to descend to his level of base animal violence?' And he answers thus:

> 'The morality of lethal retaliation versus suicidal submission must be addressed at two levels: practical and spiritual. I never understood why, within a space of eighteen months, American television correctly depicted the Guyana tragedy as a sickening, debasing case of sociopsychological cancer, yet in the TV-movie *Masada* glorified a similar mass suicide-murder as a "moral victory." Mass suicide and killing your children to make a political statement of self-righteous morality is still murdering your children, whether you do it in the name of the People's Church or Judaism.
>
> 'One wonders if the Roman legions, upon entering the corpse-strewn mountaintop fortress of Masada, ever really believed they had lost a moral victory. Suppose American forces had landed on Saipan in 1944 and found that all the Japanese had killed themselves. They wouldn't have looked at each other and said, "Aw, Jeez, we've been deprived of a moral victory." They would have said, "Yay! Thank God! None of us is going to get killed! The crazy

Japs killed themselves! Let's break out the beer and celebrate!"

'The generals of the Roman legions entering Masada must have felt the same revulsion and hatred for Eleazar Ben Yair as we all had for James Jones when we saw the bodies of those hundreds of women and children who had been forced, weeping, to swallow poison at the command of a mad fanatic. Both leaders had forced women and children who didn't want to die, to surrender their lives in the name of a "moral principle."

'The message of Masada was supposedly that, by killing your wives and children instead of letting them be captured and made slaves, you further your own righteousness and the glory of your God. But suppose instead of slaughtering their wives and children, the defenders of Masada had surrendered.

'Perhaps the men would have been executed, fulfilling their wish to experience moral superiority. The children would have been slaves, but would have been sown like seeds within the bosom of the conqueror society, each filled with a burning motivation to avenge Masada. A generation later their heritage and righteous hatred might have flowered into a Nat Turner-like rebellion. Such a firestorm could have rocked the oppressor society to its roots. Who is to say that history might not have been changed, that centuries later wars might not have been averted and six million Jews might not have been spared the horror of the Holocaust?' "

He closed the book. After a long moment Sarah said in a tiny voice, "That's moving."

"It describes Michael," the rabbi said softly. "He will not sacrifice orphaned children and a widowed wife. He began as a soldier of Masada and he has become a Maccabee. He is a righteous warrior who strikes when he must, on behalf of the innocent. It is because he is good, because he cares, because he has the same family values he had when you fell in love with him. You see, he hasn't really changed. He is the same light seen through a new prism, and if he has changed at all, it is in that he has become stronger, more protective, more compassionate for the innocent and for the people he loves."

Sarah lowered her head. "I should go to him, shouldn't I?"

"Yes," the rabbi answered. "Yes, I think you should."

BEHIND THE HIGH, ivy-covered walls and gates of the Altman property, no one but the Blizzard could see the machine rolling out of a separate building that had always been locked up and off-limits to them. Only Altman and Huxley knew what was inside.

Rolling through its door now, taking what seemed forever to emerge, was a giant Cadillac limousine, snow-white in color, stretching more than twenty feet, its windows tinted black.

"My father called it 'the monster,'" Altman mused. "He bought it toward the end, before he died, when our family was getting some threats because of some false accusations against me. It's bulletproof. The windows are Lexan. The doors are armored. There are hidden gun ports in all four doors. It cost over two hundred thousand dollars back then."

Mann and Crowther whistled in awe. Huxley said, "Unfortunately the windows don't roll down. The M-60s would be too big to get in there. Besides, you know what they sound like when they go off. Shoot them from inside a car, and you'll be deaf for the rest of your life."

"Oh, who cares?" Altman's squeal had an impatient ring to it. "We've got the regular rifles and the pistols. That's all we're going to need. What are the subhumans going to throw at us? Rocks? Bottles? Pistol bullets? My father paid for this to stop NATO armor-piercing 7.62 mm rounds.

"We'll just cruise through, shoot a few of them, leave. Set an example. Anything they throw at us will be like water off a duck's back. We'll show them!"

Wallace Crowther kept hearing "we" and "us." Ian Altman had always stayed home and let the rest of them do the dirty work. He couldn't help asking, "Uh, Ian? Sounds like you plan on coming with us."

Altman turned toward him, and Crowther saw the insane glitter in the huge man's eyes. "Of course! This time, of course! This will be my masterpiece!"

Live and learn, thought Crowther glumly. A new surprise every day.

THE VIOLENCE in Liberty City was escalating. For a four-square-block area, cars and buildings were burning. The fire trucks were coming under sniper fire, and their operators were refusing to enter the epicenter of the riot. No one could blame them. The flames burned out of control. So did a handful of overturned cars in the street.

Stakeout Team Two had been brought together by Mike Cohen. No more riding pairs: they'd run in a cohesive force of seven until further notice. The Hidden Agenda vests were gone, too. Each Stakeout cop wore the same dark blue emergency jumpsuit, flak jacket and riot helmet as did most of the other cops. Their Benelli automatic shotguns were visible now, in German-style slings that carried the weapons across their chests. The flak jackets would have blocked their access to their usual concealed-carry holsters, so each wore an SAS black nylon leg holster. Designed by the SAS, Great Britain's Special Air Service commandos, the holster carries the gun on the outside of the thigh, above the knee but below a heavy, outside-worn bulletproof vest. It gives quick access despite the wearing of bulky emergency equipment, and does not get in the way during rappeling or window entry. For this reason, the SAS thigh holster is widely favored by American police SWAT teams.

The air was acrid with smoke. The pall of smoke from the burning buildings had darkened this part of the city like some terrible storm clouds blocking the moonlight. In the distance they could hear sirens, and not so distant were the pops of sporadic gunfire.

Mike Cohen was briefing his troops.

"Looks like this is all we've got," he told the five officers in front of him. "We don't know where the hell Harrington is. He doesn't answer his phone, and dispatch says his pager isn't working. That leaves six of us. We'll run in this van over here. We borrowed it from Narcotics. No radio, just our portables. No emergency lights, just a little magnetic Kojak light to plug into the lighter and put on the dashboard.

"We won't function with the regular Field Forces. Lieutenant Bartlett wants us out and about, a rover car, still an umbrella car like you've been doing.

"Our target is the Blizzard. The chief thinks we have to take the latest threat seriously. I don't see much chance of them getting in through the roadblocks, but those people they're supposed to have blown away at the airport the other night didn't think that was going to happen, either. Keep your heads up.

"Snipers? We respond. We've got two scoped .308s in the cases in the van. Bob, you're the best shot on the team—we need some countersniping, you're the number-one designated hitter. Stan, you're our second-best marksman—you back him up with the second rifle. Everybody keep your shotguns on and ready to go.

"Vehicle rescue? We respond. You know the Field Force drill. One car in front, like a battering ram. That's us. We deploy out with the shotguns and pistols, not the rifles, while three more patrol cars come in behind us, rescue whoever's trapped and pull back out. Don't try to arrest anybody. Let them go if you don't have to shoot them. We just extricate the victims and back on out.

"Any questions?"

"Yeah, Sarge," said Bob Carmody. "Right now we've got the Benellis loaded with double-O buckshot. That's gonna spread real quick, and not be too effective against cars, either. Anything we have to do is likely to involve taking out a selected target. And if the Blizzard is in cars, we want something that'll punch through an ordinary auto body. We've all got the one-ounce rifled slugs with us for specialty ammo needs. Any chance of us loading up to start with the slugs?"

A year ago Mike Cohen would have exploded in anger against a subordinate who had dared to suggest replacing standard ammo with projectiles that weighed an ounce, measured almost three-quarters of an inch in diameter and traveled at 1400 feet per second. But that was then, and this was now.

"You're the team firearms instructor, Bob. You think it's a good idea?"

"Yes, Sarge, I really do."

"Okay, team, you heard him. Change the ammo. Four slugs in the magazine and one in the chamber. Do it now, and then we roll!"

16

Sarah and Jacob Cohen sat on the living room sofa. "The PBA called today," the mother told the son. "Between the riot and everything else, we all think the best idea is for the kids whose parents are cops to go to the PBA headquarters. They've got it all set up like a playroom inside for you. There'll be lots of cops to take care of you. Now, I want you to be a real man, Jacob. I'm going to leave you in charge of the baby. You know how important that is?"

He nodded solemnly and then asked, "But, Mom, where are you gonna be?"

"I have to see Dad," she said, and it choked her up to watch his eyes brighten.

"You mean," Jacob said happily, "you and Dad are gonna get back together? All right!" He threw himself into her arms.

She held back the tears. "Go on," she said brusquely. "Put some extra clothes, and a toothbrush and toothpaste for you and some diapers for the baby, into one of the bags. I've got to get something. Then we'll go." Jacob scampered off excitedly.

It's the right thing, she said to herself with determination. She couldn't let all those years be for nothing. Perhaps the rabbi was right.

She thought for a moment and then walked purposefully toward the master bedroom. As she stood at the wall safe, dexterously fingering its combination, she tried to rationalize to herself. Mom always said that if you at least pretended to agree with your husband, that would be enough. It's not like I'm subjugating myself to his paranoia. It's . . . it's a gesture at reconciliation. She opened the box, took out the gun. It was gray and ugly. So were the five bullets in the box.

She never forgot anything she had learned. All those years ago, she had gone through a firearms-training course as part of the department's effort to develop a sensitivity program that would help the spouses to "understand the job" and perhaps reduce the incredibly high divorce rate among its members. Nationwide, she had learned, police would divorce sooner and more frequently than people in any other occupation.

Now she knew why.

Sarah thumbed the knurled, square latch on the left of the revolver's frame and pushed the cylinder open. Its five cartridge chambers lay like torpedo tubes, yawning open.

One by one she thumbed the cartridges into the chambers. Each seated with a solid little thunk. She closed the cylinder, and it locked in place with the finality of a bank vault slamming shut. She could begin to understand how people got their false sense of security from owning one of these. She could feel the deadly power that seemed to emanate from it.

Sarah was wearing jeans and a golf shirt, with a fanny pack in front to hold her wallet. The pack had room. She unzipped its pocket, inserted the gun as carefully as she would handle a poisonous snake and zipped it closed again.

She thanked God for small favors. When Michael had been going through his paranoid period, she had indulged him by signing the paperwork he sent to the state office in Tallahassee for the permit to carry a concealed weapon. When it came back, she had obediently put it into her wallet next to her driver's license, hoping it would make him happy. But, no, he'd wanted her to actually carry the damn gun!

Well, she was carrying it now. Conciliation. Reconciliation. How could two words that sounded so alike have two such different meanings? She would never be conciliatory to someone she disagreed with outside her own family. But reconciliation? For Mike?

She remembered his tender touch on their wedding night. Remembered the blissful look on his face as he stood at the bottom of the delivery table as she gave birth to their only natural child. Remembered the glow in his eyes when they first saw their new, adopted baby.

Michael, she thought. If it will stop the pain, I'll carry this damn thing for you. You can never make me use it, but I'll carry it, just for tonight, as a symbol of my love, of my willingness for us to be a family again.

From the hallway she heard Jacob shout cheerfully, "We're ready, Mom!"

At the last moment, she remembered that MPD and Metro Dade had closed off access and egress to riot scenes. What if Michael was there now, at what the TV said was a "miniriot"? If that was where she had to go to find him, she would need an entrée.

Her mind raced back over their married life, since he had graduated from the police academy. Whenever Mike had to identify himself as a cop, he simply showed the badge. Come to think of it, no one had ever actually bothered to read the ID card that went along with it.

An involuntary smile came to her face as she remembered the early days, when she'd polish his brass for him, iron his uniforms with the sharp creases down the legs and help him pin on the nameplate and the badge and all the other accoutrements of the clothing that defined the job he loved. Mike had owned, what, two full-size badges and the little off-duty one? A big badge for the shirt and another for the jacket in cool weather. She remembered he'd taken only the big one and one of the small ones with him. He hadn't worked uniform since joining Stakeout, and his uniforms were still here.

She opened the closet and pushed some shirts away. There! The pressed and starched blue shirt, ready to go, with the gold-lettered nameplate on the right breast and the gold shield of a Miami Police sergeant on the right.

Gently, almost reverently she unpinned the badge. It was time to thank God again, this time for a gender-integrated police department. There were police sergeants who were mid-fortyish women in good shape, albeit graying.

She could pass.

THE RADIO INSIDE THE VAN crackled to life. It was on the unmonitored channel, the one the cops used inside the danger scene. Usual radio procedure was not followed when it wasn't recorded.

"Stakeout Two," a masculine voice barked. "Northwest Twenty-fourth Avenue and Martin Luther King Boulevard. Got a report, car full of Asians, under attack, they're trying to drag 'em out. We've got three marked Field Force cars rolling."

"Responding now," barked Cohen into his portable in the right front seat. Frank Cross, beside him at the wheel, spun the van toward the scene. Cohen shoved the plug into the cigarette-lighter socket to turn on the dashboard police light. "Places, guys," Cohen said flatly.

They were ready. Bob Carmody and Tom West were poised by the van door, their hands on their chest-slung shotguns, ready to slide the door open and go. Behind them, coiled and ready, were Stan Baranck and Melinda Hoffritz. They all had their helmets on, with the Lexan visors up for better visibility.

As Cross came out of the corner and toward the cross street, his high-beam headlights bathed the scene. A copper-colored compact car was stopped at the crosswalk, surrounded by what had to be ten good-size black men. They were rocking the car back and forth, trying to tip it onto its side. Even as they watched, the car went over on its right, quivered and stayed like that.

The Stakeout cops could hear the sirens of the patrol cars coming in on their flank to assist.

Cross swept the van around and in front of the copper sedan that lay on its side. His left door was facing the vehicle and the men around it.

Cross didn't get out of the van.

He didn't have to.

He simply raised the chest-slung Benelli automatic shotgun and aimed it out the left window as he barked, "Police! Don't move!"

The other cops were bailing out of the van now, first Carmody cutting left and around and West buttonhooking right and around, then Baranck and Hoffritz doing the same thing. Sergeant Cohen was already out of the car and coming in around the front of the van.

Perhaps four of the ten men were holding tire irons or ball bats. They dropped them as they looked down the barrels of half a dozen automatic shotguns.

And now the other Field Force cops swept in. One cruiser pulled up parallel to the copper car on the right, the other on the left, the third in behind. More cops were in the street now, two carloads of Miami cops in blue with Glock pistols or Remington shotguns out and racked, and a carload of Metro Dade cops wearing tan and leveling assorted 9 mm automatics.

"Hey, man," one of the rioters squeaked, "we was only tryin' to scare 'em, ya know?"

A cop barked, "Anyone hurt inside?"

One of the three Cambodian women in the car said tentatively, "No, not really."

"Hang on tight," yelled one of the Metro cops, and in moments several strong arms had pushed the car back upright, bouncing on its wheels. The cops hustled the three frightened women out of the vehicle, pulling each one into every squad car. Each car backed up, spun in a J-turn and left, one-two-three, like the Blue Angels flying in formation. When the last was gone, Sergeant Cohen and his people were alone with the rioters.

"You got a freebie," Cohen yelled, his voice as cold as it was loud. "Take advantage of it. Get out of here. *Now!*"

Nine began to back off. One held his ground, staring at the ring of Stakeout cops, his eyes burning into Tom West's.

"How can you be doin' this shit, man?" he asked indignantly. "You s'posed to be African-American! You s'posed to be blood!"

West took a step forward, his Benelli automatic shotgun aimed at the loudmouth's chest. "You're no blood of mine, punk," he growled back.

"Shit," growled the rioter. "You a Uncle Tom, is what you is!"

Tom West's voice was even colder and harder. "You're not black, you little bastard, you're just yellow. How many stores did you and your scumbag friends rip off tonight that are black owned? Probably all of them!"

The man looked down sheepishly.

"Get out of here," West roared contemptuously. "You make me ashamed of the color of my skin!" West took one more step forward. The rioter cringed backward, then turned and ran, following the others.

"Back on board, team," yelled Cohen. "Mission accomplished! We're out of here!"

WHEN SARAH COHEN dropped the kids off at the PBA's makeshift day-care center and safehouse, the place was bedlam. She had to block one ear as she talked into the pay phone after dialing her husband's number at the police department.

"Stakeout Team Two is all down in Liberty City, ma'am," she could hear the secretary say. "That's all I can tell you. We can't beep them except for priority-one emergencies. Do you have an emergency?"

No, Sarah admitted, not really, and she hung up the phone.

She was glad she had taken Michael's badge.

THE COMBINED FORCES of ARM, CCC and SOLID deployed out of the Everglades in four vehicles, two vans and two sedans, equally divided with seven per squad. Before they headed out, the heavyset commander from ARM gave them one more pep talk.

"Remember," he cried, "we ain't there to shoot Nigras! It ain't the time yet. That day'll come, make no mistake, that glorious day will come! But today we got to avenge the deaths of our great patriot brothers, who done been backshot by them coward Blizzards! We gonna just kill bad whites today, so's y'all can preserve yer right ta string up Nigras an' Jews on thc lampposts tomorrow, like in the Newest Testament! Y'all with the program?"

"Yes," they chorused. "Yes!"

Satisfied, the ARM leader piled into his van. He had mostly his own people, khaki-clad activists of the Aryan Revolutionary Movement. They had their 9 mm automatics as personal-defense weapons, and H&K MP-5 submachine guns just like intelligence indicated the SWAT team of Miami PD and the Special Reaction Team of the Metro Dade police would have. The guns had been sold with the approval of the West German government to the antiterrorist police of Colombia, and had been taken from dead Colombian troopers by some of the militant dope dealers that ARM bought guns from.

The leader and his cohorts didn't let the rank and file know where the guns came from. They were politically naive, and wouldn't understand. It was better to just let them go on with their fantasies of an all-white nation where their skin would make them successful in a world where their minds and bodies could not.

Of the six others in the van with him, four were elite ARM citizen-soldiers. The fifth man was the lone SOLID survivor of the Blizzard ambush at the airport. As soon as the ARM head knew this guy was available, he knew he wanted him at his side. He was, after all, the only one who could pick out the enemy on sight. His SOLID counterpart had loved it when he was invited to ride with the ARM leader; it made him feel all warm and fuzzy and accepted.

The fool.

The sixth man was a former City of Miami cop who was currently suspended without pay and awaiting trial for extortion charges. Somehow when the police department people had picked up his gun and badge and ID, they had missed a duplicate badge and duplicate MPD ID card. That was going to be their ticket into the scene tonight. Maybe the others wouldn't get in to kill the Blizzard, but this crew would.

Sitting in the right front seat, the ex-cop turned and said, "You know, guys, I'm really having second thoughts on this."

Sitting behind him, the ARM leader grinned broadly. "Well, shit, boy, I unnerstan' that. An' I got some advice for y'all. When yer feelin' like crappin' out on us, there's just one word y'all need to remember."

He drew his stainless-steel Smith & Wesson 9 mm from under his khaki shirt and thrust it viciously under the ex-cop's ear.

"One word, boy! An' that word is—*don't!*"

THE GOVERNOR WAS STALLING on the troops, and Kearn called him to find out what was going on. "Chief," the governor said, "I understand your concerns, believe me. I want to help. But as the governor, I have to have the request come from the mayor of the involved city. Orlando Hernandez just called me and told me emphatically, very emphatically, that the situation does not require either martial law or National Guard troops. Chief, my hands are tied! I hope you understand my position."

Kearn forced himself to keep a level voice when he answered, "Of course, sir, I understand. Please stay available for the next ten or fifteen minutes. I'm going to need to have the mayor call you back and get this cleared up."

He put the phone gently down in the cradle and, as soon as he did, stabbed his finger into the intercom button that signaled his indispensable chief secretary, Charlene.

"Get my driver here now," he said coldly, trying to keep a lid on his already boiling temper. "The mayor and I have a few things to discuss. You know his secretary. Call her. Tell her to keep him there till I arrive."

LIEUTENANT TIM CALLOWAY, Miami PD, supervised as his officers examined every vehicle entering the southeast checkpoint into the riot scene. He loved the feel of his Kevlar flak jacket and his heavy riot helmet, the sweat notwithstanding. He felt a singing adrenaline high that he had never felt at Harvard. Of course, at Harvard he had never made any of the teams, either. Nonetheless, for an administrative lieutenant who normally dwelt in the office and away from the street, riot duty was definitely a walk on the wild side. It would be something to tell his kids about.

A red Volvo drew up to the checkpoint. Behind the wheel was a white woman about forty-five, still good-looking even if her brown hair was going gray. Calloway heard a patrolman tell her the usual: "Ma'am, if you don't live inside the cordoned perimeter or have a very good reason to be there, we have to ask you to turn back."

Calloway saw the woman flash the badge, the gold shield of a Miami sergeant. He heard her say crisply, "Sergeant Cohen. I need to liaise with Stakeout Team Two. Where will I find them?"

The patrolman looked skeptical. Dumb flatfoot, thought Calloway. Probably only has a high school education. Doesn't know the voice of authority when he hears it. Calloway leaned forward and said, "No problem, Sarge. In two blocks straight, and two blocks left. They're running out of the gray van. Keep your head down." Calloway saluted. The woman looked nonplussed for a moment, then returned the salute and put the Volvo in gear, moving forward rapidly into the riot scene.

The next vehicle up was a big van with tinted windows. The man in the right front seat leaned forward, flashing a Miami patrolman's badge. "We're bringing in the new pepper-gas generator for SWAT," he said crisply, and asked for the SWAT team field commander. He knew the right name. He was obviously one of them.

"He's at the command post," the lieutenant said. "Left here, all the way down. Good luck."

The man in the front seat nodded, and the van went through.

The patrolman said, "Sir, if you don't mind my saying so, it might be a good idea to be checking ID cards and things."

The lieutenant turned toward him haughtily and sneered, "Well, thank you for the advice, Patrolman. If and when *you* ever earn promotions, one of the things you'll learn is that the advanced supervisor learns to distinguish command authority by sight and sound, not by ID card."

He turned away. His nostrils flaring in contempt, he wondered, Where do they get patrol-level personnel from these days?

SLOWLY, FUZZILY, Dan Harrington became half-awake. It took him a while to orient himself. He realized that he was facedown on the carpet. This was not anything new to him.

He wasn't aware of any pain from the gash his fall against the edge of the table had opened in his forehead. Cops didn't call being drunk "feeling no pain" for nothing. Alcohol is an extremely effective general anesthetic. During the Civil War, military surgeons got their patients drunk before they sawed their mangled legs and arms off.

The floor was wet, sopping wet. Harrington tried to look around, but he couldn't see much. The alcohol had affected the pupils of the eyes, bringing him a narrow tunnel of vision that was dark at the edges. He couldn't see the blood pool around him.

Besides, the eyelids were sticky. Blood had run into the eyes.

But it had not yet coagulated. That was why he was still bleeding, the red fluid not spurting, but oozing regularly into a flow like many creeks coming together to form a river.

Alcohol was also an extremely effective anticoagulant.

He wanted to get up, but he seemed terribly tired and weak. The floor was wet? All right, he'd pissed himself. Big deal. That had happened before. It came with the territory when you had to purge yourself of the pain of the day, the pain of being hated and ridiculed and held in contempt. At least, if you managed it right as he did, it only happened in the safe privacy of your own home and no one ever knew the difference.

He chuckled to himself. His wisdom had kept him safe once again. He lowered his face to the soft, sticky carpet and let the welcome, restoring sleep come back. Soon, he knew, he would be strong again.

Beneath him his blood soaked into the pile carpet, the huge crimson puddle growing wider, steadily wider.

THE SECOND VAN of CCC, ARM and SOLID people was stopped at the southwest checkpoint. A cop asked, "Do you have any need to be here, sir?"

"I don't need nothin'," the driver responded. "It's a free country, ain't it?"

The Miami cop stepped back. "Sir," he asked, "I want you to step out of that vehicle and keep your hands where I can see them." The cop's hand had fallen into a drawing position on the butt of his Glock 17 service pistol. Behind him the nearest officer—a brown-clad Metro Dade patrolman—took the cue. That officer took a drawing grasp on his Smith & Wesson 9 mm service automatic and thumbed off the holster's safety strap.

Suddenly the door of the van was kicked open.

The cops saw the black-clad man coming up with a blue-steel automatic pistol.

They started firing as soon as their own automatics cleared leather.

The Miami cop hosed eleven shots from his Glock. Nine Silvertip hollowpoints hit the suspect, mushrooming as they went, lodging in his back. The Metro Dade cop ripped off eight rounds, six of which hit, half of the 147-grain subsonic hollowpoints just ripping right through and one of them wounding the man in the right front seat in the leg, the other three staying in the first man's body, which slumped to the ground, bleeding like tomato soup out of a sieve.

The man in the front seat clutched at his bullet-broken leg and screamed, "Don't shoot me any more!"

All the cops outside the van ducked. Two of them leveled long guns, an AR-15 rifle and a Remington 12-gauge shotgun, at the windows. More than ten firearms were now pointing at the van, and the cops were screaming, "Police! Don't move! Show us empty hands!"

On the other side of the tinted windows, five more men clutched M-16 machine guns and MAC-10 submachine guns. One of them whispered, "We can shoot right through the sides, kill these ZOG dogs in a second, then get outa here!"

Another whispered back, "Yeah...an' who's gonna drive us?"

In less than a minute, all five had filed out of the van, obediently, with their hands straight in the air. The cops handcuffed them, along with the wounded man in the right front, after they were all disarmed. They even cuffed the corpse of the man who had been shot fifteen times, just to make sure.

The Metro Dade sergeant in charge of the checkpoint called the command post. "We've got 'em," he said exultantly. "I think we've got the Blizzard!"

JOHN KEARN WAS STILL wearing the dark brown suit pants and sweat-stained white dress shirt he had come to work in. He had thrown the necktie somewhere in his office, and his collar was open. If you didn't know the strong face by sight, you would have to look to the belt, where the black-banded police badge was clipped in front of the right hip, just ahead of the Glock compact 9 mm automatic in its black plastic holster.

That was how he looked when he strode into the mayor's office. No one could stop him. The bodyguards outside the door were, after all, Miami police officers assigned to the Executive Protection Unit. They just raised their hands, palms upward in a submissive gesture, and let the chief walk by.

Although the mayor could fire them from bodyguard duty, the chief could fire them from the whole damn police force. They hated working for the mayor, anyway.

Kearn was now into the one last buffer zone before the inner sanctum.

He saw Annette, the mayor's secretary-receptionist, guarding the door like Cerberus guarding the gates of Hell. Annette was the best friend of his own secretary and strong right hand, Charlene. He couldn't let her get hurt.

Kearn throttled back his own momentum and stopped at the oak door of the mayor's inner office. He looked down at Annette. Other people were looking at him, from the right, catching his right profile.

They couldn't see his left eye, which closed in a conspiratorial wink.

Annette jabbed at the intercom button and said, "Mayor Hernandez, the chief of police is here to see you."

The mayor's voice came back. "Tell him that'll be a cold day in Hell!"

Kearn winked again. "Oooh, Mr. Mayor," she squealed in mock terror, "I don't think I can stop him!"

That was his cue. John Kearn flung the door open.

In front of him was the broad expanse of the mayor's mahogany desk. On Orlando Hernandez's left sat Bruce Yount from Miami Police Department's Professional Standards Unit. Yount's jaw dropped open in horror as he realized his commander was standing there looking at him, behind enemy lines.

On the mayor's right sat a tiny, elfin man, white, his cheeks slightly rouged. The little guy wore a fancy French-cut suit and a floppy straw hat. He was cringing back in his chair, his mouth as wide open as Yount's.

"Mr. Mayor," boomed Kearn cheerfully. "I don't believe I've had the pleasure of meeting your friend here, but it's good to see you with Detective Yount. And to think there are people out there in the media world tonight who think my police department doesn't interface with your office."

There was a long silence.

The little man said, in a frightened and defensive tone of voice, "I am Oliver Teasdale! I write for the *Miami Crier!*"

Kearn looked down, stunned. So this was the man who had tried for more than a year to make a mockery of him, of the Miami Police Department, of the Stakeout Unit.

The mayor snapped, "What do you want?" There was panic in his voice, and his eyes were darting back and forth.

Kearn grinned broadly. He felt better than he had felt for days.

"Are you looking for your bodyguards, Mr. Mayor? I can get them for you, if you like. They're just assigned to you . . . but they work for me."

The mayor's jaw dropped. His olive skin seemed to turn pale.

"I said, what do you want here?" The mayor's voice was cracking in fear.

Kearn moved ominously forward until he was leaning over the mayor's desk. Orlando Hernandez cringed back in his swivel chair. He thought the chief was going to hit him again.

"I just got off the phone with the governor," Kearn said. "The governor was a little puzzled. He knew we needed the National Guard in here. He knew we were going up against people tonight who've used heavy machine guns and LAW rockets, and he didn't seem to understand why the mayor had expressly told him that National Guard assistance wasn't wanted.

"Now, Mr. Mayor, the deal is this. Those people *are* coming in tonight to face our cops. They've done everything they said they would so far. We need a National Guard level of weaponry to deal with them. If that isn't there, and these weirdos who call themselves the Blizzard run amok, every single person hurt will have a lawyer suing you and the city, jointly and severally, for failure to stop a predictable threat that you were responsible for stopping.

"The phone is on your desk, Mr. Mayor. Pick it up. You know what you have to do."

After a long moment Orlando Hernandez picked up the telephone in his shaky hand and stammered, "Annette? Get me the governor. There, uh, there seems to have been a misunderstanding...."

MIAMI HAD three full SWAT teams, each with its own big, armored step van to carry all the equipment. An unfortunate TV show in the 1970s had referred to a SWAT team's support truck as a "war wagon," and that was how the public saw them now.

The commander of Miami SWAT Team Bravo brought the war wagon up to the Red Cross truck that was adjacent to the northeast sector checkpoint. Two groups of people blessed the Red Cross: disaster victims and the emergency-services personnel such as police, fire and paramedic rescue teams.

SWAT Team Bravo blessed them tonight.

They'd been in the field for more than three hours, without food or coffee or candy, when SWAT Team Alpha had offered to cover for them if they took a twenty-minute coffee and washroom break.

The men were grateful. They knew that for the next twenty minutes, they would be covered by the best. Two other teams like themselves ... three more of the same level—or, dare they admit it, maybe even better?—from the Metro Dade Special Reaction Team group...and, for good measure, those upstart SWAT wanna-bes from the Miami Police Stakeout Unit, all divided between here in Liberty City, and Overtown.

The men of SWAT Team Bravo relaxed. But they kept their MP-5 submachine guns slung across their chests in the West German counterterrorist GSG-9 webbing, just in case. So did the two men who handled the long-rifle portion of the mission: their guns were match-grade SG-I 7.62 mm sniper rifles, capable of firing full automatic like incredibly accurate M-60 machine guns.

Two of the men were in the Porta Potti cubicles, and eight standing around sucking up hot black coffee, when it happened.

Two sedans drove up to the checkpoint. The cops gave them the usual bit about emergency in progress, need to enter, have a nice night and so on, the usual treatment of nonsuspect citizens, firm and courteous.

Then the team leader saw the Colt .45 automatic emerge from the window, saw the small, round fireball, saw the Metro cop at the checkpoint go flying back from the impact of the slug on his bulletproof vest.

He didn't need to tell his people to punch up. He saw from the corner of his eye that they were already dropping their foam coffee cups and swinging their H&K automatic weapons upward.

All he had to say was two words.

He roared, "Green light!"

Even as his own MP-5 vibrated from the recoil of the fully automatic fire, even as he saw the doors of both sedans flying open and strangely dressed men coming out with guns, the air was filled with the unearthly din of eight fully automatic police weapons going off at once.

The sedans rocked back on their rubber tires from the onslaught of the bullets. The windows disintegrated into a cloud of glass shards. The men who were already outside the cars with guns in their hands seemed to come apart in slow motion, their clothing puckering from where the police bullets went in, and fragments flew away.

Fragments of cloth. Fragments of flesh. Fragments of bone.

The deafening barrage lasted for perhaps four seconds. By then every SWAT weapon was out of ammunition. The team leader heard the clacking sounds of his men reloading and cried, "Hold fire! Cover position!"

In the background other people were yelling and saying things like, "Oh, my God!"

The team leader edged toward the cars, his freshly reloaded MP-5 up and ready. Behind him he heard someone shout triumphantly, "SWAT got 'em! SWAT got the Blizzard!"

But the team leader knew better. He knew it wasn't over till it was over. With the muzzle of his submachine gun, he edged one bullet-shattered car door open and felt the deadweight of a corpse fall onto the ground in front of him.

He and his people had emptied eight magazines of twenty-eight shots apiece on full automatic. Two hundred and twenty-four bullets in perhaps three seconds. There had been seven members of CCC, SOLID and ARM in each of the two sedans.

If you had asked the team leader beforehand, he would have told you that no one could survive an onslaught like that.

Now, as the car doors were prodded open, he could confirm it.

No one had.

17

Lieutenant Tim Calloway stood, tall and macho, his face visor bravely up on his riot helmet as he sipped his sweet, light coffee from the foam cup. A lesser leader might have abandoned his post for coffee, but no, not he. All it took was sending a patrolman to get it for you.

The big white Lincoln limousine approached the checkpoint. Some of his cops started moving forward.

Calloway barked, "Stay back!" He threw the coffee cup away from him, out of sight, not caring that the hot liquid splashed on another officer. Anyone running a car like this in here tonight was *heavy*. The kind of person an up-and-coming lieutenant needed to meet!

The driver's door window hummed down on the Lincoln, and the lieutenant bent solicitously forward.

The driver flashed a badge wallet with a Miami police detective's shield and ID card. "Executive Protection Unit," the plainclothes cop said. "The mayor wants to see the situation for himself." The man had spoken gruffly. Some of the police officers who were specially trained as bodyguards for VIPs under the mantle of police protection considered that they had a special status deserving of greater respect than your average cop. It tended to show in their manner.

Calloway peered into the darkness of the back seat. He saw the angry face of the man he recognized as the mayor.

"No problem, Mayor Hernandez," he bleated, waving desperately with a hand behind his back to tell the other cops to pass the limo through. "No problem at all, sir! You're in good hands!"

The stretch Lincoln limousine roared into the riot zone. Behind it came another white stretch limo, an older-model Cadillac. Obviously part of the mayor's retinue. Calloway waved it through, and seeing his movements, the other cops stood back and let it pass.

"Sir," said a patrolman, "with all due respect, we are supposed to be checking everyone going through this checkpoint."

Calloway exploded.

"Don't you dare use that tone of voice with me," he screamed. "You see these bars on my collars, Patrolman? That means you don't tell me what to do, *I* tell *you* what to do! Do you read me?"

Calloway expected the patrolman to blanch and gasp, "Sir, yes, sir," the way kids did at the academy. Instead, the gray-haired patrolman muttered, "Yeah, I get it," and turned away.

Calloway reached for his pocket notebook and wrote the officer's badge number down. This man was obviously not command material.

"NOW YOU KNOW why Ian's my main man," Dewey Huxley said proudly from the driver's seat as he wheeled the Cadillac limousine through the wrecked streets of Liberty City. "Tell 'em, Ian!"

The fat man smiled smugly from the right corner in the huge rear compartment of the Cadillac limo. "After the debacle at the drawbridge, I knew the mayor would have to come here to make amends to the voters. As you saw, we just waited a block down from city hall, and when his limo rolled out, we rolled ours out behind it."

"You're a fuckin' genius," murmured Tony Mann, starry-eyed.

Wallace Crowther knew better. He'd almost expelled the proverbial brick at the roadblock. His survival instinct was screaming, We're gonna get wasted in here tonight!

The limo turned a corner. Up ahead, in the opposite lane, was a dark-colored van.

The side windows were tinted, but the front glass wasn't. Through that windshield, Dewey Huxley could see four faces.

They were all white. He didn't know the driver, or the nervous-looking guy in the right front, or the big guy behind him. But the other guy peering over the seat, he did recognize.

The last time he'd seen the SOB, he had been standing at the portal of a Beechcraft KingAir, aiming a stainless-steel automatic at him.

"It's *them* guys!" Huxley screamed. "The guys from the airport!"

He realized that the man he was focused on was now staring at him from inside the van, pointing a finger and saying something animatedly.

"It's goin' down, guys," moaned Huxley.

"No," squeaked Ian Altman insistently. "I'm not ready yet!'

Too damn late, fat boy, thought Wallace Crowther as the first bullet from the van hit their bulletproof limousine and bounced off harmlessly.

THE INFORMAL VOICE of the dispatcher on the unmonitored channel said, "Stakeout Two, respond to Twenty-seventh Avenue Northwest and Martin Luther King Boulevard. Shots fired, white limo and blue van. Caller reported in from a local bar, says it's a white-on-white shooting."

In any other previous riot, that would have been an anomaly. But this was now, and Stakeout was looking for the Blizzard, and they knew the white racist hate group had already killed five other whites at Tamiami Airport this week.

"We're rolling now," Cohen barked into his portable as Cross gunned the van toward the scene.

In the back the rest of Stakeout Team Two checked their weapons. Something told them that this time it was for real. They'd heard over the air twice tonight that white armed groups had been caught—one group blown to dog meat—and that the Blizzard had supposedly been dealt with. But something cynical and subconscious in their police-experienced brains had told them that it wasn't over yet.

Those same brains were now giving them all the same message.

This time it was for real. This was it!

DEWEY HUXLEY SPUN the steering wheel of the big Cadillac and felt the rear end break away. What the hell? he thought. Why didn't Ian give me some time to get used to driving this boat? But now it was too late. The car fetched up against a curb.

The van squealed to a halt against the curbing on the opposite corner. The left side of the Caddy limo was presented to them like a perfect target as the men wearing different-colored clothing opened fire at the big white car. Huxley ducked as the vehicle, heavy as it was, jerked from the impact of the slugs hitting the side body and the windows.

Then he realized, Wait a damn minute! What the hell am I worried about? We're bulletproof!

Huxley grinned and sat back up, ripping his Colt Commander .45 automatic out of his waistband and flipping the safety catch off. He saw three lead bullets, trapped in the heavy, bullet-resistant window, lodged in the cracked glass like pregnant flies in a spiderweb.

Another consideration entered his frantic mind. Wait a minute! How do I shoot out of this thing?

Behind him Wallace Crowther had thrust the muzzle of his Mini-14 into the firing port and was pulling the trigger as fast as he could. The muzzle blast was trapped partly inside the armored door, but even so, every shot made a deafening concussion inside the car.

The theory of the gun port for return fire in an armored car was that you sprayed and prayed, hoping that you could keep the assassins' heads down until your driver could get you out of there. But this time the driver wasn't going anywhere. Even if Dewey Huxley hadn't been fixated on trying to think how to fire a .45 pistol outward from behind a bulletproof door and window, the engine had stalled and the car was jammed against the curb.

Wallace Crowther's gun port was invisible from the outside because it was covered by a layer of sheet metal. The bullets had to go through that to get out.

The bullets did get through, but as the .223 rifle bullets from Crowther's gun hit the sheet metal and tore past, they began to tumble in midair, flying awry. None of his bullets even came close to the van from which a deadly accurate storm of full-automatic weapons fire was now streaming toward the white Cadillac.

From the back seat Ian Altman screamed, "Dewey! Dewey! Get us out of here!"

But Huxley was still trying to get his .45 automatic into a gun port meant for the much narrower muzzle of a .38 revolver and didn't even hear his patron's screams. Tony Mann was thrashing like a barracuda on a heavy block and tackle, almost frothing at the mouth. And Wallace Crowther was at the left rear door, jamming a fresh magazine into his Mini-14 and hoping that this time he'd blown enough steel out of the door's outer shell to get some bullets where they needed to go.

With Altman shrieking a couple of feet behind him, Crowther thought grimly, One more clip an' I'm outa here, you fat, stupid hog!

Then he concentrated on pulling the trigger.

THE STAKEOUT VAN DREW UP to the corner behind where it was happening. The cops bailed out, their guns at the ready. All of them left their .45 pistols in the holsters. Carmody and Baranck had unlimbered the Remington Model 700 .308 sniper rifles with the scopes, and the rest were relying on their semiautomatic Benelli shotguns.

The Stakeout van was south. The Cadillac was north. The van with the avenging white supremacists was caught straight in the middle, between the two.

It was the sergeant's job to give the command, so Mike Cohen did. "Police," he yelled. "Don't move! Drop your weapons!"

Cohen could see five people at the van. They were all taking cover against the Cadillac on the other side, and were therefore completely exposed to the Stakeout cops. One was standing behind the cover of the van on each edge, two were down prone by the tires and one was standing in the right front door. All clearly visible to Cohen and his people.

That was why it was so stupid for them to turn on the officers with their guns in their hands.

Cohen didn't need to give a command. He just opened fire, as the others did.

A rifled shotgun slug has its grooves already formed in it when it leaves the ammunition factory. It cannot be traced to a specific weapon. Therefore, no one would ever know which Stakeout cop fired which slugs. All the Stakeout officers had started shooting.

The man at the west end of the van was turning, his deadly M-16 machine gun in hand, when a shotgun slug shattered his pelvis and dropped him into an awkward sitting position. He tried to bring his M-16 to bear, but then another three-quarter-inch-wide lead projectile caught him in the throat and blew his cervical spine all over the van, killing him instantly.

The man on the east end of the van swung toward the cops, fire blazing from the muzzle of his rapid-firing MP-5 submachine gun. A one-ounce lead slug from a Stakeout shotgun caught him in the forehead and blew his brains out the back of his head in a spray of red-and-gray tissue.

The man behind the right rear wheel of the van was wearing a bulletproof vest, but it didn't do him any good. As he squirmed to aim his MP-5 at the Stakeout cops, twisting into a position that had him down on his side with his feet toward the cops and his head away, a .72-caliber lead Winchester rifled slug caught him between the legs. It disintegrated his testicles, roared through his lower abdominal tract, clipped off the bottom of his heart and came to rest as it smashed his upper spinal column into something that would look like matchsticks when the medical examiner x-rayed the corpse.

The one by the right front wheel was coming up to empty his MAC-10 submachine gun at the officers when the first slug hit him in the belly. He was wearing a bulletproof vest. It felt like a punch. That was an impact he could take.

His finger curled onto the trigger.

The next Stakeout slug caught him at the wrist of the left arm he was using to point the submachine gun at the cops. The slug ranged upward, from wrist to elbow to shoulder, shattering every bone and tearing apart every complex of nerve tissue and blood vessels in between. The slug mushroomed into the shape of a flat lead washer with a hole in the center by the time it broke his shoulder and stopped there, slamming him against the side of the car.

Still, he tried with his good right hand to aim the machine pistol.

The next Stakeout slug struck him in the mouth, shattering his teeth and passing through the medulla of his brain and roaring out the back of his head into the van, leaving an exit hole more than an inch in diameter. He slumped to the ground without even a convulsion.

Four of the five men who were visible had been shot down in less than three seconds.

The fifth had not been shot because he did not have a gun in his hand. He turned toward the officers, his hands empty and exposed.

The fifth man faced them in the deadly silence of their finished gunfire. He wore khakis. He was big, solid, about fifty years old.

Cohen yelled again, "Police! Don't move."

All the Stakeout guns were aimed at him now.

The big man said, "I didn't come here for this shit! Didn't come here to kill no good white men! Jes' watch out behind me! They're the fuckin' Blizzard yer lookin' for!"

He knew that behind him he still had two more white Aryan patriots with guns, still inside the van. If he could just lure these stupid cops forward...

AMAZING no one in the Cadillac had been shot.

Wallace Crowther knew they had run their luck to the end of their string.

He had emptied two magazines from the Mini-14 through the so-called firing port of the armored limousine's door. It was a wasted effort. Useless!

Beside him the hog he had come to hate was squealing, "Get me out of here! Get me out! Now!"

He checked the Beretta automatic, stolen from Homestead Air Force Base, that Huxley had given him. Yeah, it was still in his waistband, fifteen copper-jacketed bullets in the magazine and a sixteenth in the firing chamber, ready to go. The first gun Altman had given him, the Charter .38, was still in his hip pocket.

It was time to go. But he had to leave diplomatically.

"Ian," Crowther said urgently, "I'm gonna get you outa here! Trust me, okay?"

The fat man nodded gratefully.

Crowther reached toward the right rear door of the limo. The car was big enough for two people deep, but Altman blocked the rear seat so effectively that Crowther had to climb over him.

Once he was out of the car, Altman was reaching for him, his right hand coming up in supplication, like a baby reaching to a parent. Crowther felt like kicking himself. And this is the man I followed, he thought scornfully.

Disgust welled inside Wallace Crowther. Disgust, hatred and contempt.

He raised the Beretta pistol in his hand, aimed it at the center of his former leader's mass.

Ian Altman screamed, "Noo!"

Wallace Crowther fired four fast shots.

He saw the stretched-out shirt that lay atop Altman's distended belly tuft and pucker with the shots. Saw blood come rushing up through the holes. Saw the look of horrified disbelief on the fat man's face. Saw Tony Mann and Dewey Huxley turn in the front seat, looking at him with the horror that is reserved for someone who has betrayed a trust.

And then Wallace Crowther was running, running into the smoke of the riot until he was lost in the darkness of that savage night.

MIKE COHEN GATHERED his wits about him even as he hugged the cover of the police van and shoved fresh shells into the magazine of his automatic shotgun.

In front of them was the van where four men now lay motionless, and a fifth upright with his hands raised. That didn't mean there weren't more in there.

Beyond them, like a beached whale, lay the old white Cadillac stretch limousine. It appeared that someone had just run away from it from the other side, into the darkness. Well, so be it—he and his people could handle only so much at once.

He barked into his microphone, "Stakeout Two! Fire against us has ceased for now, but we have four people down, other suspects ensconced behind cover and presumably armed and not within control. We have at least one suspect running north through the alleys in the vicinity of Twenty-seventh Avenue Northwest and Martin Luther King Boulevard."

After a moment the radio crackled back, "Acknowledged, Stakeout Two. We don't have any backup we can send you right now. We'll get backup to you as soon as we can."

Even during the radio communication, Cohen kept his eye on the scene.

He saw the big man in front of the van take a step to the side. Cohen's voice cracked out again, "Don't move!"

The big man yelled back, "Fuck you, ZOG! I told you, there's the Blizzard in that fuckin' pimp-mobile behind me, here! Ain't you gonna do nothin' 'bout it?"

Cohen glanced to his side. He saw that Bob Carmody had already moved out, the sniper rifle at his shoulder, ready to aim. Backing him up with a ready shotgun was Tom West.

Cohen yelled back, "Sir! The car behind you will be taken care of. *Slowly* raise your hands straight up in the air. Good! Now, slowly kneel down!"

The big man obeyed.

Suddenly there was movement in the van, and then a flash of orange flame.

Something close and deadly hummed past Mike Cohen's head like a hornet. He dropped forward, his shotgun coming up.

Baranck and Hoffritz were already firing.

One shotgun slug tore through the window of the van and into the face of the man who was trying to stick his MP-5 out the window. That man toppled backward, dead.

Another slug homed toward the survivor of the airport massacre. He stood in the doorway of the van, aiming an M-16. The slug flew parallel with his gun barrel, an inch above, and entered his right eye at the inside edge of the orbital socket. By the time it blew out the back of his head, sucking a spray of liquefied brain tissue behind it, the man with the M-16 was a falling corpse.

ALMOST A HUNDRED YARDS from the shooting scene, Wallace Crowther emerged from the alley onto the next street over. He clutched his still-cocked Beretta automatic.

There was no turning back now. No going back to the Blizzard. No turning himself in to the cops. Now there was only survival.

Carefully he lowered the cocked hammer of the gun so he wouldn't shoot himself when he shoved it into his belt under his shirt. There was a time to flash guns and a time not to. If you wanted to get someone with a car to stop for you and drive you the hell out of where you were, it was a time not to.

He had just tucked his shirt over the stolen Beretta when the Volvo turned the corner. He peered through the glass.

The driver was a woman. A white woman.

She was coming his way. Wallace Crowther ran into the street, waving his arms. Altman had taught him to be a good actor. He screamed, "Help me! Help me! Please!"

MORE POLICE CARS were sweeping into the shooting scene now, the officers bailing out with shotguns and pistols in hand.

The commander of ARM was the sole survivor of his van load of armed supremacists, and he knew it. It was one thing to talk the talk in a motel room. It was another thing to walk the walk when all these guns were pointed at you.

"I give," he yelled. "I give up! Jes' don't shoot me, okay?"

Stakeout cops kept him covered as uniformed personnel moved in to grab him, throw him face-down, pull away his 9 mm pistol and handcuff him. He didn't move at all. He knew when he was licked.

SARAH COHEN SAW the scared-looking bald man waving his skinny arms in front of her headlights and screaming, "Help me! Help me! Please!"

She imagined the horror of being a white victim caught up in a black riot. She pulled over and, as he rushed up to the driver's window, wondered why he hadn't come to the passenger's side.

And then her door was ripped open, the hot, ugly muzzle of the gun was thrust into her ear and she heard the man scream, "Get over, bitch! Get over! I'm drivin' from here on!"

Numbly Sarah Cohen obeyed. She would remember later that the strangest thing was, the muzzle of the gun he pressed against her ear was very warm. She had always heard that a gun barrel was supposed to feel cold.

Then she was in the passenger's seat, and the skinny, sweaty man was driving, his left hand on the steering wheel of her Volvo and his right hand waving the big, black, ugly gun around the front seat.

She would later remember thinking, Mike, where are you? I need you, Mike!

BOB CARMODY WAS YELLING, "Police! Don't move!"

His rifle was aimed directly at Tony Mann, who had stepped out of the bulletproof Cadillac so he could have some mobility. Everybody else was leaving, and Altman himself was already in the back, shot and dying, so why shouldn't Mann get out of the car?

He held his Browning 9 mm in his hand, down low at his side. The cop was yelling for him not to move.

Now another cop was running in, a black guy. And now a third one, a blonde—a woman. A woman was gonna tell him what to do? A woman pig? A pig bitch?

Mann still kept his gun down at his side, but he turned his head toward Melinda Hoffritz.

"You," he cried. "You! Get outa my face, you bitch! I'll kill you! I fuckin' mean it!"

He was tunneled on Hoffritz. She tried to do the right thing.

"Sir," she said loud and clear, "just open your hand and let the gun fall, and you can say anything you want to me. Sir, please, just drop the gun!"

Carmody knew, with a sickening coldness inside, what was going to happen. Quickly he flipped the carrying strap of the rifle over his left bicep, tightening it into what marksmen called a "hasty sling." He took a deep breath. The cross hairs of his telescopic sight came to their cruciform center on the man's head. Carmody began to take up the slack on the trigger, until only a three-pound pressure—like touching the key on an electric typewriter—stood between the silence of the gun and the launching of the high-powered bullet.

"Sir," called Hoffritz. "Please, sir, drop the gun!"

Tony Mann uttered a wordless scream.

"Yaaahhh!"

He swung up the Browning.

And even as Tom West and Melinda Hoffritz pressed the triggers of their shotguns, they saw the gunman's head explode into a halo of bloody mist from Carmody's fast-fired .308 bullet, an instant before their own high-powered shotgun slugs tore Tony Mann's heart to shreds.

"JUST SHUT UP, bitch! I'm drivin' here!"

Wallace Crowther made it clear that he was in charge of matters in the front seat of the Volvo.

He was breathing hard. He asked, "How'd you get in here, anyway? Place is supposed to be sealed off."

Sarah Cohen tried to impress him with the truth. "My husband is a police sergeant. I had to see him. They let me in."

Crowther laughed mockingly. "Yeah, right. Sergeant Rambo's gotta shoot it out with the bad white mothers *and* the baddest niggers they got, an' they're gonna let his bitch in to bullshit with him. Yeah, right."

Sarah became indignant. "Yeah! *Right!* My husband is a Miami police sergeant, and I had to talk with him! Do you know what's going to happen to you if you hurt me?"

There was no one around to see, only a few burning cars in between a few burning buildings. Wallace Crowther stood on the high-tech Volvo brake and brought the car to a stop so fast that Sarah, who hadn't had a chance to put on a seat belt, bounced off the dashboard.

He laughed with the laughter of a maniac.

"I've lost count of how many people I've killed the last few days, 'cause I'm the Blizzard. The Blizzard!" Crowther screamed.

"But I'll tell you this! I've killed four Miami cops that I know of this past week or so, an' your dip-shit husband, whoever he is, can just as easy be number five as not!"

Sarah knew, with a numb sense of horror, that he was telling the truth.

"I'm tellin' you, I gotta get outa here! The pigs got the area cordoned off. Can't get in, can't get out. *You* gotta get me out, you dig it?"

THE VAN WAS SECURED: six of the seven occupants neutralized, the seventh in custody.

On the other side, there was still the Cadillac. Someone had gotten away from it. One had died next to it.

That left two unaccounted for.

Mike Cohen yelled, "This is the police! You behind the Caddy! Raise your hands, slowly, empty, and you will not be shot!"

From behind the Cadillac, there came only a sick sound of laughter.

The six Stakeout cops kept their weapons trained on the area.

THE VOLVO ROLLED SLOWLY through the streets, Wallace Crowther holding the steering wheel with his left hand, holding his stolen Air Force Beretta to Sarah Cohen's head with his right.

"So, bitch, what's your name, anyway?"

"Sarah. Sarah Cohen."

Crowther's head rocked back, cackling in laughter. "Oh, this is *beautiful!*" And then the mirth was suddenly gone from his voice, and he looked at her and screamed, "You're a Jewess! You're a Jew cop's wife!"

There was foam at his mouth now as he said, "Cops fucked me up. And Jews an' niggers did it to people like me since before I was born. I paid my soul to do what I done this week. You understand?"

She stared at him in numb, uncomprehending horror.

"Nah," growled Crowther contemptuously. "You don't understand. But believe me, you will understand! And soon!"

KEARN'S DRIVER had brought him to the mouth of the riot scene, a block distant from the flames and the gunfire. There he met Lieutenant Ken Bartlett. Like the chief, Bartlett hadn't had time to don riot clothes. He was wearing slacks, a shirt with a loose tie and a Glock .45 on his hip.

Kearn had time for one word. "Update!"

Bartlett answered, "Stakeout Team Two just engaged the third white-racist carload that's gotten inside our perimeter tonight. You'll want to study what happened, but it looks like it boils down to one lieutenant who got sloppy at the roadblock. He let in the mayor, for one thing, and an unidentified limo behind it that definitely wasn't part of the mayor's party. Let in the assholes my team had to blow away. That was something like the third of three—the others were interdicted at the roadblocks, one by Patrol Division, one by SWAT."

"Damn," Kearn muttered.

A patrol sergeant added, "The same leak at the roadblock let in at least one other car we know about. White female, flashed a Miami sergeant's badge, running a Volvo with this license tag." Bartlett handed the chief a slip of paper with a license-plate number written on it. "I was just about to broadcast the number. You wanna do the honors? It'll carry more weight coming from you."

The chief grabbed the paper with one hand, the command-post microphone with the other. "This is Chief Kearn," he said in a powerful voice no one could mistake. "I'm going to give you a license number. I want this vehicle stopped. It's a Volvo, license..."

He read it over the air. Bartlett stood with a hand over one ear, listening to a radio transmission on another channel with the other.

"Okay. Dammit, Ken, I been hearing, 'We got the Blizzard,' and then, 'No, *we* got the Blizzard.' Ken, I gotta know. What the hell do we have?"

Ken Bartlett, who had been there all night, said, "Chief, I think we do have the Blizzard. I think we've maybe got 'em all. And more.

"The bad news is, the ones you really want maybe haven't been taken yet. Come with me. Stakeout Two is having a standoff with them right now."

DEWEY HUXLEY and Ian Altman cringed behind the bulletproof Cadillac while the cops were yelling at them. Huxley had to go down to both knees to support the weight of Altman's upper body in his lap.

"Help me, Dewey," Altman rasped in a soft voice Huxley had never heard before. "Help me like I helped you when you were in trouble. Don't let me die, Dewey!"

Dewey Huxley looked down at his fallen friend. He saw four separate bullet holes in the man's huge belly.

"You been shot four times in the guts, Ian. Don't look good."

"I weigh five hundred fifty pounds," Altman gasped urgently. "I never told you that before. But I don't feel anything deep inside. I wonder if maybe the bullets just hit my fat."

"Maybe," Huxley conceded. "So what? They're comin' in on us, Ian. They killed all the others already."

"Let them do it, Dewey," Altman pleaded. "Mommy and Daddy always got us out before. It'll be fine. They'll get us out of it this time, too. You'll see!"

Huxley said tenderly, "They're gone now, Ian. Your mom and dad are gone. They can't help us anymore."

"I don't care," Altman bleated, clutching the holes in his huge abdomen. "It hurts, Dewey!

Mommy and Daddy will fix it. They always have, you know?"

"I know," answered Huxley.

He brought the muzzle of his Colt .45 automatic to Ian Altman's head. The cops were closing in on them, and they were running out of time.

THEY BROADCAST four descriptions of cars with license tags over the air: the mayor's, the white-supremacist van's, the bulletproof Caddy's and that of the Volvo that got through the perimeter because the woman behind the wheel had said she was Sergeant Cohen.

"Oh, shit," said Mike Cohen, stunned, as he heard the broadcast. "That's my wife! That's Sarah. She's here! *Here!*"

At that moment the Volvo coasted past the intersection not twenty-five yards away from them. The Stakeout sergeant looked into it.

He saw his wife's face.

"Bob," he yelled to Carmody. "You in position to take over?"

"Yeah," Carmody yelled back reflexively.

"Okay," shouted Cohen, and he turned and ran toward the car that held his wife and a life-taking monster.

For an instant the other Stakeout cops looked at their fleeing sergeant.

Then Carmody yelled, "Tom! You there?"

"Yo," Tom West answered.

"Tom," cried Carmody, "back Mike up! The rest of you—*this* problem here, now!"

THE VOLVO COASTED gently down the street toward the roadblock. It didn't occur to Wallace Crowther to look in the rearview mirror. He didn't care where he'd been, only where he was going.

Had he looked, he might have seen behind him two very determined men holding short-barrel automatic shotguns, loping after him.

Instead, he said, "You got in with your husband's badge, right? Okay, then. Gimme the badge. If it got you in, it'll get me out."

"Okay," Sarah Cohen replied softly. "Just, please, don't hurt me. I want to go back to my son. I want to go back to my little girl."

Crowther threw his head back and laughed. "You shoulda got me yesterday, when I was feelin' mellow. Right now I got no sympathy for cops. I got no sympathy for cops' wives." He looked at her, paused and added, "And I got no sympathy at all for kike cops' wives."

THE OTHER COPS had moved in, taken the prisoners who needed to be taken and sealed the scene behind them. Now the cops of Stakeout Team Two moved in on Dewey Huxley and Ian Altman.

Behind them they could hear the affirmative roar of a largely black crowd. White cops had come into the ghetto, not to kill blacks, but to face and perhaps kill white racists who *had* come into the ghetto to murder innocent African-Americans.

It was changing the tone of everything in the background.

The Stakeout cops didn't have time to think about it.

They had to focus on the two men behind the Cadillac.

Huxley held the .45 to his friend's head. "Ian," he said, "tell me true. This is our last chance to be honest with each other. You want me to pull the trigger now, put you away, stuff the gun in my mouth and kill myself, too? I can pull the trigger now. After it's over, they'll never let me touch a trigger I can pull. Be sure, my friend."

"No," squealed Altman. "No! Don't shoot me! I'll fix it. I'll fix it!"

Now the cops were around the side of the car, looming over the cover that had moments before protected Huxley and Altman. The muzzles of the automatic shotguns were pointed at them.

"Police," the cops were yelling. "Don't move!"

Dewey Huxley asked one last time, "You sure?"

"Yes," squeaked Ian Altman. "Yes! I want to live!"

Dewey Huxley looked up at the drawn guns of the Stakeout cops.

He said two words.

"Fuck it."

Then he turned the pistol in his hand, shoving the Colt .45 muzzle into his own mouth. Before anyone could stop him, Dewey Huxley pulled the trigger.

"YOU'RE GOING TO KILL ME, aren't you?" Sarah Cohen asked softly.

Wallace Crowther laughed out loud. "Of course I am. What did you think I was gonna do?"

Sarah slumped forward, defeated, her shoulders almost coming together in front. In a tiny voice, almost inaudible, she said, "I have a husband. I have parents. I have children."

"Yeah? Well I don't! You just ain't ready to die. But that's your damn problem, not mine!"

In her mind's eye, Sarah saw Jacob and the new baby they had adopted. Saw them growing up without a mother. Cold chills went down her back.

She realized in this moment, This is what Michael faced. The knowledge that when you die, it isn't just your death that weighs the scales. It is knowing that your spouse, your mother, your children will never see you again, and you will never see them again, and being lost from them is the same as if they had been murdered instead of you.

In all the time of her arguments with Mike, if someone had asked whether she would let someone rape or kill her, she would have answered yes.

But if someone had asked whether she would watch her child be murdered, she would have cried,

No. No! I would tear his throat out with my teeth first!

The syndrome of the mother wolf. It had been there all along. Why hadn't the rabbi or the psychologist seen it?

Too late now. The man's ugly, big gun was coming up toward her face.

"Say goodbye, bitch!"

"Wait," Sarah cried. "Money, I'll give you money!"

The shaved-skulled killer leaned his head back and laughed out loud. "Oh, that's rich, that's *funny!* You'll pay me to let you live?

"Fine. Give me your money. Tell you what—it'll buy you another ten seconds. Fair enough?"

He lowered his gun, laughing.

She reached into her fanny pack, as if for her billfold.

Sarah's hand closed on the hard butt of the LadySmith .38.

The car was filled with the roaring, concussive thunder of gunfire.

MIKE COHEN WAS RUNNING up behind the slow-moving Volvo when he saw the muzzle-flashes inside. They were fast, bright, one after the other, again and again.

He heard himself scream, "No! Sara-a-ah! Nooo!"

Then the Volvo seemed to jerk to the side, bumping to a stop against the curb.

As he came forward, Cohen reflexively let go of the shotgun, knowing it would fall safely against his flak jacket, suspended by the nylon sling. His right hand drew the ParaOrdnance .45 automatic as his left hand ripped open the driver's door of the Volvo.

The corpse of Wallace Crowther spilled out in front of him, the Beretta automatic harmless now in Crowther's dead hand.

Instinctively Cohen kicked the gun away.

His eyes went back and forth.

On the left, the blind, dead-fish eyes of the Blizzard murderer.

On the right, the wide-open, terrified eyes of his own wife.

The decision was easy.

Cohen leaned down through the open door of the Volvo, over the body of the dead man whose feet were still in the car, reaching for his wife. And then Sarah Cohen was in his arms, sobbing, making unintelligible sounds, the LadySmith—empty now—still in her right hand.

He took the gun away from her gently. Behind him Tom West had already moved in, placing the muzzle of his gun against Wallace Crowther's eye.

There was no response.

Looking down, Cohen could see that at least three of the bullets his wife had fired had struck home. Blood was emptying out of the dead man from a hole in the throat that had almost certainly pierced the carotid artery. A hole in the center of his forehead was rimmed with both black gunpowder residue and bluish gray scum from the brain tissue that had been extruded. And the chest? Soaked with blood. One, or maybe two or three, of Sarah's shots had found their way there.

Tom West looked up at Mike Cohen and gave the trained head gesture, the gesture that said, No hope, this one's dead.

For the first of all the times he had seen it, Mike Cohen was happy to observe that gesture.

The woman in his arms looked up at him. She was crying, but the words were still understandable.

"Michael, I love you," she cried. "I love you, Mike!"

Cohen held her hard. And wept.

IT TOOK TWENTY MINUTES for enough police reinforcements to arrive that the paramedics were comfortable coming in. No one could blame them.

There was only one viable patient. The rest had been shot to pieces. On a routine day the parameds might have worked on one or two of them just for resuscitation practice, but not on a riot night. People were coming to take pictures, draw chalk tracings around the corpses, bag the bodies and take them to the medical examiner's office.

The one survivor from the Blizzard group was Ian Altman, even though he had been shot four times through the abdomen.

At the scene the senior paramedic said, "He's fine. We call it sandbag effect. You see it often with the morbidly obese when they suffer gunshot wounds. The layers of flab on the torso act like sandbags, redirecting the bullets and dissipating their force. Doesn't look as if anything even got into this ol' boy's body cavity. He'll be fine."

They put the wounded Ian Altman on a gurney, but it buckled. They had to resort to another strategy. They picked him up off the ground, had him wrap his huge arms around their necks and escorted him to the ambulance.

At that moment a man came out of the crowd, a slender black man.

One of the cops trying to get Ian Altman into the back of the paramedic transport truck started to say, "Excuse me, sir," but it was too late.

Radleigh Bingham swung the Smith & Wesson Highway Patrolman .357 Magnum up from behind his back, thrust it into the face of the obese white man who had brought so much trouble to the ghetto and pulled the trigger.

There was a bright fireball of orange flame. The muzzle-flash seared Ian Altman's face.

But Altman did not live to complain about it.

The bullet entered the center of Ian Altman's face just as he was about to say for the tenth time, "I'm rich! I'll pay what you want! I have the money!"

The PMC Magnum slug made its first contact at the bridge of Ian Altman's nose. The bullet tore through his medulla oblongata, mushrooming as it went, and exited through the back of Altman's skull, taking with it a two-inch-wide spray of pulverized bone matter.

Ian Altman collapsed in the arms of the officers who were supporting his huge body. He had been killed instantly.

City of Miami and Metro Dade police officers jumped on Radleigh Bingham instantly. They drove him to the ground and ripped the .357 Magnum out of his hands.

But Bingham didn't care.

He had done what the voices had told him to do.

And now, at long, long last, the voices were silent.

EPILOGUE

It was the age of the minicam. When the video footage showed the number of armed, homicidal white men who were shot by police in the wake of the Miami Blizzard fiasco, it became apparent to the black community that, at least on this occasion, the cops were not the enemy. The miniriot came to a sudden and abrupt halt.

THE DAY AFTER the disturbances were over, there was time to do things like find out where your cops were who hadn't shown up.

Dan Harrington hadn't answered his phone or his pager. Lieutenant Ken Bartlett went to his apartment house.

When he caught the smell outside the door, he called the PD and the medical examiner's office before he went in by himself.

When the door was forced, Dan Harrington was found dead on his own living room carpet. The investigators pieced it together exactly. Autopsy showed a .323 blood-alcohol content, three and a half times legally drunk, the level at which most nonalcoholics become comatose and must be rushed to the hospital when discovered, according to police regulations.

Harrington had passed out, smacked his head and bled to death from the laceration. It was hard for the Miami cops to accept at first, but it shouldn't have been. The "get drunk, fall down and split your head, be too drunk to solve the problem" syndrome had been there a long time before the late Dan Harrington, and would be there forever after.

MAYOR HERNANDEZ tried to convince the Dade County state's attorney that Chief John Kearn should be prosecuted for assault and battery.

"No way, Orlando." The state's attorney sighed. "I love you, but none of us is gonna lose our career for you. Orlando, you must have seen the videotape! Kearn's defense lawyer will show it and convince the jury that you were out of control, hysterical, and he smacked you to wake you up to reality."

"I'll go over your head!" Hernandez yelled into the telephone. "I'll take my case to the state's attorney general!"

"Good luck," the state's attorney purred back softly.

"Yeah? Yeah! Good luck my ass! What makes you so damn confident about it?"

"Well," the state's attorney told him, "for one thing I already have discussed your case with the attorney general."

Hernandez asked, eagerly and expectantly, "And?"

"And," he was told, "his office also perceives you as having lost it. Really, Orlando, would you want to be there to testify against Kearn at trial, and watch that videotape of you becoming hysterical, being shown again and again and again?"

The mayor dropped his phone in its cradle and his head in his hands. He wanted to cry.

OVER THE PAST YEAR it had become a budding tradition for Chief Kearn to get together with Lieutenant Bartlett after the conclusion of a successful Stakeout case of major proportions. This was the third time they and their wives had met for the famous seafood at the Chart House Seafood Restaurant in Coral Gables.

When the coffee and brandy came at the end of the meal, Kearn and Bartlett excused themselves and strolled outside on the pier behind the restaurant, watching the moon cast its reflection on the dark waters.

"I must have played my video of you smacking Hizzoner about a dozen times," said Bartlett. "It's a thing of beauty."

"Ouch! You made a copy of that?"

Bartlett grinned. "Me and every other cop on the job. It's a classic law-enforcement moment, you might say. The rank and file loved it. They'd follow you through the gates of Hell right now, you know. Most of them figure you'd even come up with a way to get the search warrant."

Kearn laughed. "They don't know me very well, do they? Those nut cases from the Blizzard had me climbing the walls. If they hadn't gotten too crazy at the end, we might never have caught them." He sighed. "Six dead cops. I hope to God nothing like this ever comes down on us again. How did your people take the thing with Harrington?"

Bartlett frowned. "I keep thinking how pathetically small the funeral was. You die in the line of duty, you get the parade and the rifle salute and the whole ball of wax. You die alone, drunk in your apartment, nobody shows up but the cops from your unit and your chief. Thanks for that, by the way. It meant a lot to my people."

Bartlett shook his head and added, "I keep wondering if I couldn't have done something for him. I saw the drinking signs, you know, but he always denied it. I could never actually catch him doing anything where I could mandate he go in for counseling. Next thing I know, he's dead. Not much I can do for him now."

Kearn put his hand on the lieutenant's shoulder. "There was nothing you could do, Ken. You can't help anyone who doesn't want to help himself. How's the rest of your crew holding up?"

"Not bad, but we'll be needing some replacements. The docs diagnosed a heart murmur in one of my Team One guys, Hardesty. He's got to go on light duty. I'll need a replacement for Harrington, of course. Maybe one more—Frank Cross came to see me today. He was feeling me out about an unpaid sabbatical. He wants to get involved in training and counseling cops who've been in critical incidents."

"Nothing wrong with that," Kearn said. "Have him come see me. There might be some way we can have him do it within the department, train him on company time for it, so he wouldn't have to give up his salary."

"Don't think that'll be a problem, Chief. His lady's got big bucks, bestselling author and all. I've got a feeling he might wind up leaving the job, doing it on his own."

Kearn sighed. "Kid's been through a lot. Maybe he's earned a rest. How about the rest of Team Two? What is it you call 'em, your shit magnets?"

Bartlett grinned. "Mike Cohen's walking on air. Back with his wife again. West and Baranck are cool. Jesus, they're my rocks. I wish I could clone 'em. Hoffritz and Carmody are making goo-goo eyes at each other, and Mike asked me about openings on one of the other teams. I get the feeling they might be, you know, about to become an item. I think he wants to make sure nothing looks out of line."

The chief shrugged. "Use your own judgment. I've seen them in action. Two fine young people. If they've got feelings for each other, I don't think it'll get in the way of the job. They'll use common sense."

Bartlett asked, "What about you? Hizzoner won't be making things any easier for you."

The chief laughed. "Who knows? Maybe he'll thank me for his new bodyguard. I took Bruce Yount out of Professional Standards and assigned him to the mayor's security detail."

Bartlett was shocked. "I don't get it! He's been going behind your back to the mayor, and you reward him with one of the best jobs on the department?''

Kearn winked. ''That's what everyone thinks. I guess under the other mayors, the bodyguard work was pretty good duty. Nice places to go, good food to eat, all that. But ever since I've been here, guys on the detail have been putting in for assignments somewhere else, anywhere else. Seems the mayor doesn't want bodyguards—he wants a bunch of toadies to carry his stuff, take his picture for him, do errands. But everybody thinks it's a cozy little job, which is why no one can accuse me of punishing that little rat weasel by transferring him.''

Bartlett whistled. ''Beautiful. I love it! And he's where he can't get good cops in trouble anymore. He's gotta lick boots instead of kick butt! He and Orlando deserve each other.''

''Indeed,'' answered John Kearn, looking up at the beautiful night sky. ''Sometimes, Ken, life *is* fair.''